Matthew J. Seery is the author of two novels, *Caste American* and *The Record Prophets*, and has been a high school English teacher since 2006. He earned his B.A. in English from SUNY Albany in 2004 and his MS in Secondary Education from Dowling College in 2007. He resides in a small town on the South Shore of Long Island with his beautiful wife and two sons.

This work is dedicated to the beloved memory and spirit of my mother, Debby Seery.

Matthew J. Seery

CASTE AMERICAN

AUST︎N MACAULEY PUBLISHERS™

LONDON ∗ CAMBRIDGE ∗ NEW YORK ∗ SHARJAH

Ordering Information:
Quantity sales: special discounts are available on quantity purchases by corporations, associations, and others. For details, contact the publisher at the address below.

Publisher's Cataloging-in-Publication data
Seery, Matthew J.
Caste American

ISBN 9781643786964 (Paperback)
ISBN 9781643786971 (Hardback)
ISBN 9781645364894 (ePub e-book)

The main category of the book — FICTION / Thrillers / Technological

Library of Congress Control Number: 2019907605

www.austinmacauley.com/us

First Published (2019)
Austin Macauley Publishers LLC
40 Wall Street, 28th Floor
New York, NY 10005
USA

mail-usa@austinmacauley.com
+1 (646) 5125767

Thank you Christine for giving me the time, love, and space to write and create; to my father and family for their support, especially Michael Seery for his mathematical expertise; to the indefatigable team at Austin Macauley that helped me realize a dream; to my agent, Clara Macri, whose tenacity and energy fueled me to look beyond each and every rejection letter; and to John Jacobsen for his original artwork.

1

March 2nd, 2019.

"Better move your ass, Tony! That sloppy head start's all we're givin' you!"

Anthony Palmieri, a parasite of a lawyer whose commercial slogans and legal philosophies ranged from the depraved—you're not a molester if you identify as a child!—to the racist—if you've stood your ground against a super-predator, I'll stand up for you!—to the misogynistic—her legs, like her mouth, should have stayed closed!—slipped passed his hand-crafted-by-the-Amish shed and entered the wilderness that loomed behind his isolated upstate New York home. He found the footpath that he and his Golden Retrievers had traversed many times before, but the foot-and-a-half of untrodden snow brought his sprint to a stumbling crawl.

"You don't have to do this! I can help you!" he bellowed back to the four intruders, realizing that his only chance at surviving depended on stalling them as long as he could.

Laughter echoed his plea.

"You're going to help us, huh, Palmieri? Even after we shot those beautiful dogs of yours?"

"Damn shame you sent 'em after us! What were you thinking?"

"What kind of sick bastard trains Golden Retrievers to attack anyway?"

"This piece of shit lawyer, that's who."

"Ex-lawyer, Danny. None of 'em are allowed to practice as of midnight tonight."

Palmieri couldn't hear the conversation, but he had clearly heard the fate of his loyal dogs, Mop and Bucket. He loved those animals but sacrificing them had bought him enough time to get out of his house and into the woods; the cold, barren woods in which he now shivered. He didn't know who any of these men were; he'd been scrolling through job training programs when he saw the four of them coming toward his house. They didn't even bother covering their faces, nor did they make any attempt in concealing their pump-action shotguns and bolt-action rifles. They looked like old buddies returning after a trophy-less hunt. Palmieri deduced why they were nonchalantly walking across his lawn toward the front door, ignoring the 'Keep off the Grass' signs. He knew at that moment that they were not disappointed returning huntsmen—their prey was sitting at his desk, his cooling dinner barely touched, sweating as he watched his surveillance monitors. These men had no intention of leaving him alive. They could have been working for any one of the myriad former clients or defendants who wished him dead. For all he could remember, they were the former clients. There had been too many to keep track of. As they made their way to the locked front door, Palmieri used his intercom to ask who they were, what they wanted. "Call me Zaroff," one replied; another opted for Rainsford, the other two remained silent. Palmieri, not being much of a reader, missed the literary allusions. It was at that point that the balding, fat former attorney decided to sacrifice his dogs.

"You know what, Palmieri? You've piqued my interest," the supposed leader of the foursome yelled to the darkness. "Enlighten me. How can you help us?"

The lawyer paused and huddled behind two trees, maniacally crafting an answer that might save his life. Reasonable men would not have come with weapons out; reasonable men would have started with some type of negotiations; reasonable men would not have shot the dogs. Instead of offering an answer, figuring that the last question was just a lore to figure out his position, he moved away from his cover and deeper into the woods.

"Not biting, huh? No problem, shitbag. We'll just start with the lawyer jokes and wait for you to freeze. We've got hours worth of 'em!"

At the mention of that option, Palmieri realized how violently he'd begun to shiver. He weighed the options of being shot to death or freezing. Neither met his optimal approval threshold, so again, he paused and hunkered down in the snow. *I can talk these clowns outta this*, he thought. In his days in the courtroom, he'd been able to get some deplorable specimens out of seemingly insurmountable situations, so how much harder could this be? He tried to throw his voice out of the left side of his mouth, as if it would somehow divert them away from hiding spot.

"Even if I can't legally practice, I can still be an adviser for you! For the right price, I can help you get outta any shit that comes your way! Believe me, with this new system, people like you are still going to need legal assistance. People are gonna being suing each other for everything!"

"For the right price, huh, Palmieri! I knew killing a lawyer would be gratifying but hollowing out your head'll be better than blowin' a load!"

"So, you think it's gonna be kumbaya when all the lawyers are gone! You think the world will magically become a peace-loving commune! You think—" Palmieri cut himself off as he heard two sets of footsteps from his flanks. How had they moved so quickly in the knee-deep snow?

While he fell silent and stayed perfectly still, two men with snow-shoed feet closed in on him. When they were each about twenty-five feet away from their prey, they stopped and raised their rifles.

"Stand up, Palmieri," said the one on the left. "We see you just fine."

"Please…please…I can help you…"

"The longer we let him talk," a voice came from directly in front of the victim, "the better chance he has of getting outta here alive, boys. Pick your shot, and make it count. We've got a long list to check off tonight. Lots of *t*s to cross and *i*s to dot."

"You sure it's him? I mean, we shoot up the wrong guy and we're going away forever. Let me scan his face to be sure," said the man standing to Palmieri's left.

"Of course it's him, but we might as well cover ourselves. Sure, scan his fat ass. But I don't think he's gonna pose for you, Bill," said the man in the middle.

"Well, I'm not lookin' to make Christmas cards out of it and I don't need much light at all. This new app has a flash built in—just point, click, and prosecute. And…got it. Look at how clear that came out."

"Already uploaded?"

"And synched with our case. We're going to be the first trial to stream live on the internet, boys! You're gonna be even more famous, fat boy! Give it a second, and…here we go."

The online jurors now had a first-person perspective on the trial of Reggie Barrit vs. Anthony Palmieri. Barrit was charging Palmieri with the wrongful death of his nephew. The viewership rose to over ten thousand in only half a minute.

"At least tell me who the hell you are! I don't know you! What the fuck have I ever done to any of you?" Palmieri practically cried.

The hunters in the snow leveled the barrels of their weapons at Palmieri's silhouette. Only the man in the middle began shooting, though. The muzzle flash preceding the first bullet looked like a wizard's wand casting a spell. Palmieri saw that fiery orange burst an instant before he felt the bullet pierce his abdomen. He did not know the exact pathology of that first shot (nor the others that entered him later on), but it had journeyed through his generously padded stomach, through his small intestine and liver, and come to rest in between the T-11 and T-12 vertebrae. The new paralysis sent the already kneeling Palmieri crashing onto his right side. The shooter waited for the screaming to stop before explaining his motives. He moved closer, walking around the reddening snow.

"My name is Barrit, Reggie Barrit, and my nephew recently killed himself in his prison cell. A prison cell you put him in. I get that you can't really listen right now, can't really understand much with your guts pouring blood all over this beautiful snow, but I just wanted to be the first to take advantage of the new system. Everyone can see what I've done, and I want to know who'd actually convict me for killing a lowlife like you."

"I don't think he remembers your name, Reggie. He's not even looking at you while you talk. Turn your flashlight on so he can see you better, so everyone can see you better."

"Good idea, Bill. Can you see me now, fatboy? Does my face remind you of my nephew? Still no, huh? Fine. I'll just tell you before you die from shock. My nephew stopped that school shooter in Blue Bay Elementary a few years ago. Stopped him by stabbing him with the steak knife he'd brought for his lunch. Wasn't able to protect every one of those poor kids, but he did save dozens of others by nearly killing that maniac. And what did you do? On behalf of that psycho's family you sued the school and my nephew! You ruined my sister's oldest son because that child-killer's family was rich enough to hire a parasite like you. We couldn't afford an attorney of your *caliber* to defend him the way he should've been, so what happened to that hero? Tell me, you fat fuck!"

"He was put in jail for attempting to kill a mentally-ill victim!" Palmieri screamed in defiance.

The messages in the online trial's comments section repeated one after another: *KILL HIM!*

Reggie Barrit rose from his squat. He walked over and looked at the screen in Bill's hand. He would say nothing more. He backed farther away from the dying man, backed up to avoid the splattering that was about to occur.

The torrent of lead ripped through Palmieri, tearing the flesh from his bones, ricocheting and redirecting through his organs and skull, exploding his scrotum and shredding his shriveled penis. Arteries spurted out the last remnants of Anthony Palmieri's life. The bloody parts of the former lawyer flew through the snow, but the symphony didn't end until each ammo belt was emptied. It was more cathartic than any lawyer joke any of them had ever heard.

Reggie Barrit and his associates had underestimated their chances of taking the law into their own hands. Before their safari, they had been worried that the viewers would go soft on them and demand mercy for Palmieri. Barrit was enjoying being wrong. In the new system, as the first online trial in the mid-Hudson region, they were christened the new brothers Earp.

2

June 2024, Runners' Landing, Long Island, New York.

"So, the situation I want you to ponder is this: two people walk toward each other on the same side of a narrow rural road. One is a middle-aged man pushing his two children in their stroller while holding their family dog on its leash. The K-9 appears to be obedient but begins to pull and bark excitedly as it sees an approaching woman. In the stroller sit two children in tandem. The vehicle is heavy to push and awkward to control. Coming from the opposite direction is an elderly yet spry woman who is out for her morning exercise. She's carrying a light walking stick but is not dependent on it for balance. Which person is responsible for giving way or for moving to the opposite side of the street?"

"Mr. Larkin, did you come up with this or is it another one from the script?"

"Are you honestly curious or are you just trying to avoid the task, Pat?"

"I just don't see the point to this. Who cares who walks where? I can't believe I'm actually saying this, but can't we just finish *The Crucible*?"

"We'll find out what happens to Abigail and Proctor next week, and as I explained before, this is an exercise in reasoning and critical thinking. The situation is hypothetical, and I, along with Ms. Decardo back there, want to see how you can apply these skills to this imaginary situation. Now, please begin writing your explanation. Follow the instructions on the board."

"Whatever. I get my notes printed, Mr. Larkin."

"The copies are, as they have been every day this year, up front for you and anyone else who needs them, Pat. A reminder for everyone: you have about nine minutes and thirty-eight seconds left to form an argument for the scenario. I'll remind you when you have five minutes left."

Jimmy Larkin, one of the four remaining liberal studies teachers at Runners' Landing High School, moved between the pairs of students, quickly

14

assessing who was on task, redirecting those who weren't, reading what was being typed, and making sure that, for this portion of the lesson, each student was working independently. He was trying to follow precisely what his assistant principal, Ms. Roseanne Decardo, had emphasized in their pre-observation meeting: scrap the planned lesson and design one around the skills they need to become responsible citizen jurors; the law, after all, was now in everyone's hands. She had also made it a point to him during that conference that if the school's participation in preliminary judicial competitions did not increase in the coming months, their corporate sponsor—the social media giant AbowtMe—would be making some significant personnel changes.

Larkin continued his journey through the Comp-U-Desk stations before stopping at one of his prize seat warmers. "Mr. Kours, if you put as much time into answering my prompts as you do into drawing laser-shooting rocket ships, you'd probably be an honors scholar."

"Those aren't rocket ships, Mr. Larkin...they're ejaculating penises," Tammy Goetz said with a giggle.

"Thank you, Tammy. Please get back to your response."

Larkin began to sweat, knowing that he should have just ignored Kours' sketches. Even after he had gotten used to teaching, had learned the nuances and triggers of teenage moods, had navigated the many layers of revolving administrators, had picked his battles over grades and complaints with certifiable parents, he still found himself getting anxious before, during, and after observations. Perhaps it had something to do with the elimination of tenure for public school teachers (the system had been replaced with a combination of administrative evaluations and online student/parent satisfaction surveys) or maybe it had to do with being unable to discern between what his many bosses said they wanted to see in a lesson versus what they were really looking for. He had given up trying to please them all and had, over the years, figured that most of them had no idea what they wanted to observe either. His new pedagogical dance, along with anyone else who had survived the Great Purge of educators, lawyers, and judges in 2020, was dedicated to developing these students into whatever the Big Four needed them to be.

Larkin moved to the next pair and glanced toward where Ms. Decardo sat, her stylus flying across her tablet, no doubt punching in negative comments and ineffective ratings for the Kours exchange. She was a rather new addition to Runners' Landing High School—a product of one of AbowtMe's pilot managerial universities. These company-sponsored institutions were schools in the most tenuous sense: they were online programs where the prosperous yet unemployable Ivy League graduates went to learn how to manage those who required substantial doses of re-education. Decardo had been selected to cut her teeth by monitoring her teachers' compliance to the new curriculum that Runners' Landing High School had adopted the previous spring. She had never wanted to be in education, had loathed its tediousness as a student, but having a job in these times was impressive enough and being employed through a company like AbowtMe was her idea of an American knighthood. So, keeping her bosses happy by enforcing their standards and by punishing non-compliants like Larkin was becoming rather gratifying.

"Mr. Larkin, that's ten minutes, and you said you'd give us a warning when there were five minutes left, and I'm not done and you didn't warn us, so you can't count this as a zero because that really wouldn't be fair. You told everyone that you'd warn us, and you didn't, so that's your fault, not mine, so my mom will be on the computer before the class is over, and if you do give me a zero, you can kiss today's survey goodbye," Desiree Wilton said.

He was still trying to respond to her Gatling-gun response when he turned to see Ms. Decardo packing her tablet into her bag and slinging it over her shoulder.

"Mr. Larkin, I have to meet some visitors in my office. They're here to observe and present to your eighth period class. Do not be late. We will continue this," she waved a hand toward the mass of students, "on Monday." She fumbled her way along the perimeter of the classroom, gluing herself to the wall and looking down, trying to avoid talking to or making contact with any of the teenagers.

When she was out of the room and safely out of earshot, an anonymous voice asked Mr. Larkin what had been on most of the students' minds, "So now that she's gone, do we still have to do this?"

He didn't respond. Instead, he called time. "Now, I want you to share your thoughts and arguments with your assigned partner. Read what they've written, highlight their claim, and comment on the strengths and weaknesses of their responses. You have fifteen minutes."

Begrudgingly, the students continued working on the scenario. After several minutes of silently reading each other's work, soft chatter began, only the most confident at first, but slowly, like animals that have confirmed a safe watering hole, the others began speaking with their partners. The crescendoing discussions reminded Larkin of the chaos of city rush hour. He continued his rounds and paused at a pair in the middle of the room. The angrier of the two was Daniel Hooten, an aspiring capitalist (drug dealer, who specialized in opioids), and the meeker Rajiv Chaudhri, a robotics enthusiast who, when pushed to his precipice, could assuredly stand his ground.

"Why the hell should the man with two babies have to move? He's got them, the stroller they're in, and the dog!" Daniel barked.

"The stroller's got wheels, and it's not the old woman's fault the guy doesn't know how to use birth control. Why should anyone with a family be more important than someone who doesn't have one?"

"How do you know she doesn't have a family? She's just out for a walk."

"What difference does it make anyway? She's got the right of way because she's old."

"How does being old give you any more rights than anyone else?"

"Why wouldn't it? What's wrong with respecting old people?"

"Forget it. She's got less to deal with, is obviously enjoying retirement, and should be the one to cross the road! And whatta you think about the little kids? It's not like they can tell Daddy to move across the street! Heck, maybe one is distracting him!"

"His kids can't talk! This guy knows that taking his family out for a walk is his responsibility, so he's got to be the one who moves!"

"Who said the kids can't talk?" Mr. Larkin added to the discussion before moving on to a different group. They were raising some of the same points as the others but doing so with more animation. The student to his left was Bailey Tomanicki and sitting behind her was Kristy Shine.

"If you own a dog, you're responsible for training it. The woman can obviously see that the dog is going to lunge or jump, so she should be the responsible one and move to the other side of the street," Bailey said.

"The guy has two kids, maybe he's a single father, maybe his wife cheated on him and left him, you never know, and now he's left with two kids and a crazy dog, when the hell would he have time to train it? If that's the case, I agree that the old woman should move, but I think she should, not for her own personal safety, but out of a little pity and compassion for this guy," Kristy countered.

"That's the dumbest thing I've ever heard. You can't just make things up! You have to use what Mr. Larkin gave us. That's the whole purpose for this!"

"You, uh, wanna stop yelling at me. This isn't real, you know."

"But it's ditzes like you who are going to mess up the system, Kristy. Where's your belief in personal responsibility? We're responsible for anything that happens to us, just like this woman! If she doesn't cross the street, she'll get bit by that dog, and she'll have no one to blame but herself. And forget about this stupid assignment because someday, like real soon, we're going to have to log onto trials, look at evidence, argue with total strangers, and decide a person's guilt or innocence! There isn't room for compassion and pity, just the evidence that's given. Remember that there aren't any more lawyers or judges; it's all us! That's how this new system works!"

Kristy didn't know how or where to begin her response to her I'm-here-when-it's-good-for-me friend, Bailey T. "I know how this system works, bitch. We've been learning about it since fifth grade. How about you calm down and get off your horse? We can't all have parents who do nothing but work on trials."

"You know my stepdad's a landscaper and my mom's a nurse—they just enjoy being good jurors unlike some parents I know." She let that one sting for a moment. "I'm just saying that it's going to be our responsibility, that it's, like, so much fairer now than it used to be, so we should at least agree that people who let bad things happen to themselves are just as pathetic and guilty as those who actually do bad things!"

Kristy sat, flabbergasted. "Aren't you a good little Big Four zombie? It never strikes you as odd that the only people you see in these trials are darker and poorer than you? Or it never occurred in that narrow brain that those who can afford to hire trolls and pests to bombard trials in their own favor?"

"What do you think they have Mods for? There are plenty of rules for each trial—my stepdad's shown me almost all of them—so if your lib-rant is done, I'll finish this so I can pass."

"Fuck off, Bailey."

Larkin had heard the beginnings of this exchange but had moved on to a different group, so getting back in time to play referee in the escalating row before the bell rang proved impossible. At its sounding, the Comp-U-Desks retracted into their sleep-mode positions. The students rose and moved in a staggered procession with their heads down and earbuds in, giving no thought to the congestion they would cause at the narrow doorway. Larkin fought his way toward Bailey and Kristy, making as little contact as he could for even the accidental touch of his elbow to a shoulder or, unthinkably, a softer-tissued area, would trigger almost-certain assault charges, public humiliation, and the immediate termination of his license and job. He spun, moved forward, paused, rocked back on his heels to avoid a pajama-clad adolescent, and moved through the narrowest gap between Benjamin Dimas and Angela Burrows. He was making impressive progress, but he felt like a worm writhing through the blades of a freshly cut lawn, a worm destined to lose to the radiating sun. The shuffling students ignored him as if he were any other body; the bell had stripped him of his authority.

He remembered, although too late, that he had a voice and called out, "Girls! Hold on a second. I want to—"

Bailey and Kristy left separately, not wanting to have their argument broken down and analyzed by a pseudo-psychologist teacher. Everyone in the current educational environment, even the damn lunch ladies, wanted to know how they were feeling. 'You look down. Are you feeling all right?' became more common a greeting than 'Good Morning.' Responding to these inquiries with 'I just need to take a shit' or 'I'm high as hell right now' were not viable options for the youth, so they always answered with the avoidance volley of, 'I'm fine.' Both Bailey and Kristy liked Larkin and his class, but there was nothing his two-minute intervention at the end of a period could have accomplished.

Larkin watched them run out the door. Part of him, however diminished it had become, still believed in what his early years of training had indoctrinated: he could solve their problems, each and every one of them; he could be the educator everyone rooted for in the movies, the savior, the secular saint whose vocation commanded him to right the wrongs and shortfalls of society in forty-five minute periods. Excuses for underachieving, from students or teachers, could not, at the expense of civilization itself, be tolerated. Parents divorcing? Group work will make you forget all about that.

Parents died? Oh, you poor thing! Don't fret, though, these motivational posters and Socratic discussions on the keys to happiness will be your surrogates. Boyfriend or girlfriend broke your heart? I bet you've never felt the solace that a research paper can bring, have you? You'll forget all about him or her as you become a detective and piece together the evidence of Shakespeare's early life. Impoverished because your parents' jobs were taken over by machines or modern-day Southeast Asian slaves? You have to remember that you've got a bi-quarterly test coming up, and if you don't show growth, I'll have to recommend weekend tutorials. What, you haven't enjoyed school since the first grade because all you know are tests and the word *accountability*? Read up on the billionaire owners of the Big Four: President Krauss, Richard Moss, Phaedra Reid, or Hobart Tuuthe—their fabulous wealth will inspire you to ace those exams (because that's what made them exorbitantly rich, right?). You enjoy reading modern and classical literature? Have you been tested yet? No, not more multiple choice. For special-ed, I mean, because those authors and their ideas won't lead you to money! No excuses for anything below a hundred.

As Larkin recalled the ridiculous lectures, ideals, and speakers he'd sat through in his training programs and early years of teaching, he snapped back into the moment. He realized that he was standing in an empty room, a man who had never become everyone's shoulder-to-cry-on or everyone's target of hate. As a teacher, he'd many years ago come to the conclusion that his influence on the lives of the youth was minimal at best.

The girls who'd left, the two who had been ready to tear each other's eyes out, would either calm down and reconcile or start a vituperative online assault on one another. Either way, he'd document the incident and hope for the best. He went to his desk to grab his lunch. There was no point wasting his one free period thinking any more about Bailey or Kristy or reading the class's responses and critiques, so he blocked off some time and space in his mental calendar and decided to grade some old-fashioned papers while he ate. He picked up the teetering stack that his juniors had turned in almost a month ago and made his way to the faculty lounge.

3

You're Wanted Because the People Deserve Justice.

The notification appeared on his cracked screen. Just a simple sentence that a decade ago would have been mistaken for spam or a virus. But in 2024, this discriminating sentence provoked anxious twitching, damp armpits, and the driest of mouths in anyone who received it. Jimmy Larkin's dropping stomach and clenching sphincter could now be added to the oft-surveyed response list. He sat in the fluorescently lit lounge, ignoring his colleagues' banal discussions of which students hadn't turned in homework, which students' parents were pains-in-the-ass, and which students were dating each other (he never understood why teachers cared). Larkin sat, captivated by the sudden activation of his phone. The digital voodoo usurped his mind, stopping his half-eaten lunch between his plate and face. A thin stream of balsamic dressing dripped from a loosened corner of his wrap, trickled down the hairless underside of his forearm, and met the white edge of the rolled-up cuff. It spread serpentine through the interlocked veins of fabric, expanding wider and darkening with each new drop. Holding half of the roll-up sandwich was consuming too much processing power, so it, and his hand, slowly fell back to the table, and the inane conversations at the table melded into one discordant, static-like background noise. Larkin's concentration, more focused now than it had been on any lesson he'd ever taught, any love he'd ever made, any of the three children he'd watched his wife birth, went to the newly displayed black block letters and anachronistic scales of justice that now seized his screen. His twitching left thumb swiped at his phone, first left-to-right then up-to-down, but the Proxy Accusation, commonly known as a Medusa, always had the same effect: for three minutes, the perpetrator's device, their contacts' devices, and devices of all other connected parties were frozen—the Accused with only the message, the others with both it and the summary of the alleged crime. When one of the three minutes had past, two new options were presented to the Accused: Select Guilty or Not Guilty. Below these choices was a running two-minute timer. After the timer had expired and the Accused had chosen either guilty or not—for those who made no choice, the default was guilty—the Accused was given the choice of self-defense or leaving it up to the new jury: the masses of anonymous internet opinionators.

1:59. Larkin mimicked his phone's inanimacy.

1:48. Oxygen and the foulness of deodorant-less adults and the stench of someone else's reheated salmon hovered in front of his lips and below his nostrils. Inhalation and exhalation were momentarily in a standoff.

0:57. The sweat cascaded down his back, saturating the waistband of his boxer briefs.

0:36.

0:25. He finally broke his attention away from the screen, and like prey that knows it's being stalked, scanned his environment for the perceived yet unseen threat: the phones and devices around him. Each one he saw, each in its black, blue, or pink protective cases, had been placed life-side down; each and every one was emitting a soft glow from its edges. He saw a couple of others under disorganized stacks of quizzes and some sticking out of briefcases and pocket books. Unimaginably, everyone in the room was engaged in speaking to someone else, involved in sketching a colored pencil over quizzes, scarfing their meals, or flirting with those well out of their league. The timer again caught his peripheral attention.

0:15.
0:10.
0:5.
0:0.

George Alvarez, another of the district's vanishing liberal studies teachers, thought he had heard someone smack the table with a ruler. The dissonant noise reverberated through the teachers' lounge, a room whose usual conversational volume was no louder than that of a confession booth. Prior to the smack on the table, he had been trying to explain to his wife, the talented and beautiful math teacher, Erica Primm-Alvarez, that sitting in on special-ed meetings when you didn't know the student was about as useful for the education process as ice melt was in August. What confounded him more at this last meeting, the one that had eaten up most of his one free period, was why the mother had been so irate at the fact that he had nothing to contribute to her my-stepson's-disruptive-behavior-and-refusal-to-do-his-work-is-not-the-result-of-my-refusing-to-medicate/discipline/parent-him-but-it's-the-direct-result-of-none-of-you-knowing-what-the-hell-you're-doing narrative.

"You don't understand! None of you do!" George said, mimicking the parent. "Haven't you listened to anything his psychologist has said? All of you, no matter what you're doing, have to let him out of class if he needs to masturbate! It's been on his IEP for four years! That damn science teacher wouldn't let him go—no, I don't know where his aide was—so he had to use the beakers when he finished!" George began a Vaudevillian impression at this point. "It's the only thing that keeps him focused through the day!"

"So I asked, before she went on any further, 'What grade is—I had to check the name on the file in front of Jeff Rossler—Sean in these days, and what exactly is his condition?'"

"That must have gone over gloriously with Mom," Erica interjected.

"Oh, she loved it. She practically spit on me when she told me that her darling was taking his third ride through tenth grade and that his classification was in the general realm of deficiencies in executive functioning. Before that got any worse, Rossler asked Mrs. Tomanicki-Reilly if Sean were on anything for his condition."

George fell back into his pantomime. "No, I will not put him on any more medication; Big Pharma keeps pumping out those happy pills to prime our kids for their latest and greatest opioids, so there will be no more poison put in the boy! I do not care what you think about that so please keep your ignorant opinions to yourselves and just let the damn aide take him to the bathroom so he can fully relieve his anxiety!"

Erica looked at him incredulously and asked, "You mean to tell me that she's not sure what her son's learning disability is and she refuses to try any drugs to help it?"

"Apparently, they've never had him formally tested, according to Rossler. They're just going by instinct and what they've seen on the internet. Never mind that, though. So I asked her, 'Should the aide do more than escort him or can he handle everything on his own'?"

Erica was having a difficult time keeping her smile hidden during this absurd impression, and she did not want to draw too much attention to their exchange, so she quickly looked down at her teabag and bobbed it up and down in the tepid water. When she knew her laugh had passed, when it had shot down through her shoulders and chest, made its way through her breasts and stopped at her goosebumping nipples, she adjusted, looked back at her husband, and posed the same question he had, "What kind of a psychologist would have recommended this treatment?"

"How can you question a professional like that? You're supposed to be an educator!" he chided his wife, back in the mother's voice.

George laughed harder when he saw her again looking down at her mug, again holding back her amusement. "It's the same damn question I asked!" he responded, loving her reaction, reaffirming in him that this logical, vivacious mathematician was his soulmate. "And after I asked it, she whipped her binder—the one she's been keeping since her fine stepson entered middle school—harder, I imagine, than she had meant to. Damn thing opened up like a gliding seagull, flew past my shoulder, and shattered a picture frame and two awards on Rossler's shelf. His eyes welled up before the last shard hit the floor. Pretty sure the picture was of him and his first dead wife and the two awards were educators-of-the-year from back in '12 and '15. Didn't know guidance counselors qualified for awards like that."

"He's got more than one dead wife?"

George held up two fingers. "The first one died on that picture day, six or seven years ago. Remember that? When that box of combs was delivered to the high school instead of the middle school and one of the secretaries thought it was a bomb? The first Mrs. Rossler had a heart attack when they put the lockdown code over the loudspeakers. She had always been worried that her final moments would come in another massacre."

"Ah, yes. The kids used the grievance counselors to get out of classes for months. They didn't even like her that much from what I remember, but she was always polite to me."

"It was some undiagnosed heart thing, if I recall, and she was always nice to me, too. Rossler's second wife was actually one of the earliest victims of—"

Erica was well aware of the circumstances of the murder of Jeff Rossler's second wife, a victim of mistaken identity in the early days of the new system, so she brushed her hand back and forth in front of George's face, cutting him away from the infamous topic, and he picked up the cue. He went on to finish his meeting anecdote.

"Well, I don't know what happened after the flying binder because I left. Only so much crazy I can stand, especially from a parent I don't know. Did I miss anything fun here?"

"Before Sandy and Nick left, we were having a dirty joke contest." This narrowed George's attention. "I thought I had it until Sandy blew both Nick and me away," she said, teasing her husband's near constant state of arousal.

"What was it?" he asked seductively.

"What did the sedimentary rock say to the igneous rock as the geologist approached?"

George's excitement dropped.

"We're about to get pounded," she teased, knowing how to playfully manipulate his libido.

"Watch out for those Earth Science teach—"

He cut himself short this time when he saw Erica look down to her phone. Hadn't even noticed it was in her hand. When the hell had it replaced the teabag string? She had been doing so well with curbing it since seeing her psychiatrist, and she knew she wasn't supposed to have it on her during school hours, as per Dr. Verma's orders, but before George could raise a quiet remonstration, he heard the *crack!* that sounded like a ruler hitting a table.

His instantaneous inspection of the cramped room provided the answer: Jimmy Larkin, his fellow liberal arts teacher and perennial favorite among the students, had lost consciousness while eating his lunch, smacked his forehead on the edge of the table, rolled out of his chair, and landed onto his stack of mostly plagiarized research papers. Blood poured down from the new gash, ruining the papers at the top. It didn't much matter (considering most of them would eventually be drenched in red anyway) but for the moment, those essays were providing some excellent head support for the now unconscious teacher.

When George's attention moved to the collapsed Larkin, Erica stole another look at her screen. She knew that it was supposed to stay off and in her car during the day, but she had felt something like a magnetic pull toward it in this last week. She had made so much progress with not being its slave, with being the one in control, but it had slithered back into the driver's seat after she had earned her promotion from ordinary juror to Mod/Forewoman. She had kept this from Dr. Verma, during their last session, and from George. The doctor would have never allowed her to accept the promotion, but there were so many cases, so many guilty people who needed punishment, so many innocent victims who needed justice. Figuring out how to hide it from George and her colleagues had been like solving an equation, and the reward of looking down at its glow, even though he had probably seen her at her first peek, was euphoric. During this second glance, she saw the Medusa, saw Jimmy's name and picture, but had only a second to see the charge. Before she could finish reading, George interrupted her with a shout.

"Get the nurse!"

Erica bolted into the hallway but as she passed the first bank of lockers, she stopped. Instead of sprinting in her heels to a nurse who wasn't in the building on Mondays, Wednesdays, or Fridays—this being a Friday—she took out her phone and decided to read the detailed charges against her colleague and friend, character:

As a distinguished Mod/Forewoman, you have been activated to moderate and report on the jury's decision regarding Case SR28-473-8719 and help render a decision of Guilty or Not Guilty on Mr. James Larkin, age thirty-four, of Runners' Landing, NY. As of the official filing date, today, June 6th, 2024, eighty-three percent of social media participants expressed OUTRAGE and DISGUST over Larkin's statutory rape of one of his sixteen-year-old students. The evidence found in over a dozen sites and reports is as follows: On the night of January 25th, 2024, the Accused was allegedly engaging in lewd and lascivious sexual acts with a minor at the Runners' Landing Motor Inn. Multiple eyewitnesses have documented their accounts and have posted their video evidence on their blogs and social media accounts. Further accusations claim that the girl, who will remain anonymous on this notification, exchanged sexual acts for passing grades. Those reports remain unconfirmed, but evidence gathering will remain OPEN for the duration of the trial. Larkin has expressed his innocence by selecting NOT GUILTY. He has yet to make any statements on his AboutMe or Share-It accounts.

As the moderator of this trial you will record, maintain, and oversee the discussions and verdicts from your assigned social media circles. You may not censor any part of these discussion groups, but you must make sure that each opinion is heard, that each opinion is that of a U.S. citizen, and that no single voice hijacks the proceedings. Your country and judicial system thank you. The forums for Guilty will open in twenty-four hours. Following those arguments, the forums for Not Guilty will open. After forty-eight hours, you must open the Accused's account so he may defend himself. Your reporting of the winning percentage, whether it be Guilt or Not Guilty is due in seventy-two hours. God bless America.

To her, Jimmy Larkin was no longer the bleeding-faculty-lounge victim or her long-term colleague; he was an Accused who required immediate punishment, or if his expression of innocence turned out to be true, an Accused who needed to be exonerated. Instead of continuing a pointless search for an absent nurse, Erica Primm-Alvarez signed out of the building and prepared to become the referee to hundreds, if not thousands, of irate American jurors.

Even trained professionals are relieved when tough situations are mitigated on their own. This meant that the professional, like a CPR and First Aid certified coach and teacher—in this case George Alvarez—bore no responsibility in the event that anything got out of hand. So when Larkin sat up on his own volition, George gave a brief, animated pump of his right fist and offered his steady hand to his wobbly colleague. George really didn't want anyone to know that he had cheated through his last fifteen recertification tests, nor did he want to test his rusty skills on an actual man-in-need, so he then did what he had always done for his injured football players or nauseatic students: he offered his friend a drink of water.

"George," Larkin said, still only semiconscious, "what the hell is a glass of water going to do for me?"

George was again relieved. One less thing he had to do.

"How bad am I cut?"

"Just try and take it easy. Erica went to get the nurse. It's still bleeding pretty badly. Just a second."

George took the closest thing he could find, Ashley Klepp's paper on the 2019 alterations to articles IV, V, VI, and VII of the Bill of Rights, and forcibly jammed it onto his friend's gaping wound. Once the blood saturated through the Klepp paper, Aaron Elskin's replaced it. Being someone who noticed and recalled minute details, George saw that the entire class had written about the same topic. The Elskin paper, though, added '…and How Social Media Can Steer America to a True Democracy' to its title. The papers, even Elskin's voluminous work, weren't helping the outpouring of blood. Just as the top corner of the boy's essay was saturating, one of the custodians produced a roll of paper towels, tore off a wad, and began packing it into the redness.

"Thanks, Kevin," George said to the custodian. "Stay here with him a minute. I'm going to see where the hell Erica is. You all right, Jimmy?"

"I'm fine, George, really, I'll get a bandage and get to class."

"Stay awake and upright. I'll be right back."

Larkin's reality reset, and he remembered why he had dropped away from the world. He frantically searched for his phone, searched to prevent anyone else from seeing the screen. While his fingers combed the stained rug, he tried to think of anything he could have done that would warrant the Medusa. He was not a violent man, he hadn't broken the speed limit after getting his second ticket, he was faithful to his wife, his porn searches were more or less tame, and he always paid his taxes.

He crawled under the table, pushing and knocking chairs out of his way. Those who hadn't left backed up against the walls, panicked by his increasingly erratic behavior.

Larkin wished he could get rid of as many of these people as he could; he wanted to find his phone, call his wife, and explain to her that this was just a case of mistaken identity. In a moment of catharsis and epiphany, he stopped his search—finding the hidden phone was pointless. If anyone around him was in any way connected, they would have already known what had transpired. In fact, they would know more about the charge than he did. When he accepted this truth, he sat back and felt it just under his left thigh, just lower than his wallet would sit, and his heartrate fell to an even more manageable level. He gazed at the device the way a guilty toddler looks at a parent for forgiveness, but the screen was back to normal; just a glowing surface waiting for his security code. The miniaturized scales of justice sat in the top left corner of his phone, reminding him that the preliminaries of the trial had begun. Those scales and a new message from his wife. A new message from his mother, a new one from his brother, an all-caps one from his father, and one from his... The phone died in his shaking hand. *If I don't charge it*, he thought, *maybe all of it would just disappear.*

George moved easily through the still empty hallways toward the main office; in two or three more minutes, hundreds of students would pour from their crowded classrooms into the spillways of the school, making the search for Erica impossible. He had already decided that he'd be a few minutes late to his next class but still tried to take the stairs to the second floor two at a time. While he was an athletic man, he wasn't the most coordinated, so he fell hard onto the marble steps after miscalculating his second bound. He avoided breaking his nose and shattering some teeth by getting his hands in front of his face, but he couldn't prevent gravity from dragging him back to the landing. There, waiting for him, was one of his young AP disciples.

"Mr. Alvarez, Mr. Alvarez!" she shouted with sincere concern.

He looked up at her, his heart lifting with the hope that the spritely Jessica Connors would offer her sympathies and generous assistance.

"Did you finish grading our essays, yet?"

"Miss Connors (he wanted to tell her to go fuck herself), I'm fine, thank you, and, no, I haven't finished grading the essays."

"All right. My mom wants to know why I haven't gotten my hundred, so could you please email her? Until I get that grade, I can't drive the Benz to school, and I see you've got a paper in your hand, even though it looks like you spilled something on it; that's not mine, is it? So, as soon as you have the grade, can you input into my StudentData folder? Thanks!"

She hurried away, anxious to get to her next class before she had to share the halls with any of her knuckle-dragging (that was all of them, according to her parents) cohorts. George really felt like tripping her and shoving the paper he was holding—why the hell was he still holding the Elskin kid's paper?—down her throat, but he instead watched her scuttle down the hallway. He gradually got to his feet, brushed the dirt off his hands and pants, put the now-crushed paper into his back pocket, and went to find Erica.

Larkin had composed himself enough to get through the day. *If I don't see it, it's not there* was now his new mantra. But the anxiety of the Medusa still pissed sour into his stomach. He envisioned crimes he'd never been a part of, ones he'd read about or seen in movies, and placed himself in the leading roles. *What the hell could it be about?* He'd have time to figure that out later. *But what if Decardo or Baker or Ellis have seen it?* he thought. Shauna Baker ran her building as if it were the Triangle Shirtwaist, but she would have preferred it to always be ablaze. She would have adored the sight of what she called her lazy-ass teachers crackling and popping in the flames. As flesh melted and separated from their bones, she would've been shouting AbowtMe's Core Education Standards over the loudspeakers, chastising those who dared complain about the heat. No, Larkin continued thinking, if she had seen the Medusa, he would've been in one of the building's in-school-suspension cells by now. Conversely, he wasn't sure Jackie Ellis, his chairwoman, knew how to read or operate any type of electronics, so the threat from her end was minimal. He also knew the main office had the contact information for every teacher in the building, but the chances that his admins had each of the teachers' numbers in their personal phones were small. He decided that he would go through the rest of the day and if anyone questioned him about the charges, he'd simply reply with his students' go-to deflection: 'I don't know what you're talking about. Everything's fine.'

He thanked everyone who had helped him get steady and left to facilitate his next group of juniors. He hated that description: facilitator. It made him feel like a classroom referee instead of an erudite educator. He held Masters in both World History and Adolescent Education, yet, over the years, his role in the classroom had degenerated into that of a jockey's, riding along through prefabricated lessons and scripts, whipping helter-skelter toward his students' often incorrect conclusions. Instead of enlightening them with stories they would never read on their own or introducing them to histories that would more than likely disappear in the vastness of the Web, he had become their tame handler, a stopwatch incarnate, regulating when they started one part of an activity and when they transitioned to another. It's true, he had to admit, that people do absorb more through applied learning, but early on in the professional shift from teacher to facilitator, he had encountered some oddly indignant students who wanted to know why the hell he was being paid if all he did was design and assign projects and papers and helpful videos for them to be busy with instead of actually teaching them. He'd long suspected that AbowtMe's motive was simple: create an interchangeable, cheap cog of a facilitator before the ultimate conversion to total online instruction was complete. At least he'd been allowed to design the projects and papers in those days. At that time, he thought deeply about students' questions and insights, and when he was truly at a loss for an answer, he brought them to his then mentor, George Alvarez. George had provided some advice and guidance that got the inexperienced Larkin through many layers of teenage catastrophes and, on the professional side, revolutions in administrative faces. As for the teenagers, George advised him to simply listen to them, regardless of how bizarre or benign, and offer no advice. They just needed ears sometimes, not, as hard as it is to believe, tongues. For the principals, assistant principals, chairmen and women, assistant superintendents of curriculum, assistant superintendents of instruction, assistant superintendents of special education, and superintendents, George offered this: show them what they want to see when they're watching and then do things the right way after they've left.

Facilitator. Euphemism for useless manager. You didn't need professionals as facilitators. Programs and codes (just as Larkin predicted) *had* taken over most of those positions in the last few years anyway. If you wanted someone to facilitate cumbersome group projects or have students work independently to come up with their own answers, why not sell them a program and send them to mommy and daddy for homeschooling? AbowtMe was trying to figure out this shift in the public-school paradigm, but people became quite contentious when their bedrock traditions—religion, marriage, education (ironically enough)—were tested. AbowtMe and the others knew not to push their changes too quickly.

The time Larkin had to muse over these thoughts—amazing that he had not once thought about his Medusa—was over. Standing outside of his classroom door was Roseanne Decardo, Department Chairwoman Ellis, the Assistant Superintendent of Curriculum, Mr. Fred Edmunds, and, finally, an austere-looking man in a pinstriped blue suit who wore a visitor's badge. Oh, shit. *Don't let that be now,* Larkin thought. He checked his watch, hoping that the lunch period he'd had all year had somehow changed. As cheap as the timepiece was, it still told him what he didn't want to be true: eighth period was going to begin in just under a minute.

The diminutive assistant principal spotted him, her thin lips flexing into a disapproving grimace as the disheveled mess of a liberal studies (most history, English, and social science teachers had been fired in 2020, and in their places came the all-encompassing liberal studies facilitators) drone plodded down the hall. The only sound in that corridor was the now hurrying footsteps of Jimmy Larkin.

"You're late Mr. Larkin," she said.

"I think I still have a few seconds before the—"

"If you're not fifteen minutes early for a presentation, you're late. Explain yourself!"

She tried to sound as authoritative as possible—as authoritative as anyone with no real power can ever sound.

"I'm sorry. I'm just having a bit of an off day," he responded, trying to bring some sympathetic attention to his bandaged forehead.

"In this profession, you don't have off days," she replied and looked toward the guest for approval. *See how I treat my underlings?* she thought, hoping to have some affirmation thrown back her way. No such response came to reassure her—the guest had been looking at his tablet, ignoring the short reprimand. For the FileX rep, Leo Colmsly, this petty confrontation was a waste of his time. He wanted to give his lecture and presentation to the future group of jurors, have them practice with a standard scenario, ogle some of those teenage titties, and be on his way to his gated community home.

"If it's all the same, let's get this started," Colmsly said. "Jury participation has been below average for this area, so I need to make sure that the youth are aware of how important it is to be a part of the new system. According to my analytics," he turned his screen to his small audience, "Runners' Landing has been seven participation points below the average for the last four years, so AbowtMe and FileX need to make sure that each one of their sponsored schools is fulfilling their side of the agreement. If I find that you are not," he looked downward to the assistant principal and then over to the assistant superintendent and chairwoman, "we will replace you with those who will."

In the last remaining minutes of her seventh period Human Analytics class, Wendy Chu was desperately trying to explain the importance of value-added models as they applied to a social construct. She'd been trying to convey this lesson through every technique she could think up or plagiarize for the better part of the spring semester, but all she got back at this point in the year were vacant stares and repeated questions. She had been an aspiring engineer at CenTek but a guilty verdict in a misdemeanor trial diminished her professional opportunities to public school teacher, manual laborer, or sex worker. She chose what she *thought* would be the most dignified avenue.

"Do we have to know when CenTek introduced the formula, you know, for the final?" Emma Nolan asked from the back.

"No, you don't. And it was actually the creation of the AI, interestingly enough, not any human engineer who devised the formula," Mrs. Chu responded. "But it did build on the work of—again, interestingly enough—professional sports analysts."

"So, is this kinda right, Mrs. Chu?" Emma asked, swiping the solution to her equation from her monitor to the front board.

"No, Emma, it's not. People!" she bellowed, realizing that months of hard work had disappeared into the ether, "Here it is! As it's been for years, as it's been on every assignment you've gotten since January, as it's been on every damn tutorial since March!"

The board erased Emma's incorrect work and displayed CenTek's crowning contribution to the new social order:

$$Vt = Vs + Ve + Vg.$$

"Your total value (Vt) to the corporate state is the aggregate of your Vs, or societal benefit to the state, minus your societal detriment to the company and/or state. Your Ve is your lifetime contribution to the state minus the lifetime dependence on the company and/or state funds, and your Vg represents your positive genetic predispositions minus any detrimental genetic predispositions you might carry or display. These differences are each equally valued on a numeric scale and totaled to determine each person's value. For example, a person who is healthy and incurs minimum care costs will earn high scores in each category, whereas an individual born with developmental or learning disorders, costs the corporate state money due to educational interventions, and since they will require others to work for them instead of vice versa, they will score relatively low overall."

"But how can you raise your score if there's something that's out of your control? You know, Mrs. Chu, like being born dumb?"

"Well, Javier, positives could include any social services the Big Four or the state consider valuable. Until you're old enough to be a juror, you can do well in school, stay out of trouble, play sports, participate in as many practice trials as you can, volunteer your labor, keep an eye on your neighbors, stay out of trouble…anything that won't be a fiscal burden on society. Detriments, on the other hand, could include all major and minor violations of laws resulting in convictions, arrests, fines…" she paused, seeing how few were listening, "and remember, just because you're not old enough to be a juror does not mean you're too young to be tried. In the true essence of fairness, the amended Constitution now sees us all, regardless of age, gender, race, religion, ethnicity, as equally prosecutable. I know I'm almost out of time, so I'll remind you all that your Vt is being tabulated by CenTek's AI on a daily basis, and if your Vt goes below a five, your opportunities for employment, for education, for owning a business or home, all diminish. If your Vt drops to a three or below—"

The bell rang, ending her review.

Leo Colmsly did not wait for the invitation of the next bell to enter the occupied classroom. Mrs. Chu, who was collecting her exit-ticket assignment, was about to object to the intrusion until she saw the line of lemmings that followed the man in the suit. She took her collected stack of index cards and threw them in her briefcase. Before her students could interject with questions about the stranger and his posse, the late bell sounded, and Mr. Larkin began organizing himself, stacking the mostly destroyed pile of essays out of sight on the windowsill. Colmsly stood next to him, on the side of the room, while the others found seats in the back. After thirty seconds, the last of Larkin's juniors meandered into class, wondering what they'd be learning today in liberal studies. Jillian Foster came in with a bound and asked the question that had been on the minds of those before her.

"Hey, who are you?" but before anyone could respond to her inquiry, she turned to Larkin and said, "Mr. Larkin, does this mean we're not going over the reading from last night because, dead-ass, Hamlet's annoying, and if I have to listen to him whine about what the hell he should do, I'm literally going to explode!"

"Please just take your seat, Jillian, and if you're literally going to explode, please get me an umbrella." Not even a Medusa could destroy the teacher humor in him. "Probably get a classroom management lecture later on for that one," he mumbled to himself.

Larkin felt a hand grip his left shoulder.

"Please get out of the way," Colmsly said, "and make sure that that archaic machine is ready by the time I'm done with my introduction. I will take it from here."

Degradation was nothing new to the modern educator; it was the one thing that had transitioned smoothly as teachers became facilitators, and in fact, this was far from the rudest a speaker or boss had ever been to him. Like the mindless servant he'd been molded into, he walked over to his ancient computer tower and pressed the power button. As it spurred to life, the remaining students hurried in and found their seats. Although he still used an anachronistic keyboard, tower, and monitor setup to teach, the students of Runners' Landing High School were provided (thanks to their AbowtMe sponsors) with state-of-the-art Comp-U-Desks. The virtual keyboard would light up as the students sat down, the top portion of the desk would rise up, illuminate with their day's agenda, assignments, and StudentData screens, and the recumbent-bike pedals (the part that most of them ignored) would adjust to each of their personalized settings. Students would be reminded, via red and green lights, when they needed to power their desks through rhythmic pedaling.

When Colmsly saw that each desk had activated, he moved to the center of the room to begin his lecture. He looked toward no one in particular and let the confused, uncomfortable silence linger for a few moments. Leo Colmsly was no longer interested in getting home to his gated community or spying for the plunging necklines and deep cleavage of his teenage audience; his only interest now was frightening and converting these idiot minds into obedient student jurors. He enjoyed his job. He had instantly transitioned, both in tone and expression, into something of a drill sergeant addressing a green group of recruits.

"Many of don't seem too concerned that you will never leave this town. Many of you don't think it's admirable to want do so because your parents never left this town. This is a stupid, un-American way of thinking. What's even worse than not thinking at all is believing, as many of you do, that you are too good for this town or the town over or any town in this great country. You are, in your developing minds, positive that you will somehow rise above the realities of our glorious system. This is also foolish and very un-American. Even the greatest of us, the heads of the Big Four, President Krauss, our citizen jurors, are only powerful because they belong to a well-ordered machine—a machine you don't seem to want to be a part of. You may dream of being rich, or you may dream of inventing, but no matter what you dream of becoming, you will always be a part of the first real democracy in modern history. You may dream of being rich, but without being a good citizen, you will have nothing. In fact, you have to think of yourselves not only as citizens, but as shareholders in this great American business. You may dream of inventing a piece of tech or a code that helps your fellow men and women, but without being an active member of our direct justice system, your inventions will flounder and go unused. You will become ignored simply because people do not trust outsiders. Anyone who believes that they are better than what we've done in the last eight years in this country is a poor excuse for a shareholder and doesn't deserve his stake in the Great Experiment. Well, I do have to say that this community seems to be one populated with a large number of shareholders who think they're already CEOs who can't be bothered with the menial jobs of day-to-day responsibilities. This area, particularly this district, has a pathetic rate of juror participation. It must change! Democracy cannot work if its people are not vigilant. Democracy cannot work if crimes of any kind are tolerated. You and your families and your friends and your neighbors must become the eyes and ears of justice! There are no safe communities or low crime rates. You don't get to live in an insulated, bucolic—that refers to a pleasant countryside, you idiot, don't interrupt me again!—village because there is theft in your home, violence in your friend's home, child molesters in your neighbor's home! Our job as citizens is to make this country safe again! We can't do that while crime, any crime, is being perpetrated!"

Colmsly paused to sync his tablet with the projector. Several desk pedals went into motion.

"We're now going to practice the judicial process. On your screens, you will see the latest list of Accused in your area. Give it a damn second for it to come up, will you. Are you always the moron who asks dumb questions or is today a special occasion? While we're waiting for the latest list, review the procedures for reporting a crime. After you've reviewed those, bring your attention to the trial and sentencing procedures. I cannot believe that the Accused List still hasn't loaded! After several minutes of reviewing how to make an Accusation—it's simple: you log onto CrimeReport.gov and enter your social security number and description of the crime."

Lamont Davis, although a student of the system since he was a child, was still somewhat confused on the step-by-step process of the online trial. He'd always done the mock assignments and overheard his parents and siblings discussing them, but since he had never partaken in a bonafide proceeding, his philosophy toward them mirrored those of his classmates: if it doesn't affect me directly, why should I care about it? He wanted to ask for clarification, but he had already been humiliated twice by this asshole, so he did what most discouraged people do and remained silent, ignorant, and irritated. The question he would have asked to a normal, patient teacher concerned how guilt or innocence was determined if a trial consisted of random users presenting evidence, followed by those same people hurling accusations (insults that often degenerated into vicious ad hominem attacks), and, more often than not, ending with off-topic facts, personal biases, and most looking to punish the defendant with the harshest available sentence. If someone were found guilty, who carried out the recommended punishment? Was this actually a fairer system than what had previously existed? What had happened to all of the lawyers and judges? As many explanations as his teachers had given him through the years, as many simulations as he'd ever done, he was still unable to comprehend the callousness of it all.

"What version of CenTek's OS are you running on these machines?" Colmsly asked, irritated. "Never mind. We'll run a scenario while we wait."

Colmsly swiped his finger across his tablet screen, tapped a few times, and sent the students a simulated case.

"All right. Put on your goggles."

Each student placed their VR goggles over their eyes and focused on their screens.

"One of your monitors has been frozen with a Proxy Accusation. Some of you might know this as a Medusa but that's a misnomer," he looked toward Lamont to see if any clarification on that word was necessary but only saw the lad looking back at him with his middle finger raised, "because this is no virus, it's simply a notification."

The often-outspoken Jillian Foster sat silently in her desk.

"Now that one of you has been selected, you're the Accused. The rest of you have to read the charges, log on to any one of your social media accounts, enter the trial code, and prepare your arguments. Okay, so the charge I created for the Accused is cheating on a test. The first section, usually lasting for twenty-four hours in a real trial, is for the prosecution's comments. Half of you have been designated against the Accused and half of you will defend the Accused. In the real world, the proportions are not so even, and both sides will have more facts and evidence to review, but for our purposes here, this will suffice. So, what you'll do first is…"

Before he could finish his instruction, half a dozen messages had been sent.

This isn't fake. That bitch actually does cheat on her tests.
That's not the only thing she cheated on.
Such a skank.
I know how she got the answers…she screwed Mr. Larkin.
I only got a 93, so there's no way she didn't cheat.
You think she's bad, you should see Tracy in action!

Leo Colmsly smiled. Of course these kids would be beautifully cruel when trying to impress an adult who exudes confidence and authority. Their data appeared on his screen, divided into verdict tallies, arguments and counterarguments, and types of evidence, and the information surprised him. All of it, in terms of style, voracity, timing, fell into the average-to-above-average range. *So why aren't they logging onto real trials?* he thought. They all seemed to know how to perform. Perhaps it was a question of time. Too much pointless homework being given? Maybe the school day was too long? He would straighten that out with that dwarf of an assistant principal and that automaton of a superintendent after this frenzy was over. He watched the comment numbers grow, watched the messages get more personal and malicious. *Such wasted potential*, he thought. After each member of the first half of the class had left their comments, Colmsly moved forward.

"After the prosecution period…wait, never mind. The up-to-date Accused List for Runners' Landing has finally loaded. And I thought the most annoying part of this town was people not parking in their damn driveways.

What the hell is with that? The driveways are completely empty, but your damn cars sit there on the sides, clogging up traffic and destroying my mirrors!"

Colmsly took several deep breathes and calmed himself after his tangential rant before instructing, what was now his class, to read the names of the local Accused. Within a minute, the students were nudging each other, whispering, and pointing toward their so-quickly forsaken teacher. Jillian Foster began to cry as she ran from the room.

"Mr. Larkin," Leo Colmsly said, exposing his shoulder-harnessed 9 mm semi-automatic, "please step into the hallway."

4

"I think she signed out, George," was the response Alvarez had gotten when he had finally made it to the main office. The secretary, Henrietta Allen, had not only the longest tenure in the building but was also the true eyes and ears for any and all internal gossip—a role that was equally beneficial or incriminating depending on her fancy for you. He happened to be lucky: Henrietta liked him. With her proclivity for intruding into other people's business, she had adapted like bacteria to the new judicial system. It was the second topic she had brought up to George. "She didn't say a word, but I did see her by the sign-out book, and I did see her heading to her car. Have you tried calling her? You do know what's happened, right?"

"No, I haven't heard about anything. We've got an injured teacher, Mr. Larkin, who was bleeding all over the faculty lounge but, knowing him, probably will try to go to his next period, so if you could spare the gossip, I need to get a hold of someone who can help!"

"You obviously don't know."

"Henrietta, I don't have time for thi—"

"Larkin's been accused. I got the Medusa about five minutes ago. And according to my security monitor, he is already heading back to class, so you're a bit late on the help front."

While his brain searched to give his drying mouth a response, she swiveled in her chair, bent to her right, and snatched her phone from her purse.

"I thought you were his friend? How did you miss it?"

"I—I've been leaving my phone in the car because of Erica's treatment. What the hell did they say he did?"

"Read it," she said, handing him the phone. "See for yourself."

George carefully read through the message and charges.

"Do you think it's true? I mean, the girls do prance around him like he's Casanova or something. Maybe he's a molester and we've just never known!"

George looked up from Henrietta's phone, disgusted that she could lay out her suspicions so flatly. That honesty, however, was the foundation for the new system.

"How can you even think something like that? What kind of a person says that?"

He had thrown her phone into the nearest garbage can and left the office, not listening to her barrage of insults and threats, and turned toward the nurse's office. But before he'd gotten twenty feet down the hall, the bell rang, and students exited their classes like aimless cells being pumped through hardened veins. There was no fighting this tide, so he let it sweep him to his eighth period Critical Thinking course. He hadn't been able to focus after reading that message, and he knew why Erica had left and what she was now setting up to do. *Jimmy's head'll heal quickly*, he thought, *but I don't know how the hell he'll move on from this*. George had decided that he'd leave his class a little early to call his wife and check in on Larkin. He'd let the murmuring masses push him along and at the same time, Jimmy Larkin was being berated for his tardiness.

Critical Thinking.

George had been unable to get out of his final class early; he had to quell a brawl between two kids whom he would have loved to watch beat the shit out of each other.

"Say that again, bro, say it again!"

"I just fuckin' said it! You deaf?"

"I'm gonna fuck you up!"

"All right fellas, let's try and calm down," George tried interjecting.

"Don't tell me to calm down!"

"Then you better hit him or shut up and finish the goddamn project!" George yelled.

The unorthodox answer actually broke the tension long enough for Asshole B to storm out of the room and Asshole A to compose himself and sit down. The class, when they were done recording and snapping pictures, got back to their group work. The project was of the rhetorical variety, similar to what Larkin's earlier classes had been doing, except George tasked his students with researching the ethics and morality of cyber-terrorism, specifically the 2020 attack on automated factories and refineries. In the spring of that year, one of the most coordinated groups of hackers, self-described as the Mad-Hatters, had disabled every automated factory, port, refinery, and warehouse on the eastern seaboard. By corrupting the GPS signals that operated the machinery at each facility, they had been able to shut down global trade and commerce for forty-eight hours. Their claim for the action was described as a rebuttal to the ever-increasing layoffs and the notion that technology was the infallible substitute for the human worker. Those messages, along with their malleable mission statements (they had no real leadership structure) were immediately skewed by the traditional news organizations; they were dubbed, at the insistency of the owners of those corporate factories, ports, warehouses, refineries, and news organizations, as domestic terrorists. The business coalition and their purchased congressmen/women and senators obediently acquiesced; soon, the Hatters were hunted by every level of the US government. The group went from technological-working-class-heroes to terrorists against capitalism and consumerism in the manner of a single news cycle. Some of the brashest members were caught, but most remained free and anonymous, scattered across the world. Their techniques and identities still an enigma for the Big Four to solve.

The bell rang and George followed the last student out of the room, practically tripping her as he did. With all the agility he could conjure, he weaved through the adolescent teams of twos, threes, and fours. He tried to exercise some authority by barking commands, but the herds would not give. Most of them stared at their phones and the longer they peered down, the slower their feet moved. This pace was only infuriating to those who cared about their destinations; and those were a scant few. He swore that some of the smaller ones were simply lifted, pressed between chests and backpacks, like helpless wounded soldiers carried on Jansport litters. He was almost willing to become one of these powerlessly carried when he heard the commotion behind him.

"Let me go! Dammit, get off me! Get the hell off me!"

It was Larkin being dragged down the hall by two of the school's burly FileX security officers. George saw a fourth man following the guards but couldn't make out the name or insignia on the visitor's badge. If he had to guess, he was from AbowtMe or FileX and one of more prominent cronies based on the obvious absence of credentials. This raucous scene was one worthy of parting the hallway, so the students separated like schools of fish avoiding a voracious barracuda. These dividing fish, not to be confused as potential victims, always traveled with their phones at the ready. Instead of asking any type of questions or offering any type of help, the students switched their devices to record and captured Jimmy Larkin's pleas, threats, and desperation. They watched the one-sided struggle unfold through five and six-inch screens, streaming it live to any and all platforms. Some even put little effects on the officers and their squirming detainee: one girl placed devil horns on Larkin and halos above the guards; one boy turned Larkin into a penis and the FileX men into floppy testicles; another superimposed a striped prisoner suit over him and prison guard garb over the two agents. Finally, Mr. Larkin was brought out of the main entrance, and George was able to see that the fourth man were indeed the leader of this FileX pack. The students began competing to see who had edited the best scene. They laughed at the caricatures they created, cursed one another for copying styles, and then remembered that they had classes to get to. The bell rang, and George was left in the hallway, stupefied by what he'd just witnessed. As the final classroom door closed, he stepped forward a few floor tiles and found himself at the unlocked office of Nurse Donna Wallace.

He now realized that it was Friday and the district's sole nurse was probably at one of the elementary schools or the middle school. After the thought had processed, he went into her office, turned left into the bathroom, and splashed some cold water over his face and neck. He bent over the sink and watched the rivulets of water spiral down the uncovered drain, thinking about his wife, his friend, and the boundless apathy of the people around him. He looked up to the mirror but before he could start to rationalize the last few hours of his day, he heard footsteps coming toward the still-open office door. He switched off the light, swung the bathroom door shut, stopping its momentum just before it settled into its frame, turned the knob to avoid the giveaway *click!* of occupation, and moved against the far wall. Whoever had slowed near the office had not stopped to investigate the empty room, so George took advantage of the respite. He went to sit down on the toilet, but the sound and feeling of crinkling paper paused his squat. He took the essay from his back pocket and sat down onto the narrow seat. He stared down at the folded assignment and began to read.

Amending the Bill of Rights and How Social Media Can Steer America to a True Democracy

By: Aaron Elskin

By the end of the 20th century, America's judicial system had become a complete and utter disaster. Scores of African Americans and other minorities were overcrowding the jails, judges were being convicted of corruption, police officers were being accused of corruption and murder, and the drug wars had cost this country hundreds of billions of dollars since its inception. Something needed to be changed and with the 2016 election of former AbowtMe CEO, Emily Krauss, the stage was set for the most successful merger of government and business in US history: the streamlining of the American judicial system! By eliminating the bureaucratic tiered system of police officers, lawyers, judges, insurance companies, witnesses, etc., the new president was able to transfer, through social media platforms, the power of justice and law to the great patriots of our nation: the people. The people were given the power to review the facts, conduct their own research, listen to the testimony of the both sides, and render a quick decision (as the constitution and our forefathers originally intended), on the guilt or innocence of the defendant. Of course this idea was met with an outcry by those insider politicians who didn't want or like change, but the voice of the people was too strong. In the spring of 2018, the judicial branch of government was gloriously dismantled and in its place stood the powerful yet fair voices of the masses of the American people. The people did, however, need help connecting, so a new branch of government, branch 3.5 if you will, was created. The Technology branch of the government would act as the overseer of the new judiciary; four companies (AbowtMe, CenTek, Gazelle, FileX) wrote programs and algorithms that helped simplify the criminal justice system. AbowtMe connected all social media outlets and eliminated the old, cumbersome media outlets like print journalism and television news programs; CenTek wrote the algorithms that determined which cases appeared on any person's feed, managed each new 'juror' through popularity ranks, and developed the newest AI; Gazelle re-organized the police forces to make them more efficient at carrying out the people's sentences, and along with FileX, managed the smaller, more efficient system of prisons. While these companies were technically part of the government, each operated as an independent business, thus bringing about one of the most successful economic booms in history. Recently, this group of companies has come under fire from some anachronistic politicians, politicians who only want their power back, I might add. It's too bad for the old politicians because now the AbowtMe and FileX should create a system that would make the still-drawn-out public trial a thing of the past: they should write a program that would objectively streamline the judicial process. Juries, who are usually wrong anyway, should be replaced directly with AI judges. This way, we could simply watch justice get carried and we could all truly have justice served on the evil doers. This way, we could watch this country become even greater than it already is.

George stopped reading the propagandic drivel. The language and structure were maddening, but the tone is what made him feel like retching. He had seen too much of this ignorant, hubristic writing in the last five years, mainly from his supposedly top-tier students, so he knew what to expect from Aaron Elskin in next year's discussions: the boy would attempt to dominate any topic with pseudo-intellectual bullying; he'd quote his proudly ignorant parents, his tailored AbowtMe news feed, or his own prejudicial philosophies; he'd condescend to the girls with misogynistic comments; when threatened by logic, he'd repeat his nonsense in increasingly louder volumes until the others gave up or until he was threatened with disciplinary action. As far as George could discern, Mr. Elskin was developing into a fine new citizen juror. Ignorance before knowledge and emotions before facts. *I bet he's even concentrating on becoming a professional now*, George thought.

Opting to become a professional citizen juror was not a recognized job, per se—the minutiae between being a well-known juror and a true artisan in the field was difficult to define but earning real money as a juror depended on how many repeating followers were accrued and how many positive reviews could be accumulated during trial arguments and sentencing hearings. And while defense attorneys and prosecutors were legally forbidden to practice, a juror could become as shrewd and as knowledgeable of the law as they desired. The more popular a juror became—the more they were awarded with fake icons like golden gavels or iron handcuffs or favored status updates and comments—the more sponsors they could acquire. As their statuses in the system grew, more and more Accused and Accusers would request their help, and, with that increased clout, the more money they could earn. Once the people decided the quality and popularity of a juror's judgments (how they individually came to those conclusions, no one knew), the sponsors could identify those individuals by their collections of digital gavels, handcuffs, robes, and reward them accordingly. And if a digital juror became popular enough, some of the wealthier Accused or Accusers could take advantage of a burgeoning new market: spending copious amounts of money to sway decisions in their favor. In the new system, figuring out how to make online bullying lucrative had not taken very long. To further their participation rates, the Big Four began training the new generation of patriotic jurors by heavily investing in the education system. Appealing to the selfish nature of children and molding it into cruelty was not a difficult undertaking, nor was it a new developmental concept.

George tore the paper into uneven quarters and flushed it where it belonged. He had to get home to find out if Erica knew anything about Jimmy. He'd have to go into the office again to get his final class covered, but there wouldn't be much of a confrontation: once you pissed off Henrietta Allen, she didn't say a word to you...she just made it her professional ambition to destroy you behind your back.

5

Erica made herself comfortable. She sat in front of her screen in her spring-weight hoodie, braless, her favorite pair of worn pajama pants fitting loosely over her legs, a pair of striped fuzzy socks, and her hair up in a messy bun. Her headphones channeled house music as she scrolled through the rankings of each username who'd joined in for the opening procedures of Jimmy Larkin's trial. Her home office, a put-it-together-your-self desk, a stolen chair from school, a leather loveseat, her and George's framed diplomas, and a shelved wall full of alternatingly trashy novels, histories, and classic literature, was lit naturally through the west wall windows.

Only three hundred were logged on to read and watch the evidence; the day was still young and soon people would be getting home from work. She decided to send out some notifications. She shared the case on every one of her accounts, blanket messaged every one of her contacts, and turned off her music to make some old-fashioned calls.

"George, it's me. Listen, I think this is one we should do together. I think you should really see how the process works, and I want you to understand why I have to do it. When you get this, call me. Love you," she said to her husband's voicemail.

She left the headphones and her smartphone on the desk and went to the bathroom. She came back, drying her hands, and looked at the monitor and smiled: over ten thousand were now viewing the evidence. *People still love a good sex scandal*, she thought.

"Future shareholders of America," Principal Baker began, immediately adopting the language notes Colmsly had sent, "I've called this emergency assembly to address today's incident." The echoes of pubescent chatter muted at the mention of Larkin's arrest. "Because of some fine, honest, upstanding Accuser, Mr. Larkin's awful behavior has been brought to light,

47

and we—under the privileged guidance of Mr. Colmsly—are going to work together as a community to bring justice and righteousness to this proceeding. Your parents or guardians have already been notified and at the generous behest of our prestigious sponsor, AbowtMe, scholarships are being offered to those who log on with their parents and participate in Mr. Larkin's upcoming trial. You will have to use the school password and your individual password to qualify, so do not delay. Remember, you're going to demonstrate the skills of rhetoric and logic in this case, skills that you've practiced and honed here at Runners' Landing, so you must remember to be objective, resolute, and professional in your arguments. You must follow the guidelines and obey the moderator's instructions to deliver a fair and correct verdict. If you feel too small or scared or stupid to be a part of this important event, remember our always constant and correct motto: if you are not challenged, you cannot be changed. So, I say in that spirit, that you are all now challenged!"

George stood against the left wall, watching his and other students applaud for the end of Principal Baker's speech. Were they buying it? Were they just happy it was over? Were they just getting caught up in the moment and trying to cheer louder than their surrounding friends? He didn't know for sure, but he began to see dozens of phones light up with the AbowtMe Justice System homepage. He looked up from the rows to his principal on the stage. She was scanning the room like a perched bird of prey but through the oppressive stage lights, George doubted she could see much in the way of detail. *It sums up the way she runs the school*, he thought. A latent authority who proclaims but rarely participates.

"He's so guilty," George heard a girl say from two rows in front of him.

"You think so? He's got a pretty hot wife from what I've heard. Couple a kids, too."

"Seriously? He's literally flirted with every girl in our grade. I've even caught him checking out my tits when he checks our homework. He always pretends to look at my work, but I know he's trying to do."

"And you think he could possibly avoid doing that how exactly? I can see down your cleavage now and I'm looking at my phone, and I'd bet my summer home that the perv next to you has had a hard-on since you bent down before to move your bag."

"I'm not hiding anything on this body. It's smoking hot and I work hard to keep it that way. You like what you're seeing, Evan? Wanna take a closer look after school?"

"Uhh, I, uhh…"

"Stop messing with the kid and log in already, Cassie. I'm sure we can get extra credit on top of that other shit Baker was talking about."

"Whatever. I still say he's guilty, and I'm going to any way I can to prove it."

"You still coming to watch the softball game with me and Ryan?"

"Yeah, unless Evan here takes me up on my offer."

Evan's eyes widened and he ran from his seat, hunched over with his bag covering his crotch. The dangling shoulder strap tripped him, sending him crashing through the side door.

"You have all been a wonderful audience," the masses shot up, hearing the beginnings of the dismissal speech, so Baker hastened her pace, "and the buses are waiting, so please have a great weekend, and remember to be an active part of our glorious system!"

Progress, George thought. *Progress, indeed.*

"Strike two!"

"The hell it is!"

"How about you shut up and let the man do his job!"

"What'd you say to me, asshole?"

"I said shut up and let the umpire call the game!"

"How about you both calm down and let the girls get through this, huh?" The umpire tried.

"Don't tell me to calm down!"

"Yeah, you prick. Our taxes pay your salary!"

The umpire, Harold Higgins, a fifth-grade teacher at Runners' Landing Elementary, could do nothing but send both softball teams to their dugouts as he tried to defuse the ornery fans.

"I warned both bleachers after the third, and now I've got to—"

The two mothers went back at it, ignoring Harold's I'm-in-charge voice.

"Maybe if your little whore knew how to hit, the umpire wouldn't need to make up those shitty calls!"

"Whose daughter are you callin' a whore? Yours is so loose, she doesn't even need her hands to swing the bat!"

"What the hell does that mean?"

"Whore!"

"All right, I warned you!" Harold yelled. "Runners' Landing forfeits this game. It's over!"

"You can't do that to our girls, Higgins! They've got scholarships riding on these playoffs!" another parent yelled from behind the fence.

"I don't care! It's over! I've warned you too many times!"

The rage from both sidelines culminated in a gang-style brawl. The stampeding fans met one another just between the mound and home plate, and Harold fell beneath their feet, his screams of terror drowned out by the merging maniacs. The high school sports parent. A breed unrivaled in its selfish tenacity and prideful idiocy. At this booster club Battle of Hastings, mothers, fathers, aunts, uncles, and siblings punched, tore, clawed, pulled, spit, kicked, and kneed one another right in front of their horrified daughters, nieces, sisters, cousins, and girlfriends. Pollockian splatters of blood drizzled across home plate and both foul lines; first base flew through the air, its anchoring metal pipe shattering Harold Higgins' front teeth; an unclaimed bat swung a vicious arc until it struck the-supposed-mother-of-the-whore's face, breaking her left orbital bone.

Discerning exactly who was who became difficult through the dusty carnage, but Kristy Shine scanned the infield until she found at least one of her parents. She watched her father pummel one of the opposing parents with a fold-up lawn chair. *He'll be in jail tonight,* she thought. *Probably Mom, too,* she continued thinking, but she couldn't seem to find her. As she began to look through the outfield, she heard the sirens storming closer. She turned and saw a half-dozen officers descending onto the diamond.

The police still existed except their purpose in this era had largely been diminished to maintaining order and keeping detailed video files of any incident they witnessed or were called to. The average cop on the beat no longer arrested people in the traditional sense—unless the perps were a true danger to themselves or to the other officers—nor did they any longer detain people who were awaiting trials in precincts or prisons. Each officer was now fitted with multiple cameras—front of the shoulders, back of the shoulders, hat, feet, and on both sides of the belt—and their evidence videos were immediately streamed to real-time jurors who made instant sentencing decisions. Someone somewhere was always logged on and watching, and when crimes did occur, outside of Proxy Accusations, these constant-jurors oversaw the expedited judicial process. On each juror's screen, there were four or sometimes five multiple-choice options (options created and monitored by a CenTek artificial intelligence program) for punishments and depending on the ratio of circumstantial evidence to direct evidence, the viewer made his or her choice. Any voyeur could replay the scenes of the offense, watch it from different angles, enhance and narrow audio clips, switch perspectives to other officers or security cameras, or see it unfold from any other eyewitness footage. After any incident was neutralized, the tallies of A, B, C, D, or E were compiled by a CenTek program, and the verdicts were sent to the responding officers through their earpieces, AbowtMe watches, and phones, ensuring that justice was fairly and quickly served.

So, this is what was directing the officers who were trying to diffuse and detain Kristy's father, mother, and other members of the insanity; thousands of online participants and a quantum powered AI.

Bailey Tomanicki joined Kristy at the chain link fence, watching the chaos but seeing none of it.

"Hey, I'm sorry about what happened in class, today," Bailey said.

"What *happened*—don't pull this passive crap, Bay."

"All right, I'm sorry that I was being a stuck-up bitch in class. I just get really heated by that stuff, and I guess..." she could see that Kristy didn't want to hear any excuses, "Why don't you come over tonight? We'll forget about school and just chill."

"I just don't know why you treat everyone, especially me, like shit all the time! Then, when it's good for you, you come around and expect everything to be all right!"

Bailey looked down, unsure how to respond. Her peace offering was being rejected. She hadn't planned for this variable in her equation, so she stayed quiet, looked up through the wiry rhombuses of the fence, and saw the security guards and policemen finally regaining some order.

"I just don't get any of this either," Kristy said nudging toward the filthy mass of parents.

"Don't worry. I'm sure we'll get a chance to ruin our kids' fun and dreams someday, too. But I am really sorry about today, and I don't know why I behave like that sometimes, and we've been friends for too long, so I promise to stop being such a—"

"Whatever, Bailey. What time should I come over?" Kristy didn't want to delve any further into the psychological facets of their friendship. She just wanted things to fall back into their familiar albeit annoying roles.

"Come at seven, and we'll get some pizza," she said, smiling.

"When do you think this is gonna end?"

"I don't know but hopefully someone will be able to get us outta here, and check this out," she said, showing her phone to Kristy. "While we eat, we're going to join a trial."

Kristy saw the forwarded text on the screen. "That couldn't be true! Mr. Larkin would never do that, especially with a student. How the hell did we not find out about this sooner? Besides, we're not old enough to be jurors, so why even bother?"

"It all went down after we left for the tournament, at some assembly. I'm gonna bring this up with someone, how Coach Saunders doesn't let us look at our phones on the bus or during warmups—I'm pretty sure that's illegal. Screw that bitch, because I checked my phone just before the Jets and the Sharks went at it and saw this message from Cassie. We're totally being a part of this and we're totally going to use my stepdad's account," she said. "And don't worry about it, he's probably going to spend the night getting his ass beat by FileX officers. Look. Getting cuffed as we speak."

"That takes your stepdad outta the picture, but what about your mom? She'll know if we're logged on under their account."

"She's the one who showed me how to do it, and don't worry about it. We've got permission from the school. Don't be a pussy. We're going to stuff our faces, have a few beers, and decide whether Larkin's the stand-up guy everyone thinks he is or if he's just a perv who likes to stick it in his students. I'm literally not taking no for an answer."

"Fine, but I'm just going to watch. See if you can find some vodka instead of beer. I'll try to be there a little after seven."

At 6:45 p.m. Erica had closed out the active juror list and organized—with the help of the FileX system—who would be prosecuting and who would be defending Mr. James S. Larkin, accused statutory rapist, when she heard the front door open. She didn't want a fight; she wanted him to accept this side of her personality, to not see it as a life-controlling addiction but as her new vocation, her true calling. Instead of an exhausting screaming match, she would try seducing him with the process; she would open her husband up to the rush that had so completely taken her. *He would be tired*, she thought, so his temper would falter if she countered it with feigned submissiveness, and if she figured it right, he, after a long, even-stranger-than-usual Friday, would not want a drawn-out, deleterious fight. She unzipped the front of her hoodie, exposing the inside curves of her breasts, and went to meet him at the top of the staircase.

"I want you to see something," she said, before he could say anything.

He stood on the landing, looking as tired as his untucked shirt and scuffed shoes suggested.

As she looked down the stairs at him, she lithely hooked her thumbs into the front pockets of her sweatshirt and pulled down on the light-gray fabric. "Before you yell or criticize or tell me how much I've changed, I want you to come with me. I want you to watch me do what I really love."

"But how could you just leave like tha—"

She had already started walking toward the office, her right hand raised up next to her ear, her index finger beckoning him to follow.

6

"Are you sure you don't want another slice?"

"I'm fine Bailey. I forgot my Lactaid pills, so unless you want me leaving skid marks on your air mattress, I'll stick with two."

"Well, grab your beer and sit right there," Bailey said, motioning to the swivel chair in front of the monitor, "I'm going to show you how it's done."

"I still don't like this. Weren't able to find any flavored vodka?"

"You'll never know 'til you try, and I forgot to check. I'll be right back."

"We've known him for nearly ten years, Erica. There's no way that any of this is true!"

"Sweetheart, that's why this is so great...if he's innocent, the people will tell us; if he's guilty, the people will punish him. George, don't look at me like that. These aren't our idiot students; these are experienced jurors, and can you honestly tell me you know that much about Jimmy? We haven't seen him or his family since last summer. They stopped inviting us over, his kids are nuts—"

"His kids are all under five! Of course they're outta their minds! And how can you call these morons who anonymously sit in their houses and judge strangers guilty or innocent experienced! Any asshole with a grudge can log onto these trials, hell, they can start a trial, and destroy someone else's life!"

"George, sit down," she said, turning the office chair toward him, "because I already logged you on to counter these so-called 'assholes.' Who's better to defend this Accused (she would no longer refer to Jimmy by name) than you?"

George stared at the inviting glow of the screen, saw the background picture of him and Erica on their honeymoon, then over to his wife, and followed her directing eyes to the black cushion of the chair. He thought of one more tactic he could use against Erica's well-maneuvered offensive: calling her psychiatrist, Dr. Verma. How could he, though? His phone was downstairs in his briefcase and using the old landline would be too obvious. He gave up the idea and saw that his wife had lost patience with his indecision; she moved toward him and he felt her take his hand, felt the warmth and love in that grip. She guided him into the chair like a nurse leading a frail, confused patient back to bed.

"After you sign in, you get to pick an avatar and juror name," Bailey said.

"I thought the Accused had a right to know who the jurors?"

"Nope. Only AbowtMe knows who everyone is. They know your account info but you can be anyone you want during a trial. Fun, right? They explained that it's like being one of those, like, hangmen who wore those black hoods with the eyeholes cut out because if you have to give someone the death penalty, it's better to be anonymous or something like that."

"We can be responsible for killing Mr. Larkin?" Kristy said, horrified.

"I doubt it. This is a level III crime."

"How do you know that?"

"You see that little icon next to his profile pic, tap it."

Kristy enlarged the image on the screen and double-clicked. It opened into a new window and inside, just as Bailey had said, was an explanation of the level III offense: the maximum sentence for a guilty verdict was exile with a concurrent loss of digital identity.

"Exile? What century is this? How would that even be enforced?"

"I'm pretty sure that AbowtMe and CenTek can erase you pretty quickly from the internet, and I guess FileX and everyone in your community make sure you leave town."

"Whatta you mean 'leave town'? Can your family come with you? How much time do they give you to get out? Are you allowed to—"

"Kristy! I'm not an expert! You have to read about these details during the sentencing part of the trial. I've only watched my mom and Frank do that part a handful of times."

"I'm sorry. I never paid attention when they went over this in school. They usually just have us go after each other like animals during the simulations, so I just put on my music and play games. What's next?"

"Don't worry about it. Now that we're logged in, look at the accusations and the evidence—yup, just click right there for them—it's really not hard. Any idiot can do it."

Kristy tapped the screen where Bailey had directed her to do so, timidly touching it as if someone were judging her on that as well. *Who do I want to be?* she thought as she scrolled through the thousands of options of thumbnail pictures.

"Now that you've been assigned your first-ever avatar, decide whether you want to prosecute or defend," Erica guided.

"Which one am I, again?"

"You ran out of time during the selection process, so you're the black silhouette with the red question mark."

"Oh. Is that bad?"

"It's absolutely fine. Like I said before, most beginners choose the question-mark-head. I guess it makes them feel even more anonymous," she reassured. "Because it's your first time, and because you know the Accused, I think you should go with the defense."

"Guess so," he said.

"You want to go with the prosecution, huh! Good for you, you sadistic bitch! I knew you had it in there somewhere," Bailey said with a sarcastic laugh. "Guess he's not your absolute favorite teacher, huh?"

"He's all right, but Jillian Foster! That skank! She probably was doing him! He's so chill, doesn't care about homework, will help you with anything, and he is kina cu—"

"Relax! Jeez, jealous much? That's only what Rachel told me, so I don't know if it's true. Let me go ask Sean if he's heard anything," Bailey said.

"Your stepbrother's gross. Do not let him come up here."

"Relax. He only convinced my parents that he needs to constantly jerk-off at school because he hates that place. By the time he gets home he's too raw and tired to do anything."

"Bet you would know, you filthy bitch," she teased her friend.

"That's gross, and screw you."

"So, he isn't mental?"

56

"Not as much as my parents think. He's definitely got his issues and he really should be on something, but he's getting a little better as he gets older. When my mom and Frank went new-age, they banned medicine in the house, kinda weird for a nurse, right? I can't even take a Midol when I need it, and Sean had a rough time for a while. I think he's learned how to self-medicate on top of all the..." She was at a loss for words, so she just bobbed a clenched fist up and down and made a face she assumed was reserved for male orgasms.

"Whatever. Just don't bring him up here, please," Kristy pleaded.

"But he tells me that he thinks you're hot! Might be strokin' it right outside the door, for all we know. Relax, sit down. I'm just kidding. Drink your vodka. I'll be right back."

Bailey had gotten a few steps out of the bedroom before Kristy heard her scream, "Sean, if it's out, put it away, I have to ask you something!"

"According to Henrietta's group message, it was Jillian Foster. You know her, George?"

He cringed at Henrietta's mentioned name as if it were a hex that needed to be exorcised from the room. "Yeah, I know the Foster girl, but only from lunch duty. There's just no way this is true. The girl's got some troubles— shit, I think her family's been living in that motel for months—and Jimmy would never to that to his wife."

"We're not up to that part, yet, so don't jump ahead. This process only works if each part goes in order. All you have to do at this point is review the presented evidence and videos. Look at the texts they sent back-and-forth to each other; the messages seem to get more personal as the weeks go on."

"He was tutoring her. She had missed a lot of school, Erica. I'm not saying it's appropriate to text a student, but you're drawing conclu—"

"I'm not drawing anything, dear. I'm showing an amateur how to look for details in the massive amount of evidence and testimony. You could pay attention and learn something or you could keep interrupting me."

He had only ever seen her take control like this when they had role-played in bed. Now he was wondering, after all these years, which of these Ericas had been the performer. "I'm sorry, sweetie. I just learn fastest when I ask as many questions as possible. I'll save them for when I'm really confused."

Her eyes remained on the screen. "It's fine. Just try and keep up because the clock is moving. Next, take a look, an objective I-don't-know-this-man-from-anyone-else look, at the cell phone videos of Jimmy entering the motel room at 3:15 p.m. and not leaving until 6:38 p.m. From what I know of tutoring, our sessions are only supposed to last two hours."

George didn't want to point out that Erica was beginning to speculate just as he had earlier. He stayed quiet.

"George!"

"What, Erica?"

"Are tutoring sessions no longer two hours at the high school?"

"No, they're still two-hour blocks, once a week. That is a little strange now that you mention it…"

"It is, but let's move on to the other clips and testimonies."

"So, what if he was there late? Jillian's a dumbass, nice set on her, but still a dumbass," Sean said. Bailey's stepbrother, the nineteen-year-old self-made rebel had joined the pizza party sleep over—even after Kristy's vociferous objections—and had begun reviewing the written and recorded evidence with them. "I've had tutors stay over-time before. Remember when I messed my knee up, Bailey? I even tried to screw that math tutor who came around, even with my torn-up MCL, but, nah, she wouldn't go for it. She ended up staying late bunches of times because I couldn't get geometry."

"You don't get anything, you dumbass," Bailey said, sounding more nasty than playful.

Sean stared at her for a few moments and said, "I get enough to know that this juror system you like so much is totally fucked up. How the hell are groups of morons supposed to understand the law, argue so it makes sense, and then decide someone's guilt or innocence so quickly? You know how many people are probably working their lives away at those labor camps because of dumb ass little girls like you two who wanna play juror? Whoever agreed to change it all to this were some real suckers."

"There are no such things as labor camps, Sean. Reform groups, rehabs, and special detox hospitals help anyone who's guilty get themselves straight. Or, if they are truly deranged or dangerous, they're kept in Gazelle's open-nature facilities until they can be released back into society or kept until they're dead. And how was it any better when only super-rich people could pay good lawyers to get away with practically anything! You remember that millionaire who lit his own mansion on fire 'cause he thought his wife was screwing their live-in chef? It happened a few miles from us. The rebuilt house is in the same place overlooking the Sound."

"Yeah, I remember that. Happened when we were kids. Some electrical fire, right?"

"Yeah, 'cause most electrical fires conveniently happen when both your wife and her supposed lover are drugged and past out? That fire burned through the property and jumped to the house on the west side of them and killed two kids and their au pair. The rich-arsonist husband got off with nothing because he could afford lawyers good enough to convince at least one of the twelve schmucks on his jury that it was all an accident. That's the type of system you think is just?"

"Was it perfect, nah. Is this better? Not a chance."

"If it's so screwed up, how come you're hanging out with those losers down at the militia clubhouse so much?"

His right eyelid twitched a little as the correct answer bounced around in his brain. It was in there, careening around like those lotto balls waiting to get sucked up and read aloud, but just like most people's luck with the winning numbers, Sean's correct thoughts never made it out. This was true with much of his thought processes, so in lieu of trying to explain to her that the support and camaraderie he had found at the Long Island Freedom Fighters militia had been more stabilizing for him than anything he had with his family or his school or his few friends, he just threw out an automatic diversionary response, "You're as naïve as you are hot, Bails."

"That's gross. You're my brother."

"Just by a step," he said, getting up. "I think I'm going to do something more productive anyway with my boy, Lamont. Lemme know what happens to Larkin, will ya? He's actually one of the few teachers I can stand."

"Try to stay out of trouble. And we're out of hand lotion thanks to you, so don't hurt yourself," Bailey said with a sneer.

Kristy watched as Sean left the room. He wore his pants a little too low for her taste, but he was definitely not as disgusting as she had previously assumed.

"Pay attention," Bailey said, focusing back on their evening entertainment. "It's time to start the opening arguments. This is where it gets fun!"

"What you have to remember when you're arguing at this point are the facts. There are going to be so many imbeciles spouting so much nonsense that you will want to shut down and leave. Don't. Don't be led into straw-man arguments; don't fall for red herrings; don't accept specious reasoning of any kind. You're here to follow the facts to their conclusions," Erica commanded.

George now sat like an eager pupil at his very own tutoring session. "You're not allowed to kick out the people making those types of arguments?"

"Only if they repeatedly make violent threats or if they try to expose anyone's true identity. Other than that, the other jurors decide who gets the most exposure in the threads by clicking on those little happy face icons next to the usernames. If they don't like what someone's saying, or if they're just trolling, the people will click on the frowny face next to the username. The more times the happy face gets hit, the more your posts are broadcast. If your frowny face gets hit too many times, your comments won't be read by anyone. Eventually, if you really suck, all you'll be able to do is log onto trials and watch. You'll always be allowed to type, but what you type will never be seen. It's kind of an incentive to not be an instigator."

"That makes sense, I guess," he said flatly.

"Of course, it does. Now, select a username."

"How about this," he said and typed on the keyboard. "I've always admired who he was."

"ImNoClarenceDarrow it is," she said.

"All right Kristy! Are you ready? We'll do the first part together. Don't get too distracted by the bullshit; if there's someone you really want to get into it with, click to comment directly under their username and go to town. That's the username you chose? Really? WhatsRightIsRite?"

"I don't know, it's kinda a reference to a character I liked named Piggy. You remember him from that book we read in Larkin's class, *Lord of the Flies*? He was the weakest and he was only trying to help and he got killed when he finally had the guts to stand up for himself. It pissed me off! Whatever, leave me alone?"

"No, it's, uh, fine, just don't be surprised if you get shit for it during the trial."

"Why would anyone make fun of me for that?"

"Doesn't sound a bit righteous to you? Never mind, forget it! I'm excited for you! Take another sip and let's get into it. Yay!" Bailey said, clapping her hands.

You are now joining the opening arguments for the People against Jimmy Larkin, Case No. SR28-473-8719. The Accused is being tried for one felony count of statutory rape, one misdemeanor count of endangering the welfare of a minor, and three felony counts of misuse of a Gazelle device to commit a crime. By clicking on the box below, you're confirming that you have read and agree to the Citizen Juror Terms.

Be aware that any violation of these terms will result in immediate arrest and prosecution.

You May Now Comment in the Opening Arguments:

– ImNoClarenceDarrow: Ladies and Gentlemen of the jury. I've known Jimmy Larkin for nearly ten years, and I can adamantly say that he is a caring, honest, law-abiding family man who would never do anything like what's been described in the charges. His professional record is nearly immaculate, he's an active member of his community, and he is renowned among his students and colleagues. If you look at the evidence, and some of it is very hard to evaluate because the quality is so poor, you will see a dedicated teacher who stays beyond the required tutoring time to help a disadvantaged student.

– Kill'emAllandLetGodSort'emOut: Excuse me, but you sound like a pussy who was hired by this molester to buy his freedom. Most teachers screw their students and this lowlife is no different. You saw the videos! If you watched the same videos I did you saw that he came outta her room and his fly was open, and his dick was still out. I SAW IT! YOUR JUST SOME

ASSHOLE WHOSE PROB BONING HIS OWN STUDENTS AND DOESN'T WANT TO HAVE LARKIN BLOW UP YOUR SPOT!!!

– *LooserLips: Im sorry, but 'evidence that's hard to evaluate'? Please. The videos are as clear as any FileX bodycam, I should know because I once worked at FileX, and even thought I didn't see his dick hanging out, I did see his shirt out of his pants, and now that Im looking again, his fly is definitely open. That just might be his shirt sticking through his fly, tho, Kill'em. Are you telling me that Larkin stayed late every week to help this girl? Please. Teachers don't do anything unless their being paid, so don't tell me he wasn't forcing himself on that poor girl.*

– *MakeUSgreatAgain: Why do we even have teachers anymore? Taxes are high enough on Long Island as it is!!! The only reason anyone would want to still be a teacher is 'cause they wanna have sex with teenage girls!!! Let's get rid of this pervert and lower our bills!!!!!*

– *Inothelaw: Darrow, do you even no the law?? I doubt it. Try looking it up before you join a trial. Fucking newb. You're literally giving me a rage headache and its only the opening statements! And Clarence Darrow, srsly!? Can you choose a more privileged, old, white male as your name? Take your racist username and go fuck off!!! Kill urself and let people who no the law take care of this.*

– *IFillAllHoles: Racist name? Are YOU serious Ino?? Did you even spell Clarence Darrow right in your search?? He was the farthest thing from a racist! What, are you just finishing your first sociology class at Suffolk Community?*

– *Inothelaw: STFU ^ asshole. White-male privilege is over in this country and where going to prove that by sending Larkin the kid-toucher to wear he belongs! OR U CAN JOIN HIM AND KILL URSELF 2!!!*

– *WhatsRightIsRite: Um, I don't know exactly what happened and I guess none of us but Mr. Larkin and Jillian Foster do, but she's pretty well-known around school as being a slut, and who knows, maybe Mr. Larkin did screw her, but I don't think he should be kicked out of town for it. Maybe just fired.*

"Jesus, Kristy! I leave to pee and that's what you type! You can't name the victim! It's against the rules for this trial! And you slut-shamed her, a girl who was possibly raped! What the hell is wrong with you? How much did you drink?"

– OodlesofPoodles: Ummm, what kind of sicko are you? Did you break into Mommy's computer? Is that it? And how dare you name the helpless victim!? You need to leave, dirtbag, and you need to leave fast. Can we please downgrade this idiot as much as possible, pls? Someone wanna tell the Mod, thanx!

 – NeilBeforeMe: Downgraded. What a tool. Mod notified.

  – KeepsItHairy: Downgraded. I hope he or she kills herself!

  – Justice4All: Downgraded, and ^ why don't you use a gender neutral identifier like "they" instead of he or she? Maybe WhatsRightIsRite doesn't identify as strictly a male or female?

   – KeepsItHairy: Oh voice of the gender oppressed! Fearless guardian of the ever-offended! Maybe you offend me by using the Oppressor's English. In fact, don't talk to me until you use a language that hasn't been used to oppress minorities, women, gays, lesbians, trannies, etc.

   – Justice4All: ^ Fuck you

"Erica, can't you do something about this thread? That person WhatsRightIsRite did violate the rules of the trial."

George got up and she slipped into the chair. They had been sitting and sifting information for hours in the same uncomfortable positions. He stretched his back as she tapped on her settings icon but the usual tools would not highlight. She tried several different commands but nothing seemed to work. "I don't know. You see that grey icon? It should be black, and I should be able to highlight and click it. Nothing changes when I hit it or drag the mouse over it. Let me notify a manager."

Erica clicked on the little phone icon and after a few rings, a voice came through her speakers. Usually a video window would accompany the audio, but that too had malfunctioned. Not the most fortuitous of starts for her first trial as a Moderator.

"This is Colmsly."

"Yes, hello. This is Erica Primm-Alvarez, Mod No. 8016-F, and there seems to be something wrong with my settings. I need to remove a juror who's both violated the trial terms and has been downgraded by the thousands within 20 minutes."

"You are no longer authorized for removals of any kind, 8016-F."

"But, sir, the terms clearly say—"

"Don't you fucking dare talk back to me! You are no longer authorized to remove any citizen from anything. According to our video display, you are not the one moderating this trial. I assume that twat standing behind you is your husband. You, dear boy, need to grow a pair, and you Mrs. Erica Primm-Alvarez, Moderator No. 8016-F, should be more concerned with knowing your terms of service than what some idiot citizens are saying in a pointless trial!"

"But, sir, I have been closely monitoring—"

"You've been giving your husband a happy little tutorial when you should have been doing your job! If you really had read those terms of service, you'd damn well know that we monitor everything you say, see, and type in your first year. Yes, it's not just in the trial itself; wave to the camera on your monitor! Smile and blow me a kiss. If you feel like it, you can pull that zipper down some more. If not, you can just sit there looking shocked. And you can also consider yourself demoted. Have a nice night."

George tried as best he could to embrace Erica, but she was hunched forward in the chair, as if getting closer to the computer might reverse the sudden rejection that had just happened. Erica started when George's arms wrapped around her.

"I'm sorry for barking orders at you like you were some slave, honey," she said as she turned to see him. "You didn't deserve that. I'm really tired, though, so I'm going to turn in."

"It's all right. We'll talk about it more in the morning. It's been a long week. I'll meet you in there in a few. I'll shut this down and feed Shinnie."

George went downstairs to feed and let out their yellow lab, Shinnecock. The four-year-old dog was huddled by the door, minutes away from having his first accident in over three years.

"I'm sorry, boy," George said, scratching Shinnie's ear. He opened the screen door, and the dog contorted through the narrowest opening between the door and its frame and darted for the backyard. George looked to where the dog had run but saw little through the screen and obfuscating back porch light. As he waited, he thought he heard a faint scream from down the road followed by some lower-pitched yelling. *It might've been from much farther,* he thought, but it was very difficult to gauge; he never understood how people were able to tell the distance of an oncoming or outgoing thunderstorm, something about counting the seconds between booms he could never remember, and he found that trying to discern where the voices had come from was impossible. Screeches in the night were infrequent in Runners' Landing, especially what he had just heard; the shriek had sounded, he decided, like someone in pain.

He switched off the light, as if it would help his hearing, and listened again. Silence and darkness seemed to expand and his eyes seemed unable to focus on anything except the mesh of the screen door. He opened it and stepped out onto his deck; he could no longer hear the dull jingling of Shinnie's tags.

"Shinnecock! Come 'ere, boy!"

Shinnecock bounded toward his voice, and George turned to open the door. Just as he touched the handle, he heard another scream. This one sounded much clearer, and the pitch and tone told him that it was made by the same person as the previous one. He thought it sounded like, "My baby" or "My lady." He listened for a few more moments, heard nothing else, and went inside to join Erica.

"Kristy, you've got to stop crying. Please, stop. It's all right, I'm sorry I freaked. Have another drink."

"No! What the hell's gonna happen now! Are your parents gonna find out! I'm so sorry!" She said through sobs.

"Please calm down. Look, nothing seems to be happening at all. You've been downgraded more than anyone I've ever seen, but you're still in the trial. That's actually really weird—you should've been booted by now."

"I don't care about the trial anymore, and I don't feel well. Can we please just go to sleep?"

Bailey was listening to her friend like she often listened in school—with only one ear. She had seen plenty of people banned from the trials she had watched with her mother and stepfather, and those people had been excused for much less. If you just went off on a tangent or if you randomly harassed people and if you got reported enough times, you'd get barred from the proceedings.

"Bailey, can we please turn that off and go to sleep?"

Bailey looked down at the digital clock in the corner of the screen. How was it already 11:34 p.m.? "Sure, just let me make sure we stay logged on; I want to see the updates as soon as we get up."

7

1 New Message from Unknown Number: You're a slut!!!!! How could you cheat on Marcus!!! I H8 U!!!

2 Messages, 1 New from Unknown Number: Don't eva show ur face in this town again SKANK!!!

3 Messages, 1 New from Unknown Number: You and your family are disgusting!!! U should of burned with your house!

4 Messages, 1 New from Unknown Number: Did you think he'd get you into college if you put out, u slut! He's got a wife and kids. Just Ewwww!

5 Messages, 1 New from Tyler: You won't even give my boy Marcus the pussy but you give it up to a teacher!?!?

6 Messages, 1 New from Valerie: A girl in Boston got caught doing something like this and hung herself... I think you should do the same. Nothing worse than a homewrecking slut!

7 Messages, 1 New from Unknown Number: Everyone knows that you did it, so just spare urself the embaresment and slit your wrists!

8 Messages, 1 New from Marcus: We gotta talk. Text me when U get this.

9 Messages, 1 New from Unknown Number: How much U charge? Is it by the hour or can I have you on ur back all night for a flat rate? Don't worry about the rubbers, I'll bring plenty for your filthy ass.

10 Messages, 1 New from Sam: U were always tryin' to get me to watch porn at those sleepovers!!! I knew you was a slut!! Maybe being around wouldn't be the best idea U should leave and do it quickly...

Jillian's phone had reached its capacity for text messages. She couldn't bring herself to check her AbowtMe page or any of her other accounts. She flicked through her favorites, found Marcus' picture, part of the selfie they had taken together at the beach, and pressed it. After three rings, she heard his monotone voice, "I told you to text me. I'm at work, and I can't talk.

Shift's over at eleven, so I'll pick you up at eleven fifteen. Be ready, and just get in the car when I pull up."

"None of this is true, I don't know why it's…" His end had gone quiet. She cried even harder and buried her head into her folded forearms.

"Jillian, honey, please open the door!" her mother pleaded. "I only want to help you, but you have to tell me why I keep getting all these messages! Please open the door!" she yelled, helplessly twisting the knob.

Just as she'd done since she ran hysterically crying from their take-out dinner, Jillian ignored her mother's inquiries and offerings of help. Her mother was strong and resourceful, but she could never fix something like this—no adult could in teenage logic. Jillian had spent the evening scouring her social media accounts, before being frightened away by hecklers and trolls, trying to figure out why the fading rumors, the ones that Victoria Slake had started after winter break, had returned like some vindictive adolescent Phoenix. She and Vicky, as she had always addressed her friend until recently, had been close all through middle school and most of ninth and tenth grade, but then Vicky became Victoria, started hanging out with a popular online crowd, and had for some baffling reason, chosen her old friend Jillian as her new whipping post. Jillian tried to maintain her old I-don't-care-what-you-think-about-me persona in school, but the herd turned against her like T-cells against a virus. She loved her family, her boyfriend, and tried as best she could to avoid drama unless there was no alternative. She and Marcus had been planning and looking forward to, like most other juniors, the upcoming prom; she started searching for colleges; she endured, along with her two siblings, living in a dilapidated motor lodge while their scorched house was razed and rebuilt, and she was maintaining an honors level GPA through all of it. Despair and disgust poisoned her blood, filled her stomach with what felt like gallons of acid, and froze her mind as she sat in her temporary room. The more she tried to make sense of what was happening, the harder she cried.

"He'll under…he'll understand," she said through sobs, looking at the digital clock on her phone, willing it to move to 11:15 p.m. "This is all a mistake," she said to the metallic and plastic rectangle in her hand.

8

Bailey—and across town, George and Erica—fell into their respective sleep patterns. Only Kristy's was disturbed, once by the incredible pressure alcohol puts on a drunk teenager's bladder and once more by the need to guzzle as much water as she possibly could. Bailey had masturbated herself to sleep, a tactic she pretended not to have adopted from Sean's advice. George Alvarez had only partially awakened once to nudge his interloping wife back to her side of the queen size mattress. Shinnecock got up, spun twice counterclockwise and once clockwise before laying down in exactly the same position. Sean Reilly skipped bedtime and a masturbation session to meet up with his friend Lamont Davis to see what adventures could be found on in the sleepy town.

The world exists in both active and dormant periods. It might not seem that strange, therefore, to think that all things wake and sleep in normal cycles. It is seen in the night and day, in the spring and winter, in sickness and health, and in life and death, this pattern of off and on and on and off, but this way of understanding the world cannot be applied to the indefatigable internet, nor can it be used to correctly describe cerebral activity: neither the brain nor the internet, in the courses of their existences, ever stop firing. In creating the interminable Web, engineers invented the closest thing they could to a sentient mind. In 2019, though, an intrepid coalition of AbowtMe, FileX, CenTek, and Gazelle engineers had created the next step in the Web's development: a preternatural system that was incapable of malfunctioning, that ceaselessly grew and adapted to every piece of data it calculated; one that could begin to make decisions on its own. This, however, still wasn't the pinnacle of their achievements. Within the following year, these engineers and mathematicians, supported by the limitless wealth of the Big Four, developed newer, ever-shrinking hardware and increasingly faster software, and when they thought it was efficient enough for everyone's use, those crafty men and women modified it again to have it function at the quantum level. It was a miraculous achievement. The celebrations in companies and countries alike were raucous when the Web began solving even more adverse equations and calculations on its own. Decisions like how wars could be won before they were fought, how trade partnerships should be outlined, who should work where and what type of job they should perform, where cars should be driven and how fast they should go, how long anyone should stay with a significant other, who that significant other should be, and who should be allowed to reproduce and how many children they ought to have. And even though the system worked out the best chances for each scenario, the companies and governments, at that time, still had the control to ignore the preferred results. Even more surprising, especially to the paranoids of the world, was that these monumental breakthroughs in artificial intelligence failed to evolve into Frankensteinesque creatures that turned on and slaughtered their creators. The AI simply performed, and as the new governor of the Web, the world, really, it was neither malicious nor benevolent by design; it had and still has no understanding of right and wrong. In that sense the AI was considered, at least by some of its coders and a dozen or so philosophers, to be the closest thing humanity would ever understand as a divine consciousness.

The leaders from all areas, business, government, education, law, medicine, criminal justice—and through old fashioned corruption, organized crime—could all access the AI's information and best-case-scenario functions, but its applications were determined to be the most beneficial for the United States in reforming the criminal justice system—a system that had become overly cumbersome, corrupt, and unjust. While it was far from being the most violent or politically retributive in the world, the exuberant costs of maintaining both private and publicly run jails had become a topic of reform that garnered support from both major parties. Democrats could claim that they were advancing social justice in their local and national campaigns and Republicans would finally have an opportunity to win over a larger portion of voters who had any type of pigment or accent. The third and minor parties cried foul over the desecration of the Constitution and civil liberties, but like it had always been when libertarians or the Green Party constituents objected, nobody listened. And while the AI achieved monumental results in potentially solving energy and religious conflicts throughout the world, the Middle East in particular, the industry and religious leaders of those areas spent millions to ensure that America's elected officials ignored the reports and statistics. The private prison firms did not have the capital to lobby congress like the energy and technology fields had, and the judiciary branch, from the federal to the state levels, had alienated too many on the left and right over the years, so the bench was left alone to try and fight for its own existence. Budgets were slashed, names were slandered, and court vacancies went unfilled. What easier target for the public's rancor than judges and lawyers? So criminal justice reform it was.

The proposed alterations to the Constitution and the loss of thousands of honest lawyers and judges were the primary obstacles to overcome, but the social outrage and ubiquitous feelings of insecurity that existed in the late teens and early twenties of the 21st century mixed to form the perfect broth for a revolution. With the combination of a bursting student-loan bubble, rampant crime, high levels of mistrust in authorities of all levels, high unemployment and underemployment, crumbling infrastructure, and ever-increasing poverty, companies like AbowtMe, FileX, CenTek, and Gazelle recognized an opportunity to solve those pressing issues and to make absurdly lucrative deals for themselves in the process. Emily Krauss, then CEO of AbowtMe, united the tech and security companies and designated herself and her staff as the liaisons who spoke before the Senate Judiciary Committees and the Justice Department representatives. As the chief negotiator, Krauss offered the government agencies AbowtMe's solution: to help deflect the public's outrage away from Congress's willful indecision, the company would guide their users' attention towards a judicial system modeled after the court of public opinion. Keep the masses distracted by trials streamed through new social media add-ons. This tactic would also produce a new market for AbowtMe's fading social media users—a market which had a dissolving, apathetic base—by implementing a strategy right out of the educational handbook: make the users take *ownership* of their internet lives (they even pulled the nonsensical jargon from the teaching world). Let each person be, even though they always had been, an active member of the criminal justice system. No more ignored jury summonses; no more lying about why you couldn't serve; no more feelings of inferiority in front of corrupt judges and litigators…the people would be free to follow their moral

71

upbringings and implement true, unabashed justice. Let them become the all-in-one judges, jurors, and executioners. After this impassioned sell, Krauss and her minions presented another possible scenario: change absolutely nothing and let the vitriol and hate spread across the states until open rebellion and chaos ensued. Although far from unanimous, the Senate approved the Big Four's first solution in a sixty-six to forty-four vote, and the House approved it in a two hundred thirty-three to two hundred two decision.

The proposal was alluring, especially to cities on the edge of bankruptcy, and within a few years, the Big Four promised and were able to produce successful small-scale results. The first two cities to launch the pilot programs were Detroit and Phoenix. Gazelle was, above the others, adept in the realm of public relations, so the first thing they did to placate the loudest, angriest throngs of objectors was to repurpose the courts and police departments. Many people in those cities, according to the statistical data provided by the AI, mistrusted the men and women who had sworn to serve and protect them. Sometimes their distrust was warranted, as was the case with the Phoenix human trafficking and prostitution scandal, but more often than not, the notions of completely corrupt police departments was fueled by generational mindsets, biased media coverage, and old-fashioned propaganda and paranoia. Regardless, the traditional systems of professionals, systems that had been essential in the creation of the United States, were replaced with the AI system's suggested Peoples of Judgment Program. AbowtMe's and Gazelle's social media platforms were integrated into a trial website and each member of the community became a proxy lawyer, judge, and juror. Practice programs and courses were set up in state-of-the-art schools (schools built and sponsored by the Big Four), and re-education programs as well as jobs were set up for those too old or too busy to attend the traditional brick-and-mortar institutions. Anyone could now be a member of a jury, anonymously accuse anyone of a crime—making the fear of retribution for informing on your drug-dealing neighbor a thing of the past—and anyone could defend him or herself with a true jury of their peers, not just twelve people selected by crafty, disingenuous lawyers. The program's early successes had other cities that were financially troubled lining up for the conversion. Local and state leaders were enamored with the savings in taxes, and the citizens who were finding it impossible to make ends meet were too tired or apathetic to protest against it. These leaders helped sell it to their constituencies by playing to the lowest common denominator. Their generalized slogans targeted anyone who had ever been sued after a traffic accident, anyone who had ever been sued after claiming an eatery had made them obese by not labeling the calorie counts, anyone who had ever gotten sick from smoking and sued, anyone who had ever gone to court over a property dispute with a neighbor, and on and on. The loudest proponents of the overhaul, typically the ones who led despicable, private lives—the philanderers, the tax cheats, the pimps (of all genres), and unsurprisingly to anyone, the Fortune 500 executives and shareholders—ate up and regurgitated the propaganda, bullied it all over social media, and in many instances, became violent, or paid others to do so, with those who tried to refute their claims.

With the success of the new judiciary, The Big Four expanded the program even further, showing it off at college campuses, trade shows, town halls, parades, festivals, and conferences of all kinds. They claimed that the AI didn't make judgements on prejudices, like lawyers, judges, or jurors did; it would not present egregious sentences on low-level offenders; it would accelerate the pace of the archaic courts; it would leave the decisions in the hands and minds of the people; and it could not be compromised because it merely follows the adaptive algorithmic path of the system. It determined the ends to trillions of complex equations each second of each day, yet it would not grow to love or hate. The AI simply *was* and had its place in the social order, not as a governor or dictator, but as the new avenue to take towards a just and good and peaceful world. It would not let the people corrupt the new order.

It was the overwhelming success and expansion of this process, though grossly simplified, that Sean Reilly and Lamont Davis were discussing as they passed a vaporizer back and forth. Lamont had summed it up as best he could through his growing high.

"It's fucked up," he said, holding his inhalation of vaporized marijuana.

"I don't know, man. My dad used to be a lawyer, worked with AbowtMe and Gazelle for a while, and he's been trying to explain it all to me and Bailey for years. My stepmom was a paralegal in the same place, so she's all into it, too," he said, waiting for the pen-like device to come back his way. "What time you got?"

Lamont exhaled. "You got somewhere else to be? It's almost 11:30. Anyway, how'd your parents avoid the work farms? I thought anyone who had anything to do with the law was sent out as slave labor?"

"I don't know, but I think if you had the money, a lot of damn money to give to the right people, or if you'd been a lawyer or judge or anything like that and agreed to register as a law-offender and gave up practicin', you were allowed to switch to a new job. That's why my dad opened a landscaping business and my stepmom switched to nursing."

"I still remember my neighbors getting dragged off in the middle of the night. Pass that back. Both of them were some typa public defenders or somethin'."

"Shit! Put it away. Someone's coming."

Two sets of running feet were coming from the east side of the tracks.

"Leave me alone!" screamed a girl as she stumbled down the rocky embankment.

The boys heard no response to her plea, but what they did hear was another set of crunching footsteps approaching where she'd fallen. Sean and Lamont pushed themselves up against the concrete supporting wall of the trestle, thinking they could either become part of it, or if the people above had vision like a T-Rex—information they'd ascertained from one of their favorite movies to watch while stoned—they could avoid being seen by standing absolutely still. They heard one final scream and saw the girl's body fall into the shallow stream in front of them and go limp.

"Holy shit! Holy shit!" a man's voice said from atop the trestle. "Jill? Baby! Are you okay?"

Whether it was the weed or the adrenaline, Lamont ran from his hiding spot to confront whoever was now coming down the rocky slope. Being one of the few black teenagers in Runners' Landing gave him the advantage of intimidating almost anyone in the neighborhood.

"What tha fuck did you do, asshole!" he screamed at the incoming silhouette. "You betta fuckin' bounce outta here before I go wild!"

Lamont's outrageous bluff worked better than he could have hoped for; the small man halted his descent, turned, and scrambled as fast as he could back up the gravel and onto the tracks. Upon reaching the railroad ties, the stranger sprinted away, his feet hitting each piece of wood like a long jumper planting perfect steps before liftoff. Lamont heard a car engine start. *It must have been parked on Fairfield,* he thought, and then the screeching of tires filled the silence.

"Lamont! Man, this is Jill Foster," Sean said, having moved next to her body. "We gotta get outta here."

"Is she breathing?" Lamont asked. "You think that was her boyfriend? What's his damn name again?"

"She doesn't look like she's movin' and I don't know, man. Whatta we do?"

"We gotta call the cops. But we can't be here when they come. My dad would end me."

"Isn't your phone still blocked?"

"Yeah, and that's another thing I don't wanna explain when the five-o shows up, so we gotta make the call and bounce. Go, man! I'll catch up with you."

Instead of running upstream, Sean did what any teenager in 2024 would do: he took a series of pictures of the dead body. After the close up shot, both boys heard another set of screeching car brakes. The car parked at the end of the same Fairfield cul-de-sac as the girl's pursuer had. The sounds that followed were those of a car door slamming and a woman's voice desperately calling out for Jillian.

Lamont, having listened to the interloper make her way down the train tracks, turned to see his friend, a friend who should have been a hundred yards away by now, playing photographer. "Man, why are you takin' pictures! How high are you!" He grabbed Sean by the shirt and pulled him away from his model. They ran in the little brook, soaking their socks and sneakers, hoping that the water would cover up their footprints.

When they reached the path to the baseball fields, they made the left and slowed their pace.

"Why the hell were you taking pictures? The second you're clear of my blocker, those shots'll be all over the Web. They'll be traced right back to you!" Lamont chastised.

"I thought you said we were fine with your app! Oh, shit. What was that, man? Did that guy push her or what?"

"That's what it sounded like to me, but I don't know! I was standing right next to you, remember? The cops are on their way, but I don't know how that other bitch showed up so fast. It must've been her mother or somethin'.

Whoever it was must've been tracking her phone, man. We gotta split, now!" Lamont said, and they ran single file, like boot camp cadets, down the overgrown path that led to the community baseball fields.

Shortly after splitting up, Sean exited the 50-yard protective radius that Lamont's self-designed signal-blocking app provided. With Sean clear of its cloak, his new pictures were accessed by the Gazelle operating system and instantly uploaded to his AbowtMe-controlled social media sites. Phones no longer needed permission to access any piece of information, or any feature for that matter—waiting for a user's consent, the Big Four had argued years prior, had the potential to obstruct justice in criminal or civil trials. A phone's purpose evolved, in legal terms, to become an extension of the person.

In thousandths of a second, Sean's phone disseminated the images across the wireless world, to every connected device and watching eye…and the transmission could be traced right back to him. He ran home, wheezing the entire way, unaware that his name and profile were already in the possession of FileX agents.

It was a CenTek judicial process program, operating within this system of quantum reactions, that augmented—while Kristy, Bailey, George, and Erica slumbered—Jimmy Larkin's charges from statutory rape to involuntary manslaughter. The actions of wrong-place-wrong-time tag team members Sean Reilly and Lamont Davis, along with the official pictures and reports given by the police, enabled the CenTek's AI to cross-reference the images with the hundreds of traditional poses and selfies that Jillian had taken or had ever been a part of. The entire process of updating the trial happened, like the uploading of the pictures themselves, instantaneously, and in those moments, between Katherine Foster's two tortured cries, both of which were heard by George Alvarez when he let his dog out to relieve himself, dead Jillian Foster had been correctly identified, the trial information updated, and the jurors given the opportunity to view their new options. The reports that spread through the trial's message boards were that Jillian Foster, after being exposed by Kristy Shine, killed herself. Jillian's mother, Katherine Foster, the boards continued, found her daughter's body on the muddy bank of a small stream that ran under the crumbling train trestle. Like a game of telephone, the story got more dramatic and grizzlier as it was retyped.

According to juror Kill'emAllandLetGodSort'emOut's post, *"She (Katherine Foster) ran to the once lovely, once vivacious body of her daughter, her daughter whose neck was now broken, whose organs now bled, whose corpse now lay beside the gentle flow of Jette's Stream, and cradled Jillian's lifeless head in the crease of her left elbow. She screamed louder than her own ears could tolerate, swept the wet strands of hair from Jillian's face, and smacked her cheeks, trying to bring the blood back to where it should have been."*

The stories became increasingly histrionic, and the sympathy for Jillian snowballed into vengeance for her death. As the venom spread, the sensible jurors began logging off. Any attempt to remain as a rational, objective member of the jury was met with relentless trolling, hellacious threats of violence, rape, or both, and taunts of getting doxxed. The harassed fled because the thought of being exposed was more frightening than the other intimidations; with the advent of the private enforcement militias (financed by the Big Four), many honest jurors had been identified by their vindictive trial counterparts and beaten or worse. FileX and Gazelle tried to stymie the backlash of these occurrences by presenting the statistics that proved their rarity. Few people were willing to risk their chances of being on the wrong end of the majority's opinion, so when most were presented with a scenario like they found in Larkin's trial, they listened, like Sean and Lamont had, to their instinctual flight response.

With the immediate upgrade in charges and the new images of Jillian Foster displayed, the two new options were presented for the purpose of expediting Jimmy Larkin's trial: (1) continue the proceedings as previously planned; (2) move forward to the deliberation/judgment stages. The overwhelming majority selected to move the trial directly to the deliberation/judgment portion. The right to a speedy trial was paramount— one of the cruxes that led to the demise of the old system was its stultifying speed—so anyone who was still viewing, commenting, and participating in this first-ever AI governed trial, was given two more options: Guilty or Not Guilty. A sixty-minute timer began, and when that timer expired, Jimmy Larkin, twisting in a restless sleep, was found guilty by an 84 percent margin. Subsequent to the verdict, the jurors, who numbered in the hundreds of thousands in the early morning or late-night hours (depending on time zones), were given four sentencing options to vote on: A. Exile on a labor farm with no possibility of paid return; B. Exile with possibility of paid return after fifteen years; C. Twenty years in a psychiatric facility; D. Retrial.

 – *Lives4Justice: No death penalty option? Can we write that one in?*
 – *RecoveredStillNotRecovered: Yeah, what's going on? The guy's now responsible for her death? Why should he get to live?*
 – *Inothelaw: Where is the moderator? I voted for the harshest one, but this is a joke! What the hell is…*

Each sentence was contrived and delivered by the AI after it had instantaneously cross-referenced thousands of data points of evidence that were circumstantially similar to previous trials. None of the compiled information that the program filtered was capricious; the AI was not capable of caprice. Nor was any of the data manipulated, as many skeptics believed, to determine an outcome; complete objectivity could not be biased. If the AI presented sentences that were too lenient, as it had done early in the transition period (between 2019–2021) when humans were still in control of determining the verdicts, the public would lose faith in the system; if the penalties were too harsh, the public would try and compensate by being compassionate to those who did not deserve it. The newest version was fair, fast, and efficient.

Leo Colmsly sat in his modestly furnished den, watching the evolution of the Larkin trial take place. What he noticed through all his data, what that the nebulous mass of jurors could not see, was that human moderators were no longer needed at all. The program, as it was presently performing, no longer needed the layman's touch. He smiled and watched the sentencing votes tally on his projection screen. He thought about intervening; he didn't know if a trial could be considered legal if there were no human administrator (he'd have to check with President Krauss and the other heads of the Big Four about that), and he was certainly within his rights to terminate the proceedings, but he was just too curious. He needed to see what the people chose when their only given options were ones that had been created by advanced intelligence software. He watched for hours, and when the vote closed, at what would have originally been the end of the opening statement period, he sat back in his recliner and smiled.

"I'll be damned," he said to the screen. "Now, we just wait to see if Larkin's final plea makes any difference."

"Daddy, I want martianpillows for breakfast," Jimmy Larkin's oldest toddler pleaded.

"Jack, you can't have marshmallows for breakfast. You need to eat something healthy, like oatmeal or a banana," he replied.

Larkin looked at his son, awestruck by the physical changes in the boy's face and overall build. He thought that it was impossible for Jack to look so much older after only one night. He kneeled down and motioned for his first born to come in for a hug.

"How'd you get so big, little guy? It's only been one night!" he said, while laughing and tickling the boy's bony ribs.

"Hahaha, Daddy, that tickles," he said, throwing his body backwards.

Larkin paused his loving assault so Jack could catch his breath. The boy brought his head upward, again standing upright, and smiled playfully at his father.

"Again," Jack said, "again," momentarily forgetting his breakfast request.

Larkin tickled the boy's underarms and ribs as if he were Fats Domino flying over the ivory keys. Jack howled, contorted, and collapsed toward the tiled kitchen floor. Larkin knew this progression, so he caught his son, lowered him with his left hand, and kept tickling with his right. The laughter was a wondrous chorus of high-pitched squeals, rhythmic undulations, and unfettered joy. It echoed through the hallway and into the living room, draining both their minds of anything malicious or threatening or ominous.

"Daddy," Jack said, breathlessly, "I need a break."

Larkin paused, and the boy looked back at him, panting but smiling, anticipating the next round of play. He brought his dancing fingers close to Jack's ribs but halted an inch above. Jack felt the phantom touch and convulsed in an outburst of new laughter. Larkin withdrew the hand and Jack's body relaxed, his loud laugh falling back to a chuckle.

"Again, Daddy!"

He gave the boy another round of tickling, hoping the boy had been distracted long enough to forget his earlier sugary-breakfast request. "Jack, it's time for your oatmeal," he said.

Jack looked up from the floor, his face transforming from absolute pleasure to steadfast determination. He rose from his father's loose grip, looked him in the eye and yelled, "I want martianpillows!"

Unbelievable, thought Larkin. Anything in the world can distract him from going to sleep—too bright a night light, too dim a night light, shadows from the night light, made up mosquitos buzzing his head, needing a drink of water, wanting gramma's watch, wanting another story—but when the boy's mind was set, nothing in Larkin's arsenal would divert his resolve.

Larkin stopped smiling, lowered his voice, and said, "You may have oatmeal, a banana, or waffles, and that is all, Jack."

The little red-headed boy screamed in his daddy's face and stormed off in defeat. His third attempt would happen in several minutes, and Larkin's wife, Susan, came downstairs toward the kitchen. He listened as she came down each carpeted step. She was still trying to be quiet even though the house was awake, and he was still trying to pretend that he would be fine, that his fellow prudent men and women would see through this absurd Accusation and find him innocent. *They might even dismiss it in the preliminary conversations,* he thought. From years of teaching, he'd developed and honed a stoic façade, a front that he now tried to hold up for his family. Early in the formation of Teacher-Jimmy—a persona who had infinite patience with his pupils and bosses and colleagues, but not for the people whom he cared for the most—he had unleashed his bottled-up rage on his then-fiancée-now-wife, Susan. He'd never struck her, never even considered doing so, but his outbursts scared her enough to threaten to break off the engagement. He learned, with help from the veterans in the profession and his therapist, to channel his anger in healthier ways and to deal with his conflicts as they happened. After a while, Jimmy and Teacher-Jimmy merged into a healthy husband and father and educator. Now, though, after having been informed of the charges against him by the FileX agents who had ripped him out of Runners' Landing High School, he was trying to put on a failing performance; he was trying to get his family and his wife to believe that he was fine and that he had complete faith in the system. He was repeating this hope to himself when Susan came into the kitchen. She pulled out a barstool from under the counter, pulled herself into it, and poured a cup of coffee. She looked at him. He was even worse than he had when the FileX men had brought him home. *Who wouldn't be?* she thought. She believed that her husband was innocent, believed that he was not the lecherous type, in fact, she was fairly certain, based on how long his pubic hair had gotten, that he hadn't had sex with anyone, herself included, in quite a long time. She thought it was one of his hilarious idiosyncrasies, his dedicated attention to his trimming: any time they planned sex, he would meticulously prune his crotch hair. In the beginning it never had a chance to grow too long, but as children appeared and life progressed, both his and hers started getting wilder and wilder. It was true of any hairy part of the body that needed maintenance: if it can be postponed for just another day and still be tolerable, it can wait. Last night, before he had gotten into the shower, she'd made a point to interrupt him and take a gander. It was nearly impossible to see his penis, so she deduced, along with the detailed story he told as they loaded the dishwasher, that he was not having sex with anyone, especially a minor whom he was tutoring.

"Have you logged on, yet?"

"No. I'm still thinking of how I can defend myself; it's her word against mine, if she's even the one bringing the charge, so who's going to believe what I've got to say at this point? Besides, it should still be in the opening phase of the trial, and there's no point reading the comments of some of those nutballs. Logic is like poison to them. Better to wait until I can speak and actually be heard."

"You should just check to get a sense of what you might have to say and how you'll have to say it."

"I will after Jack eats. He should've been back by now for round three."

"Sweetheart, Jack's not going to starve. Please check what's going on."

"I just can't believe she'd do this to me! I spent so much time with her! She passed the Regents because of me, and this is the gratitude I get!" He said, his agitation growing.

"I'm turning on my phone. You'll be fine. We'll all be fine after you tell your side of the story."

"Daddy! Mommy! I want martianpillows!" Jack interjected, returning from his hideout in the den.

Susan threw the plastic bag of marshmallows at her four-year-old son and brought her phone in front of Jimmy's face. He read every update that had transpired while he was asleep; the window of time he had had to appeal to the teems of ingenuous jurors was over. His pupils narrowed and his forehead perspired. As Jack struggled to get the twist-tie off of the bag of marshmallows, Jimmy launched the phone, his coffee, and anything else he could grab, at the French doors that led to his patio. Susan ran to him, trying to comfort and quiet him while Jack sat on the white tiles, a mess of tears, cries, and marshmallows.

9

"You're not getting bored just sitting there, are you? Have any of the other parents charged us?"

"No, they have not," said FileX Agent Sanchez, staring at his catch through the iron bars.

"Has the school charged us, yet?"

"It has not."

"So why are my wife and I still sitting here? So, we're being held here for no reason, without being accused by proxy? According to the modified sixth and seventh amendments—"

"Mr. Reilly, the information I have reviewed says that you are in no way, under any circumstance, allowed to practice or proselytize law, and regardless of every citizen being entitled to know and recite the modified Constitution, you should be careful how you phrase your part in this dialogue."

"Who's being careless or preaching law? I certainly wasn't. I just happen to have been paying attention when our rights were stolen from us."

"And whom do you believe stole these rights from you, Mr. Reilly?"

"Have we been accused by anyone, yet?"

"Are you planning on accusing anyone from the other team's side? There sure were some vicious things said and done. It is your civic duty if crimes were committed," Agent Sanchez said.

"There was too much dust and dirt in my eyes. I was only defending myself, anyway."

"That would be for the jury to decide…but no, neither you nor your wife has been accused. As per protocol for violent arrests, you will be our guests for the full twelve hours, leaving just under two hours to go. If you haven't been accused by then, that would bring us to 8:48 a.m., you will both be free to go."

"We have two teenagers at home! Who knows what my son is up to! We need to get home to make sure they're all right."

"Something you both should have considered before brawling like Vandals. If you want anything to eat or drink, please let the officer know."

"You really should watch what you say to them, Frank," Paige Tomanicki-Reilly said from the rear of the cell. "I would've shut you up, but I'm pretty sure my ankle is sprained. This ice pack isn't doing anything, and I can only raise it so high on these benches."

"Why didn't you attack him like you told me you'd gone after Sean's teachers in yesterday's meeting? You told me that you had them shaking in their seats. One even left, you were so tough!" he said, mocking her. "I'm pretty sure that's what you told me before the game, darling."

Paige sat with her ankle elevated on a small pile of towels. She looked at her husband, hurt and angered by his sarcasm.

He looked down at his phone—depriving anyone of their phone, tablet, computer, or VR goggles, even when they were placed under arrest, was strictly illegal—and tried again to track Sean. "I got him!" he said, still looking at the phone. "He's home, thank God."

"That's great, Frank. And I'm sure Bailey's doing fine, too."

"I'm sorry, Paige, I'm just exhausted, and of course I'm worried about Bailey, but you know Sean. Bailey probably spent the night watching movies or gossiping online; Sean could've spent the night breaking into cars or getting stoned. I don't know how his phone disappeared, but we'll figure it out when we get home."

Paige stopped listening to him. She had spent years fighting school battles for *his* son, convincing neighbors not to bring charges against *his* son, convincing herself that *his* son was just in need of spiritual adjustment, not psychological or medicinal help, and she was getting sick of Frank never reciprocating the same concern for her daughter's well-being. She knew he loved Bailey, he'd been her father for nearly ten years, ever since Paige's first husband disappeared overseas, but she also thought that too much of his attention fell onto Sean and too much of his neglect fell onto Bailey.

He saw her fumbling with the wrap on her ankle. She was undoing it, pulling it tight, releasing it, and then repeating the process. He put his phone in his pocket and tried to help. "Here, let me redo it. If you can't get comfortable, you could lie on the floor and put it up," he suggested.

"I would just assume chop it off than lie of this floor. You're an asshole, by the way. You shouldn't have said anything to that man about stolen—"

"Paige, don't say anything in here. It's all being recorded for any possible trial."

"You think I don't know that? You're not the only one who's studied these procedures, darling," she said irritably.

"I just want to get home. I'm exhausted, and I know you're tired and hurting, too. I'm sure Bailey's fine, but Sean could be anywhere. He still isn't answering my calls, and the last search I put out for him came back blocked. How the hell could his phone be blocked? Drugs are one thing, but if he's messing around with Wi-Fi disrupters, he'll be disappeared to one of FileX's camp forevermores."

"It could be one of the dead-zones in town. There are still places I don't get reception."

"Impossible. More signals around us than air. Any device can be located at any time, on or off, even if it's dead. It's as simple as that."

She knew that was true, so she decided to let the conversation fade away. She also knew that since every device had been made free by the executive order of President Krauss, any piece of information from any of those pieces of tech was the sole property of the Big Four. Any search you made, contact you stored, place you visited, call or text you sent or received, any picture or video you shot, anything that defined who you were—your own electronic, digital progeny—was now owned by the information gurus, so she hoped that whatever Sean had been doing while she and Frank were in jail wasn't going to get him into serious trouble.

"What time is it anyway?" Paige asked.

Almost on cue, although coincidences were scant in these times, being that almost every word spoken and image created was captured by some type of technological ear or eye, the FileX agent opened the entered the fluorescently lit cinder-block room and stood in front of their cell door. "The time, Mrs. Tomanicki-Reilly, is 8:00 a.m., but we have something interesting to discuss before you leave. Depending on who wants to do the talking this time," he paused to let the couple exchange a silent decision, "you can either be our guests for quite a longer stay or be home as scheduled."

"We want to get home to our children," Paige said, "so please tell us how we can help you."

"Mr. and Mrs. Reilly, how often would you say your son frequents crime scenes?"

"What's happened to my son? Enough with all this bullshit! Is Sean all right?" Frank screamed.

Seeing that his circuitous method of questioning wasn't working, Agent Sanchez switched tactics and continued, "As far as we know, your son is fine. As you probably know, he, or at least his phone, is at your residence. But last night, Sean, and possibly several others, were present and/or witnesses to the death of," he fumbled and scrolled at his tablet screen, "a Miss Jillian Foster, age sixteen, and the subject of a now-ending trial. It was, in fact, your son's pictures of the corpse," both Frank and Paige flinched at the word, "that helped elevate the charges and bring a swift conviction against the Accused, Jimmy Larkin. Perhaps you know him?"

"Mr…" she began, but stuttered, "Mr. Larkin's one of the teachers at the high school. I think Bailey has him for…" she said, her thoughts drifting away with the image of Sean standing over a dead teenage girl, taking her picture for the internet.

Seeing that Paige was adding shock to her list of ailments, Frank asked, "Why would Sean have been there?" He got up and went to the cell door, went up to the bars and as close to Agent Sanchez as he could.

"That's exactly what you're both going to find out for us, Mr. Reilly, because if Sean was a witness to a senseless suicide, then he needs to be commended for bringing an Accused, this Jimmy Larkin, to his proper punishment, but if he was somehow complicit in the death of Jillian Foster or if he witnessed any other type of foul play, he needs to be questioned by FileX, and Mr. Larkin's trial needs to be scheduled as a redo. Mr. Reilly, the pictures were uploaded when his phone activated on Canyon Avenue, almost a mile from where Miss Foster's body was found. Those images should have been available instantly. We can only figure that your son had or was with someone who had a signal blocking device that our programs cannot detect, and that by itself is a very serious crime, so for all those reasons, we need to know what your son knows, and we're going to give you and your wife the chance to get that information before we interrogate him. No one can afford to have innocent people going to jail—that was what helped destroy the old system—and if what was said in the trial was correct, then no harm, Mr. Larkin goes to camp, but if your son is withholding information and obstructing the signals of justice, then there is foul play, and you are all going to spend the rest of your lives in the worst getaways we can provide."

Agent Sanchez left the room without waiting for a reply. He wouldn't have gotten much if he had stayed anyway. Frank and Paige sat on the steel bench, dumbfounded by the overnight transformation of their lives. Their cell door buzzed open, a woman in scrubs came in with an old pair of wooden crutches, handed them to Paige, and led them both out of the building.

"Please, where are you taking me! My wife, my boys! You hurt my son, you assholes!"

Al Flynn glared at his partner and said, "I told you to gag him. Pull the damn car over so I can do your job!"

Roger Johnson downshifted and pulled the car over to the shoulder. He and Flynn were part of the Long Island Freedom Fighters, a scattered group of conservative-leaning weapons enthusiasts, end-of-days-preppers, men and women who believed that Long Island should break away from New York and be responsible for its own affairs. Along with their bi-weekly meetings, combat training vacations, and alcohol and drug consumption, the members of the L.I.F.F. were deputized by FileX to remand those who were found guilty by trial into custody. They were glorified bounty hunters, competing with other groups for law enforcement contracts, and during their trial period, they were licensed and encouraged to carry firearms—a privilege they relished. They, and the other militias across the country like them, weren't the first line of defense in this type of duty—the Big Four still preferred the local authorities or FileX agents to make the initial arrests; this gave some semblance that life was just as it had always been for the people of the United States—but Flynn and Johnson had been at their headquarters drinking cheap beer and even cheaper moonshine when their chapter president, Mason Miller, sent the arrest notification to their phones. Larkin's house was in the vicinity of their clubhouse, and even as drunk as they were, they still managed to swerve and weave unharmed to their prize. Three rodents and one marsupial weren't as fortunate, however. The men had arrived, apprehended, and were gone with their perp 20 minutes before anyone else had a chance to respond.

Flynn got out of the passenger seat and opened the door directly behind him. Jimmy Larkin sat handcuffed, eyes covered by a thin piece of fabric, bleeding from his nose and mouth. "I told you to shut the fuck up," Flynn said through clenched teeth, "and this is what I said would happen if you didn't." He crushed Larkin's cheekbone with a ferocious right cross.

Larkin fell toward the middle seat, but Flynn hoisted him up. "Don't cry, you pussy," Flynn said as he fit a ball-gag into Larkin's mouth, "your faggy son'll be better off without you."

Flynn sat back down next to Roger and ignored the beeping seatbelt warning. "Drive," he said.

"What the hell are you doing in here, you pervert!" Bailey screamed at her brother. "Sean, what the hell are you doing in my room?"

"I-I didn't mean to scare you, Bails. I think I might be in some deep shit and I can't find Mom or Dad. They didn't come home last night?"

Springing awake, Bailey had instinctively pulled her sheets up to her neck. Her grip on the fabric loosened, and she dropped it to her lap when she realized that Sean wasn't trying to sneak a peek at her or Kristy; he looked like someone who'd seen something he shouldn't have or hurt someone seriously or stolen something from someone he shouldn't have. "What the hell is the matter with you?" she asked swinging her legs over the side of the bed, "and no I haven't seen or heard Mom or Dad yet. They probably spent the night in jail with most of the other softball parents, so I'm sure after the FileX agents or the cops scare the shit outta them, they'll be home."

"What the hell are they doing in jail?" he said, moving to the desk chair that Kristy had occupied the night before.

"They decided to take the playoffs into their own hands, and—"

"I-I'm in—"

"Serious, shit, I know, you've said. What happened? Why wake me up if you're just going to babble the same sentence?"

"Bailey, Sean…what time is it? What the hell is going on?" Kristy asked, waking with a dry mouth and a pounding head.

"Sean and I will get you some water, Kristy. Come on, Sean," she said, walking through the bedroom door. He followed her without so much as glancing back at Kristy and her air mattress.

Kristy let her head fall back onto the pillow, but she couldn't get back to sleep. Closing her eyes just made her head pound harder and the room revolve quicker. She lay there until her bladder, again, forced her to the toilet.

Grabbing the pitcher of filtered water, Bailey poured a glass for her friend and one for Sean and again asked him, "What happened to you last night? You still look lit, so I can only guess that you and Lamont were together, and I can—"

"Bailey, do you ever shut up or do you talk through the night because, holy shit, you never stop! I'll tell you what happened but give me a few more minutes!"

He took the glass of water from her and explained what he had seen the night before. He told her each detail in the sequence he could best recall.

"What the hell are you talking about? This is the same Jill Foster who's a part of the trial?"

"That's what I just said!"

"The same girl who Mr. Larkin was having sex with…allegedly?"

"Yes, Bails, the same damn girl! Are you sleepwalking or something?"

Bailey didn't answer that idiocy. She walked past him to find her phone. She spoke to it and its voice recognition security feature gave her immediate access. She went to the trial page, refreshed it, and stared at it, incredulous at what was displayed.

"Sean. You're going to tell me, no I don't care if we have to be here all morning, exactly what you just said. Don't skip a detail or change a thing. Tell it to me again, and after you're done, I'm going to show you what you and your stoner friend have done."

His mouth was as dry as a marathoner's as he retold the night's events. Bailey listened, only throwing her you-idiot-eyes at him twice: the first time when he'd mentioned the vaporizer and the second when he'd told her about Lamont's signal blocking app. He'd noticed her second condescending look and said, "The fact that I saw a girl get tossed of the train trestle doesn't rattle you, but the signal blocker does?"

"You said you saw her hit the ground, not that someone threw her, and you don't know if she jumped like it said on the trial page."

"There was someone, a guy, chasing her down the tracks. I think he caught up to her and pushed her off!"

"Do you know how much trouble you and Lamont will be in if they find out you were disrupting their Wi-Fi signals? Forget the drugs, hell, even forget Jillian Foster. If you two are getting stoned and you've figured out a way to get off the grid, they will probably kill you!"

"So the dead girl and Mr. Larkin's being guilty don't really bother you? You're telling me that you're worried about *Wi-Fi signals*!"

"You should be more worried about that, too, dumbass! Larkin had his fair trial and Jillian Foster made her choice."

Sean smashed his glass on the floor. "Haven't you listened to a fucking word I've said?" He stepped closer to her, "She didn't kill herself, and if there's someone else involved with this, there's a damn good chance that Mr. Larkin didn't do anything! Two lives are fucked, and your advice is to make sure we don't get caught messing around with Wi-Fi!"

"Don't try to lecture me. If there's more to Mr. Larkin and Foster, there will be another trial to clear him—that's how it works! And if you don't make sure that Lamont gets rid of that app, two more lives are going to be fucked right up their raw asses! And you can clean that up," pointing at the shattered glass, "because I've got a hungover friend to take care of," she said and left Sean alone in the kitchen. When she reached the staircase, she heard the front door open. She turned, saying, "Going to that loser group of dirtbag bikers isn't going to help you!"

From across the house, Sean responded with the only thing his mind could get out, "Fuck off!"

He slammed the door and went to see who was hanging around at the Freedom Fighter's clubhouse.

"Start from the beginning, son, and don't you dare keep a single detail from me or your mother."

Lamont sat on the loveseat in the den, his parents standing over him like menacing totem poles. The dwarf couch was a fine piece of broken-in furniture, Lamont's favorite to sit in while playing video games or binge watching hours of pirated shows and movies. It now, however, felt like an interrogator's chair with his parents playing the roles of both the detectives and the blaring lights. Everything else in the room, the paintings and sculptures, the two desk lamps, and the other pieces of furniture, seemed to lose focus as his parents loomed over him; they were two scowling, brown, sleep-deprived parents who were waiting for plausible explanations from their youngest son—and if they were in anyway dissatisfied with his answers, they were strongly considering the option of a fourth-term abortion. The first bit of information they had demanded when he stumbled through the door and awakened them was why he had broken his curfew; the second was whom he had been with; the third was why they had been unable to track his phone before they had turned in for the night. They had conceded to Lamont's pleas to continue the questioning in the morning, and now, at about the same time Sean was trying to reason with Bailey, the bell was tolling for the youngest member of the Davis family.

"Answer us, son, or this will get a lot messier a lot quicker," said Mrs. Davis.

Lamont spared nothing from his Friday-night narrative. He turned over his phone, the vaporizer, and any bit of teenage freedom he might have enjoyed while still under their roof. He showed them how the app—the one he'd created while ignoring his homework—worked and how he had thought it up and designed it. They had been angry with the marijuana and the vaporizer, but Jordan and Latoya Davis, both of whom worked as software engineers for CenTek and Gazelle, were captivated by Lamont's program.

"Son, this...you thought this up all on your own?" Mrs. Davis asked, having a difficult time disguising her intrigue.

"And you wrote the code by yourself?" Mr. Davis followed, also enamored.

"I kinda borrowed a little bit of your advertising program, Mom. I rewrote the aggregate code to hide my phone from the signal pings. Sean synched his phone with mine because I wouldn't let him download it, so his was able to disappear, too."

"How did you keep it from being found, son? The second you sourced it, it should have been detected," Mr. Davis asked.

Lamont, dipping his head to avoid eye contact, "I wrote it and compiled it with your Abyss password."

"You did what? I don't think I heard that, so please, say it to my good ear." Both of Mr. Davis's ears were in perfect working order.

"For the last couple of months, I've been logging onto the Abyss with your passwords, writing my program, and logging off without any problems. Nobody knows, Pop, I swear it's all been good—"

Jordan Davis had rarely resorted to violence in his life; the time he had spent training in the mixed martial arts was more for exercise than actual combat but moving his feet into the correct stance and throwing his fist into the left side of his son's face came as naturally to him as did manipulating thousands of lines of Java or HTML. The impact sent Lamont's head spinning backwards to the right. His shoulders slackened and his body sagged like a deflating balloon. Bright points of light appeared and disappeared as he slouched into the cushions of the loveseat. He was only able to catch the tail end of his parents' argument.

"Forget about being fired! We'll be in the camps!"

"What if we call them first, try and get ahead of…"

Lamont blinked out, going into his own style of sleep mode.

Noticing her unconscious son, Latoya remarked, "He needs some ice. You didn't have to hit him so hard, Jordan!"

"I didn't mean to put him out, Latoya," he said, shaking with adrenaline, "but if they find out he was on the Abyss with our passwords, they're going to shoot us where they find us. We've gotta think, and we've gotta think fast. I'll call that dirtbag friend of his, Sean, and get his side of this, then, damn it, I'm not sure what's next. We haven't gotten any notifications yet, so there's a chance they don't know about Lamont's app, but I don't know what Sean's going to say if Colmsly and his boys show up at his house and question him."

"*Call*? Did you just seriously talk about making phone calls? Any call you make's got a damn good chance of being recorded! For a smart man, you're lackin' some common sense right now! No, I'm not suggesting we text him instead. It's not that far a ride, so I'll bike over there. It's time for my morning exercise anyway, so it won't raise any suspicions for anyone who might already be watching if I get out for a ride. I'll talk to Sean. Get some ice for Lamont and make sure he wakes up," Latoya said as she left.

Being employees of two of the largest, most surreptitious programming companies in the world brought spoils and restrictions: both Mr. and Mrs. Davis had access to the Abyss, the final frontier of anonymous, free internet. In the early 2000s, it was known as the deep Web. It was the digital equivalent of a sordid speak easy; a network originally developed for clandestine military and intelligence communications, but as its users multiplied in the twenty-teens, it evolved into a bazaar for child porn, snuff films, bestiality clips, money laundering, terrorist recruitment, and human trafficking, so the government turned to the Big Four and contracted them to help create a new, darker facet of the internet. Gazelle and CenTek had developed the Abyss, as part of their new multi-tiered system, through their quantum advancements, allowing its strictly regulated users unfettered access to any piece of information that had ever existed. It stored the programs and codes that made up the AI; it recorded and monitored every data point for every communication and search as they occurred; it would grant its users whatever they wished to know as long as they knew the right questions to ask. It was beyond the cloud. It was a functioning, evolving system, one that was no longer confined to any manifestation of fiber optic cable or storage center. Its information was condensed to the particulate level, negating the need for palatial storage units. The data could then can be reconfigured as fast as it is was asked for, from anywhere in the world. With this ability, it could take a user through proverbial time and space, all while hiding identities as they worked or played. It was the genie and the bottle, ever-present and omniscient. Only those who had permission to use it were aware of its existence (or so it was thought), and if any unauthorized citizen discovered or entered it, the government had the immediate right to declare them an enemy combatant, strip them of their rights, and punish them in any way they deemed appropriate. Of the half-dozen Abyss Access Violations to date, each offender had been executed on the spot.

All Jordan Davis could think about as he walked back from the kitchen with a bag of frozen mixed vegetables was his youngest and most promising child and how he might now save all their lives. He entered the den and looked at the unconscious boy. There he slumped, and with this scene in front of him, Jordan's mind projected an image of Lamont as a toddler, curled up on that very same couch, his index and middle fingers in his mouth, his blue blanket with its satin edged draped over him, Sesame Street playing in the background as he napped. Prowling behind that beautiful memory was a surge of guilt, and as it flooded his mind, that picture of his son became even more innocent and precious, and Jordan felt horrible for having struck him. That sweet child still existed in this maturing adolescent, and what he needed now was his father's pathos and ingenuity, not his rage and remonstrations. He placed a folded towel over the swelling cheek and balanced the frozen vegetables on top of it. Before the tears could break free from his welled eyes, he heard a gentle knock on his front door. He let the inquisitor rap on the brass knocker for another minute while he tried to balance the organic ice pack on Lamont's face. When Jordan was confident it would not slip off, he answered the door.

"Mr. Colmsly," he said, stunned at his boss's appearance, "what can I do for you?"

"Hopefully provide more information than Latoya has, Jordan. She's in the car, and whether or not you want to join her depends very much on what you can tell me about last night's breech of the Abyss."

Jordan wasn't surprised that Colmsly or the people at FileX had deduced the illegal access, but he wasn't sure if his boss or his company knew anything about his son's involvement. "There's no need to keep her in the car, Mr. Colmsly. Please come in. I'll explain everything. Please let her—"

"She'll join us if I think you're telling me the truth. Until then, she's comfortable where she is. The air's on and there's an agent in the front seat. I'll take a black coffee before we get started."

Leo Colmsly's words and commands were deliberate and seldom trivial. The coffee request was meant to spark a reaction from Jordan Davis and it achieved the desired result.

"I guess mine wasn't the face you were hoping to see on the doorbell monitor, huh, Jordan? Probably pretty relaxed. Took your time walking to answer my knocking—couldn't have been the missus because she was on her way to the Reillys. Who could it possibly be?"

Jordan spooned ground coffee into the filter as Colmsly mused aloud. As the fourth scoop hit the paper, Colmsly made his way into the den and saw Lamont.

"Rough night for your boy? He out and about doing things he shouldn't be?"

"I will explain everything, Mr. Colmsly, including Lamont's involvement in it. Please have a seat," he said motioning to the recliner.

Colmsly ignored the invitation to sit and said, "My other team is escorting Mr. and Mrs. Reilly back home as we speak. Their son, whose whereabouts are unknown at the moment, is responsible for some impressive detective work, so please make sure this story has a quick point. We know your son was at the scene of a possible suicide last night—thanks to the photo uploads and the glorious street-by-street surveillance cameras—and I'm running out of patience with the people in this idiot town, so please, don't lie to me. Don't keep me here longer than I have to be."

Jordan forgot about the brewed coffee and relayed Lamont's story exactly as it had been told earlier.

"Aside from breaking laws that warrant immediate judgment and execution, your boy's quite the little coder." Colmsly pulled his gun from his holster and pointed it at Jordan Davis's chest. "Have a seat next to him, Davis."

Jordan did as he was commanded, and as he sat next to his son, Colmsly spoke aloud to his latent partner, "Richards, are the audio and video feeds clear enough? Good. Transcribe it into a Proxy. Loop the video to his admission of his son's drug use and to his admission of knocking the boy unconscious. Use the close up of the boy's face. No, don't leave anything in about the Abyss, you moron. The charges? Negligent parenting, endangering the welfare of a child, and child abuse. Once it's ready, upload it and begin the trial."

"Mr. Colmsly, please! This isn't necessary!"

"How isn't it necessary, Davis? Exactly how would you have me handle this?"

Jordan hadn't had time to work out the variables of this equation, and he didn't know how to appeal for pity from a man who barely ticked on the emotional register, so he remained silent, sweating on the love seat. In his years working for Leo Colmsly, Jordan had learned that avoiding his boss was the most prudent strategy. Jordan would write his codes, work out the bugs, report to the required meetings, and keep his name and reputation on the outer edges of Colmsly's awareness. For nearly six years, it had been a successful technique.

"Still nothing, Davis? All of that brain power rendered useless because it's your kid involved?"

"You have any children, Mr. Colmsly? You know what it's like to care for them, to love them?"

"What's that like, Davis, that love for your kids? How's that workin' out for you today? Fascinating that something so aggravating is the result of something so goddamn satisfying. Twisted damn joke if you ask me. To think that if it were any other process, we'd have died out millennia ago, but nature's so very sly at keeping everything ticking away. No, to your question, though. I chose to make my work my jailer, not some dopey offspring."

"They don't imprison you..." He stopped himself at the anticipation of Colmsly's correction, but it didn't come.

"Coffee's ready, Davis. Like I said before, I'll take it black. You know what, throw it over some ice so you don't get the idea of trying to scald or blind me with it. Try anything and…you know the rest of that, so just leave it on the step when you come back in."

Before he could plead any more, Jordan Davis felt his phone vibrating in his left front pocket, the ominous notification of the Medusa. His eyes widened and his forehead glistened with a new layer of sweat.

"Ah, that's one of the fastest field conversions we've ever done," Colmsly said and then added to the air, "Well done, Richards."

"You didn't have to do this…"

"That coffee smells good, Davis. Black and over ice, please."

Jordan went and fixed the drink to his captor's specifications. When he returned, Colmsly was in exactly the same position he'd been in, an insipid statue. Jordan placed the glass on the step and took his seat next to his now rousing son.

"I've been mulling this over, and I've figured out what's probably still very new to you and your wife: the boy's talent isn't something that should be wasted. It seems damn impressive for someone with only a high school level of training—especially that wasteland you send him to—but your negligence with your Abyss access is criminal. I thought you and your wife were sharper than this, but I was wrong…and I hate being wrong."

Jordan thought about lunging at Colmsly—there was a chance of wrestling the gun away from him, but it was a very small chance, and this wasn't a movie. If he lost the struggle, his family would be murdered and their bodies would disappear. The only questions his neighbors might ask about the newly vacant house would be its asking price. They'd be curious to know how much their own home values might rise or fall. Jordan went on imagining escape scenarios—perhaps he could whip the frozen bag of vegetables and take down his deputy director with a double leg grapple or maybe he could sprint to the kitchen, grab the coffee pot, toss it at Colmsly's face, and then—

"No, Davis, you're not going to get out of this like that, whatever scenes you're dreaming up. Turn off that engineering brain of yours and accept the fact that I'm in total control of this. In a moment Agent Richards will be in with your wife." As he finished the sentence, Latoya and her escort came through the front door. She was fettered around her ankles and wrists. Jordan sprang from the couch when he saw her encumbered, shuffling footsteps moving to the den. "Sit down, Davis. We're not going to hurt her. Richards, sit her on the recliner." He did as he was ordered, and when Mrs. Davis was seated, the underling FileX agent brandished his pistol, too.

Jordan remained still but did not sit down.

"I think I've come to a resolution. Yes, yes, I have. And I'm quite happy with it. We're taking the boy with us."

"The hell you are!" Latoya interjected. "You're not taking my son away from me! You can't just set up that bullshit trial and then do whatever you want!"

Colmsly moved next to the protesting mother and put the barrel of his gun to her left temple. "Richards, take the boy to the hospital and then into FileX custody. Davis, if you so much as flinch in his direction, her brains will become a tribute to Pollack. That's perfect. We wouldn't want these abusive parents to have any contact with him during the trial, now would we? Sedate the kid when you get to the car."

Lamont had been regaining consciousness, but he wasn't yet awake, so Richards had to throw him over his shoulders, like a wrestler preparing for powerslam.

"Don't you let him take our boy, Jordan!" Latoya screamed. She jerked forward and was met with the butt end of Colmsly's pistol. She fell sideways and Colmsly immediately repositioned the gun to halt any retaliations from the would-be-hero-husband.

"Get him outta here, dammit! If anyone but me comes after you, kill them," he said to Richards. "Deadweight's always a bitch to carry, eh, Davis? Now, your trial is going to be fast, and it's going to end like this: your boy is going to become our property—yes, just like the good ol' days. You think the Abyss is deep? We'll bury him so far into the company that he'll eventually forget all about you two, and if he ever becomes inquisitive, he'll die. Now, you have a choice, and I'd offer it to your wife, too, but it seems she's decided to take an inopportune nap. Plead guilty, don't worry, I'll open the Proxy back up for you to do so, and continue your life with a permanently downgraded Vt score—you'll keep your job—and, maybe after some reconditioning, your family will be happily reunited...or I can execute you both right here and now, and keep your kids as well-trained FileX slaves."

"When will I see him!" Jordan helplessly screamed.

"For fuck's sake, Davis, when I tell you it's time. You better be at the office bright and early on Monday and be sure to get her something for her head when she wakes up."

Colmsly thought it better to wait for his underling to return before making his exit. If Davis felt a final, desperate surge of strength, it would be better to have another gun to use, or in the absolute worst case, another body to sacrifice.

"How much did you give him," Colmsly said after he shut his car door.

"Enough for him to stay quiet while we find his buddy, sir," he said, indicating the drooling adolescent in the back seat.

"That shouldn't be too hard. From what the records said, his compadre's nowhere near as sharp as his tech-friend, here, and his parents are already cooperating. We'll save time by skipping the theatrics." Colmsly checked the latest updates from the agents at the Reilly house—his stepsister and a friend were found at the house, along with Sean Reilly's phone, but no sign of the boy. She claims she doesn't know where he went, but the AI was projecting a 96 percent chance that he'd be at the local militia clubhouse. "Let's start there," Colmsly said, swiping the information from his screen to Richards'.

"Yes, sir."

"You been hangin' out around here more often, kid. People don't overlook somethin' like that these days," said Mason Miller as he restocked the soda machine with cans of warm, cheap beer.

"I tried telling my sister about—"

"How about your folks?" he interrupted, still keeping his back to Sean.

Sean sat at the bar that would have been recognizable in any volunteer fire station. That was, in fact, what the Long Island Freedom Fighters called home. Some members played cards at a raised round table, a couple of others played a haphazard game of eight ball, and even though no one would have cared if he had, Sean chose not to join his buddies for a tepid one; it was still early and he didn't need to add to the growing list of offenses that bore his name. "My parents got arrested for some fight at my sister's softball game or something, and I don't know any more than that, but it's strange that they haven't tried calling or messaging me. I mean, they always try and get in touch with me, even in school when I'm sitting in class or between periods they try—"

"Kid, if you're going to talk this fast this early, you gotta wait 'til I get a few of these in me," he said, displaying a can but still not turning from his task.

"I'm sorry, Mason, but I think me and my friend really fucked up last night. I mean, I'm talking *really* fucked up."

Miller, a fifty-one-year-old retired defense attorney and veteran of the Afghan conflict, finished stacking the cans in their narrow slots, closed and locked the door, and turned to speak some wisdom to his probationary member. He knew that most of what he would say would not register with the boy—as an attorney he'd dealt with too many clients who'd pretended to want his professional guidance but had only wanted advice on how to curry favors with the judges. He hoped that his military tone might not only help the boy with his current problem, but draw him further into the fold of the L. I. F. F. The lore of their secessionist rhetoric and independence-focused messages were powerful and easily broadcast in the era of total connectivity, but their most recent recruiting events had been heavily attended by middle-aged men who fashioned themselves as great military leaders or action-movie heroes or untested patriots who would take the country back. In reality they were desperate, out-of-work, off-kilter, low-scoring Vts. Miller knew he'd have to work some discipline into the group, along with recruiting more youths, if they were going to vie for a FileX enforcement contract. If they were awarded that job, which ordained them as an official supplemental police unit that searched out and arrested lower-level offenders, Miller stood to personally make over one hundred and fifty thousand dollars with bonus options for each successfully captured or convicted perp.

"Kid," Miller said, "as a lawyer in the days before my judicial discharge, I recognized how much people hated what I did, even though they really had no goddamn clue; guess they figured that all of us stood up for child-rapists, crooked CEOs, and drug dealers because we got a kick out of it. I always loved to argue, and I'm damn good at it, but I got into it because at one point I did believe that everyone could get a fair chance in court. I quickly figured out that was garbage, but by then I got sent over to the Middle East. Seeing that mess kinda helped me realize that our system—our old one that is— wasn't fucked beyond repair. It just needed some TLC, but by the time I got home and back to the grind, the markets had taken another shit and people were losing their damn minds. It hadn't been exactly hard for the Big Four marketing groups to turn the public's anger—the growing unemployment, the differences between those that had and those that didn't and the growing numbers of bums and vagrants leaking out of the cities to the 'burbs—toward authority figures like politicians, cops, and lawyers. People hated lawyers almost as much as they hated cops but nowhere near as much as they hated politicians. Funny how *they* didn't go anywhere, ya know?"

Sean looked vacantly back at Miller.

"Guess not. Well, you ever meet someone who didn't know a lawyer joke? Whatta you call a lawyer neck deep in sand?"

"I-I, uh…"

"Not enough sand! My personal favorite. My Uncle Mike told me that when I was a kid. Anyway, it had been pretty damn easy for the grande cuatro to turn people against my friends and I because we were low-hanging fruit," Miller paused to see if the boy was following.

Sean shifted in his chair, but unlike his classes in school, he was looking attentively at Miller. He did have one question, though. "Whatta ya mean by 'low-hangin' fruit?"

"Easy targets, kid. We lawyers were easy targets for people to despise."

"Oh, gotcha."

"After I was outta work, I decided to try to set up a discreet advisory business—that means a secret job, kid. Jesus Christopher Christ, don't you learn anything from school or the Web? Well, that business was advising people who'd been accused by strangers get through their proceedings. It was keeping me afloat until people really stopped givin' a shit about the details of the law. When the trials changed from civil arguments to comment-section free-for-alls, I knew my services would, yet again, no longer be needed, so I decided to use some of my other talents to get by. That's how this club got started."

"That's actually a lot like my dad," Sean said, letting his brain distract itself from the night before, "but he started cutting lawns, not starting a group like this."

Miller was pleased the boy had calmed down. He handed him a beer before opening his own. Sean decided that it might help calm his nerves, so he tapped the top with his thumb and popped it open.

"Well, your dad's probably a better man than me. Nowadays, the people who beat the charges are the people who can pay trolls to argue for them. So many leeches makin' money by doing nothin' but harassing and threatening other jurors. What a system, huh? That's why I don't try and rise above the shit anymore, to be noble or good," a contrast to Quixote balanced on his tongue but he knew it would necessitate another explanation for the teen, so he skipped it and continued, "Even when I tried to do the right thing, helping people when I wasn't supposed to, the universe, or karma or whatever, never rewarded me, so now I'm set on surviving, 'cause who knows how we're gonna get it in the ass next time."

Sean mulled his and Lamont's chances of being found not guilty in the trial that most certainly awaited. He hadn't put too much thought into the lopsided nature of using an online legal system, but at the realization of his diminishing chances at being found innocent, he took a long gulp from the can. The beer flowed down his throat, the carbonation burning all the way down, and he winced before saying, "I can't afford to pay for help! I can't afford shit. They probably won't even let me talk to my dad during it 'cause of what he used to do, so I'm done, man. I'm fucking done!"

"Now, what the hell did you actually do, kid?"

"Can I have another one?" he asked before telling Miller the whole story.

Miller listened as if the boy were a confessing client. "Kid, the first thing you need to do—"

The front door slammed open, sending pictures and their frames crashing to the floor. A tall man entered and instead of introducing himself, said, "Sean Reilly, why is your phone not on you, and why did I have to waste my very valuable time questioning your sister, her friend, and your parents about your whereabouts?"

"What tha fuck is this?" one of the billiardsmen yelled.

"Wrong fuckin' house Goldilocks!" yelled the other as he drew his cue above his head and started toward the door.

Miller's eyes hadn't yet adjusted to the blinding light, so he couldn't make out the man he was about to threaten. "This is a private club, asshole, so unless you—"

"And unless you wanna lose any chance at that FileX contract, Mr. Miller, I'd shut the hell up and tell that burly bastard to put down his little stick!"

Miller realized before his vision did who stood before him. "Sammy, relax. This ain't someone we need to mess with. My apologies, Mr. Colmsly.

Didn't realize you had business with this boy. We'll cooperate any way we can."

"Probably the best answer you could've given, Miller. I'll be sure to make a note of that on your organization's application. Now, if you'd leave us alone, I'd appreciate it."

"Just do whatever the man says, kid," Miller said before patting Sean on the shoulder and leaving.

Sean's legs were beginning to go numb as he sat, or rather, as he perched on the once-cushioned stool, yet no matter how many times he shifted or lifted his hamstrings to relieve the pressure, the discomfort would not abate—the pain reminded him of the periods he'd spent on the school's toilet seats, scrolling through porn or messages, slowly losing feeling in both his feet—but his interrogator, this man who'd introduced himself only as Agent Colmsly, seemed to welcome Sean's increasing agitations.

"There's no point looking at them for help," Colmsly said, indicating the militiamen exiting the scene, "because if any of them so much as adjust their balls, this little club will disappear like you and your friend Lamont did last night."

Sean was hoping that his secessionist brethren might change their minds and knock this suit-wearing prick back to his little office, but they offered no such assistance, and while the Freedom Fighters adored any excuse for a brawl, they knew better to trade words, blows, or bullets with FileX agents, specifically ones who could bankrupt them.

"I don't know how his signal blocker works, so why don't you just find him and leave me alone!" Most of Sean's experience dealing with authority figures was limited to whining until he got his way or offering pathetic attempts at posturing, so he'd figured he'd try the latter with Leo Colmsly— he was feeling the effects of the liquid courage he'd chugged before.

Colmsly laughed at Sean's pathetic attempt at bravado and said, "You already belong to me, you pissant. Your friend already belongs to me, to my employer, and he's actually got something to offer our company, but you...you load that should've been swallowed, the only thing I need from you is a simple answer of whether that girl from last night was murdered or if she committed suicide."

"Why," he checked his tone from confrontational to more cooperative, "why would that matter?"

He maintained his distance from the boy and began. "Last night's trial, Sean, was the first of its kind, a trial adjudicated. That means conducted—goddamn, is there something in the water in this town?—by our AI system."

"But what does that—"

During Colmsly's last part of dialogue, he'd moved closer to the boy, and instead of listening to Sean's next asinine question, deftly picked up a pool cue that had been left on the table, cocked it for a backhand strike, and whipped the taper of the shaft across the boy's right cheek. The blow sent Sean and his stool crashing to the floor. He waited until Sean's wailing and cursing ceased before continuing.

"If our AI can manage our trials, we'll be able to drop," he swung the shaft across Sean's ribs, "the idiot moderators who seem to fuck up more than they help." He let the boy scream before striking him again. He also waited just long enough to know that the feeling, those horrible pins and needles, had returned to the boy's legs, and then he struck the right and the left as if he were hacking through jungle foliage. "We'll be able to make the whole process even more efficient, so," he swung down again, "was the girl killed," another strike, "or," another, "did she kill herself?" he bellowed at the thrashing teen.

"She jumped to get away from someone who was chasing her!" Sean screamed. "Jesus, stop hitting me!"

Colmsly stopped his assault and knelt next to his victim, his property, and spoke, "If that's the truth, and so help you it better be, it means that jurors will have even less to do in future trials; it means that our system is learning and adapting quicker than we've calculated." He dropped the cracked cue and stood up. "With that last bit of information confirmed, you have thirty seconds to get up, out, and into my car. If you want to continue living, you're going to prove that you're worth FileX's investment. You and some of your circle-jerk buddies are going to come with my associate and me to arrest the country's soon-to-be final human moderator and her nutless husband. Good, I'm glad to see you've still got something left in you."

Sean staggered his way to the door, simultaneously crying and clutching his ribs as he went. The sunlight blinded him and some of the militiamen balked in protest at the sight of what they thought was their property's condition.

"What the hell you do to him?"

"He's just a kid, you maniac!"

Colmsly ignored their comments but had left the building anticipating their frustrations, so he made sure to brandish his handgun. "Choose a friend, Mr. Reilly," he said as they made their way to the black FileX sedan.

Sean looked at Miller who turned his head. Sean then pointed a shaking finger at no one in particular. "You," Colmsly said to Harry Vinks, "are going with us. The address is on your screen."

Harry looked down at his phone and saw Erica and George Alvarez's address, their profile pictures, and the description of their Medusas. He offered no objections. He went to his motorcycle and waited for the head of the parade to exit.

"Sir," Agent Richards said after Colmsly had closed the car door and fastened his seatbelt, "perhaps we should let Mr. and Mrs. Alvarez shit their pants for the rest of the day before going over there. Maybe the interrogation will go a little smoother that way. It's been a long one, even if it's still early, and they're not going anywhere."

Leo Colmsly rarely took suggestions from subordinates, but he too was fatigued from the day's activities, so he agreed with Richards and added his own addendum, "You'll go far, Richards, with ideas like those. You hear that, Reilly, you're going to spend the night in a prison cell instead of in your bed. Say thank you to Agent Richards."

"Thank you," Sean mumbled from the back seat.

"Now, Sean, if you decide to fully cooperate with us, you won't need to hang around that shack anymore. If you decide to fully cooperate with us, we can offer you an auxiliary internship that might one day lead to an enforcement position with FileX. If you fully cooperate with us, you won't spend the night being beaten and sleep-deprived. How does that sound?"

Sean only cried from the backseat.

"And, I promise I'll get to my point, Sean, but if you and your buddy on the bike work with us, your parents and lovely sister will remain perfectly safe and happily free. Ponder that while we drive because I can just as easily leave you to rot in that cell for as long as I like."

Sean knew that a snide response would not serve him well, so he said the only thing that he thought might help. "I'll do whatever I can," he said through a whimper, "but can I please call my house? I have to let them know that I'm okay."

"I've got no problem with that. As soon as you're printed and secured, you may call whomever you wish."

10

Bailey Tomanicki lay on her bed, a full-size plush mattress covered with an unhealthy menagerie of animal throw pillows, her phone and its wireless charger, and three layers of sheets tucked precisely enough to make any drill sergeant brim with pride. She was on her left side, staring at the blank flat screen TV on her wall, replaying the conversation she'd had with that cyborg of a man, Leo Colmsly, hours earlier. She blinked, and the movie in her mind's eye began from the moment he'd quarantined her in the dining room. Her parents, who had just gotten home from their internment, were being questioned in the finished basement, and Kristy had been placed in the second-floor guest suite.

"Not a bad place for a landscaper," Colmsly had said, gesturing around to nothing in particular.

"My parents work really hard," she'd responded.

"They have to...now that they can't peddle snake oil, sweetheart. Daddy and Mommy look like they've learned the value of an honest day's work. Spare me the don't-talk-about-my-beloved-parents-that-way eyes, cupcake. I know exactly what your parents used to do, and I have a very good idea what your bovine brother was up to last night, but I'm not quite positive where you and your girlfriend fit in this, so you can either help me by filling in any gaps of his activities that you can or you can direct me to where he is."

"Stepbrother."

"Come again."

"Sean's my stepbrother."

"Wow! That'll crack this case, Miss Bailey! Damn! If you're going to give me info like that, let me make sure the mic is working! Test one, two. Testing! Now, say that again clearly, right into my lapel."

Bailey had slouched, her gilded teenage confidence melting in front of the crucible that was Agent Colmsly. "I just mean that I have no problem, like, telling you what he told me this morning."

If she could have done it over, she would've tried throwing the middle-aged man off by slipping another button on her blouse. It had worked in one way or another with every guy, be it a teacher, boyfriend, or boss she'd ever manipulated, but this interrogation had felt different—it felt like one of those truly grown-up moments that define the transition between messing around as a kid and taking responsibility for something real. She'd left her clothes as they'd been and had recounted every word she and Sean had exchanged from that morning.

Back in her bed, blinking again at her blank TV, fast-forwarding the film in her mind.

"Is that everything, Bailey? You're sure you're not leaving anything from me?"

"Word-for-word, that's what he told me."

"Your friend upstairs would be able to tell me the same thing?"

"No. She was still in the bedroom. Sean kinda creeped her out when he came home, and she was pretty hungover."

Colmsly had decided that the girl was telling the truth. He had no hard data to prove this, but on rare occasions like this one, he enjoyed trusting his instincts. She had relaxed as her story had progressed, reminding him of what a guilty conscience must look like in a confessional. He'd maintained his stoic stare through it all, believing that it was the only healthy way to interact with a suspect. "So, your stepbrother is now in a little less trouble because what you just told us pretty much matches what he did. That's good for him, and you, Miss Bailey…you're quite interesting. I spent yesterday with a class full of your mouth-breathing contemporaries and not one of them showed a fraction of interest in the system that you seem to. Why is that?"

"Because I'm sick of people not taking responsibility for themselves."

"I could put you on trial right now. You used your stepfather's trial ID— hard for him to grant you permission while he was detained all night—and accessed a proceeding that led to a young girl's death. I respect that you took the initiative, but are you ready to take responsibility for yourself?"

"I was just trying to get my friend's mind off of our shitty game—"

"Are you ready to take responsibility for what you did?"

"Kristy was the one who outed Jillian Foster, not me, so if anyone should be in trouble right now, and besides, we had permission from the school—"

"I won't ask you again."

As much as she hadn't wanted to, she began to cry. "I don't want to go to jail! Why is there an age limit anyway?"

"Ms. Tomani—"

"Fine! Yes, I'll take responsibility for what I did!"

"Excellent. This is my happy face, if you couldn't tell, and as a happy man, I want to extend an offer to you, in exchange for your detailed cooperation. Are you in the accepting mood? Because it's pretty much the only chance you have at growing up as a free woman."

She'd never been referred to as a woman, yet she'd imagined it being much more flattering than the way Colmsly had expressed it. "What could you possibly need from me?"

"Absolute loyalty. If what you and your friend have started is something that is here to stay, I will need ambassadors…salesmen and women, if you will, so I need to know that what you've told me about your love and respect for the system is true and unconditional. You're going to show me your devotion by going out and creating your own trial, from Proxy Accusation to final Guilty or Not Guilty for our AI to execute. This can't be any nonsense accusation either. Find something worth my time if you want any of yours to be free again. I will give you a week, which is more than enough time for you to think this over, so please, do whatever teenage girls do and go to wherever teenage girls go to make life-altering choices, and," he reached into his wallet, slipped out a business card, and placed it on the table next to her, "message that number with your decision. There's also a password and username you can use to access some of the other crevices and levels of the Web if you'd like a taste of how much information we really have on you and your fellow sheep. Don't look so shocked. I don't think you're dumb enough to even think about screwing around with my information or with my company's property."

Back in her bed, she blinked to the present and saw her vapid reflection looking back at her from the curved screen. She flipped Colmsly's card over from his name and number to his account info on the back. Her thoughts wouldn't congeal; she kept reorganizing them, attempting to arrange them into a solution, but each new equation that came into her head came with a glaring variable. Needing some help, she sought comfort in her rechargeable, updatable steadfast friend: her phone. It came to life at the affectionate squeeze of her hand. Her AbowtMe page was visible behind her passcode screen, but she wasn't in the mood for socializing. The phone's sensors followed her eyes as she entered her password. What she needed was some outside inspiration; she would start by scouring the popular trends in current trials, and if that didn't ignite the powder, she'd need to search the message boards for rumors, leads, or gossip for assistance. She swiped her screen and sent her hand toward her dormant computer monitor. It came to life at once, mirroring exactly what was on her phone.

"Show me the trending trials," she said to the plastic and metal.

She wasn't logged on or participating as she'd been the night before, couldn't be with both her parents at home, but like any other person in the country, she had the right to read and witness any proceeding she liked. Part of her graduation requirements, in fact, required that she and every other high school student across the country view and keep a log of two hundred hours of viewed court analyses.

"They're lucky they didn't just get shot in the head," she said, referring to Colmsly's discovery of Sean and Lamont, "and Kristy's even luckier that she's not in some dungeon right now."

Her phone's primitive communications program had originally been designed to help Autistic children understand basic non-verbal communication cues, but it had inadvertently become the closest friend and confidant for legions of insecure and introverted youths. Responding to Bailey's statement, it sent a thumbs up emoji across the top banner of her computer screen. Rarely, if enabled, did a phone's AI disagree with its user's comments, wishes, or commands. *They should have known better*, it typed as a follow up.

"Yeah, they should have, but they'll all get fair days in court," she said, starting to feel normal in her routine and banter, "so I'm not going to lose any sleep over it. Show me what's trending locally versus nationally. Try to find something juicy."

What exactly do you mean by juicy? it typed.

"Don't you have access to my search history?"

You are not yet of a legal age to view those trials, Bailey.

"Yeah, 'cause clicking yes on the *Over 21* option is really difficult—besides, I've got my new tool," she said fingering the corner of the card. "Sync open trials with search history from the last two months," she commanded.

There are *twenty-eight thousand four hundred seventy-six open trials matching your most searched keywords: sex, abuse, murder, politics, and drugs.*

She scrolled through the categorized, descriptive lists until she came to a love-triangle murder case that could have been written as a made-for-TV drama. She clicked view and when prompted by the age filter, she clicked yes as she'd done hundreds of times before. She was surprised and annoyed to find an additional blocker: *Enter Juror ID and Password for Verification.*

"What the hell is this? I can't even watch the trials anymore? Stupid updates."

She peaked, out of habit, toward her shut door as if her parents were both spying on her through the key hole. She then moved forward on her chair and looked out the window to make sure they weren't hovering just outside, arms folded in condescension, holding their phones to record her every discrepancy. The air was clear of floating parents, so she entered the username and password Agent Colmsly had provided and brought her knees into a criss-cross position, propping her phone up on her pressed calves. She didn't need it at all, but feeling its contact was soothing. Her eyes kept darting from the screen to the door, from the screen to the window, her ears perceiving every creaky board as either her mother sneaking down the hall with a memorized speech on her tongue, or Colmsly crawling up the walls and ceiling in the hallway, skittering toward her room to ring her neck. But resisting the rush she felt during a lascivious trial, the venom from the jurors, the pleading of the Accused, the suspense of the verdict was akin to being blindfolded and teased to the cusp of an orgasm, so she'd risk being caught again by anyone who wanted to burst through the door, in order to satisfy the urge. Even in her addict's trance, the danger of logging back on was lucid. Was Colmsly just trying to trick and incriminate or discredit her? Her mind screamed dozens of warnings, begged her to delete the username and password she'd typed, showed her images of prison bars and orange jumpsuits, but none of these projected images or fantastical warnings could overcome the glow of the efflorescent screen.

Shall I set the timer? typed her digital pet.

"Yeah, and log Colmsly's number into my contact list. Yeah, C-o-l-m-s-l-y. I'm doing this and it's not going to be some stupid little trial about a teacher clappin' cheeks with his student. I've gotta find something that makes him believe," she said as she entered Colmsly's information.

The loading icon spun for a second before a new screen appeared. "Holy shit. He really wasn't lying about the access," she said, referring to the new message board categories that filled her screen, ones that had never been visible before.

She bent backwards and stretched her arms toward her ceiling, as if performing a sensual yoga pose, brought them down, and with her left hand, fished her headphones out of the top left desk drawer. Preparing for a dedicated hour, she put her chestnut brown hair up, plugged each earbud into its respective ear, and eased her tense body back to its relaxed position. With her mind focused and her music loud, she began clicking on and searching through menu after menu. First was the murder category. There were celebrity murders, average-Joe attempted murders, cult-murders, jilted-lover murder/suicides, but nothing struck her as momentous—nothing like what Colmsly might think of as impressive. She abandoned the killing category for the moment and clicked on drugs and drug related cases, read dozens of descriptions of pending trials, and again, nothing seemed to pique her interest. She moved on to sex crimes and then politics, and after an hour, she realized that her frustration was growing about as quickly as her expanding bladder. She pushed her chair out and unfolded her legs.

"Damn pins and needles," she said, punching her thighs.

She lurched to the bathroom and peed. She meticulously washed her hands, scrubbing her palms together six times in violent succession before alternating to her knuckles, and their vein-pathed backs. As she rinsed off the lavender scented soap, she stared at herself and thought about her next moves. "I know I've got time, but this is real. You can't leave this shit for the last minute. But what the hell can I start? Any major scandals in this town happen every ten or twenty years, and this Larkin shit is probably the only one that's gonna happen while I'm young, so what the hell am I gonna do?" she asked again, expecting a reassuring response from her phone. "I could throw Sean under the bus, but who's gonna care about that anyway? People'll ignore that like most other domestics. Fuck!"

The thought of Sean, not his physical stature or depraved personality, but his impulsive right-handed hobby made her realize that she needed to relax, and unlike most of her friends who weren't comfortable enough with their sexuality to gratify themselves, she came to a solution to clear her mind and said plainly, "I need my fans." With her decision made, she parted and puckered her lips, tilted her head, and turned toward the mirror with her right hand on her right hip in her best model pose, conjuring her persona for her webcam show, *Posting Bail*. She sauntered back to her room, deciding whether she needed to be a sub or a dominant for her next show. She couldn't decide, so she'd let her loyal audience choose for her.

11

George Alvarez was again waiting for Shinnecock to get back from his lavatorial wanderings when the phone rang. He really didn't feel like taking another survey or donating clothes or volunteering money to any type of organization, so he let it ring. He wasn't a man of the Christian faith but out of habit he'd come to respect Sunday as a day to ignore his professional responsibilities. It was a day to rest his head from the myriad voices of teenagers who needed, who always needed. He had come to realize that the daylight hours of the Lord's Day gave him the perfect amount of time to reflect on his current professional situation, to convince himself that it was exactly what he'd always wanted. He'd figured out over the years that one day out of the week to take for yourself was one too few. He'd also sometimes daydream during his lazy Sunday hours that his life and its course were in the hands of a witless creator. Even worse, he'd imagine it was being directed in a programmed simulation—perhaps his real self was an inanimate vegetable waiting in some freezer or storage center to be cured of some horrific disease—and he'd assume that the assigned writer of his life's story (if the author were even human) was a product of an educational system devoid of the arts. He'd concocted this my-real-self-is-elsewhere scenario when he was a much younger man, but he'd also had the horrible thought that perhaps the programmer was giving him every chance to change his life yet he was too much of a coward to capitalize on it.

George had spent many Sundays silently meditating or pondering the fantasies of what life possibly had to offer after he finished teaching. He'd learned to meditate from one of his physical education colleagues years earlier, and he'd found it not only helpful but necessary in order to stay clear and sane. Now, as he sat in his remodeled kitchen, sipping his mid-afternoon French-pressed coffee, he realized that he still hadn't let go of the belief that someday he'd be free from any obligations he had to his job, exonerated from any balance of love he still owed his wife, and pardoned from any obligatory need he had to be polite or tolerant to absolute strangers and students. After Friday night's trial session with Erica, he was finally ready to admit that while he saw her as his soulmate, she did not see him as hers. Now he was just waiting for the new casting call to be announced in his AbowtMe feed. He knew that one day he'd be called away from his life and a new role would open up, the one he'd always been preparing for. He'd all of sudden hear some distant director yell, "Cut!" from far away off set and then he would quickly disappear to parts unknown. He'd take Shinnie. There was always a dog in the roles he'd seen himself playing, but that would be all he'd bring along from his previous life.

The phone kept ringing. Cutting through his daydream and the rising vapor from his favorite coffee mug and the escalating barking from the backyard. As he slowly woke up, he had a different, self-deprecating thought. "Am I the only idiot in this town who still has a landline?" he said. The relic he questioned was the one he and Erica had bought years ago at a tag sale. It didn't have an HD video display or dual connectivity capabilities. It was a novelty from his childhood and he relished its simplicity. It was from the days when each area code and seven-digit number had to be recalled from the dialer's internal rolodex.

He thought it was bizarre that the caller hadn't been directed to the voicemail. Hell, maybe he or she had. Maybe he or she had kept calling back while George had been lost in his mind. He hadn't noticed. It was like a sonorous cricket, the lone ranger in the basement that heckles you as you scour every square inch of battleship-gray concrete floor to annihilate it. The incessant ringing. He moved to the end of the counter and looked down at the basic caller ID display. *Jimmy Larkin* was visible in the tiny rectangle. Even though he had a free hand, he put his coffee down to answer it.

"Jimmy! Are you all right? What the hell is going on? Why was your trial changed to Accelerated?" George asked before giving the caller a chance to respond.

"They took him, George! They took him in front of me and Jack! They took him!"

"Su-Susan! Calm down. Why would they take him so soon? He wasn't labeled as a flight risk or as a combatant, so why would they arrest him so quickly?"

"I didn't exactly have time to ask them, George! Put Erica on the damn phone! She knows how this shit works better than we do. I have to know where they're taking him and when I can see him!" she screamed.

From behind her terrified voice, George heard Susan's children crying hysterically. At each one of her bellowed demands, he heard their shrill cries rise, as if some sound producer were matching levels at his board, ensuring that the audience experienced the maximum amount of guilt and stress.

"Erica!" George shouted up the stairs, hoping to break through the noise of the powerful showerheads.

"Did you say something, honey?" she shouted back.

"Erica, pick up the phone! It's Susan Larkin!"

After her conversation with Leo Colmsly and hearing the fear in her husband's voice, she skipped her follow up question and jogged naked to the nearest receiver.

"Hello," she said, completing the conference call, "tell me what's going on and how we can help."

Shinnecock was barking more fervently at the back door but not to be let in. Several cars and one motorcycle had just pulled up, invading his clearly piss-marked territory. Both George and Erica ignored the dog's notifications, the way most people ignore car alarms, the kids who cry wolf, or the ringing of house phones on Sunday mornings.

"Susan, have you tried tracking Jimmy's phone? Anyone, whether they're free or under arrest is completely entitled to—"

"Of course I did, but I'm getting nothing! I called the police, but they have no record of an arrest. Help me, Erica! How could they just change everything so quickly? I know how much you're involved with all this shit! Isn't there anyone you can call?"

Erica thought back to Colmsly's lecture from the night before. She tried to think of anyone she might know, but with her access as a moderator terminated, she felt isolated and afraid. "If the police don't know where he is, he must've been taken by the local militia. As soon as I hang up, I'll call them, I'll—"

"There won't be any need to call anyone, darling," Leo Colmsly said, interjecting into the conversation via cell phone, "because you'll be joining him soon."

"Who the hell is this?" Susan screamed.

"Keep up that tone and you'll never know where your husband went, Mrs. Larkin," Colmsly calmly replied as he entered through the front door. "There's nothing Mrs. Alvarez can do for you at this point, so please, hang up the phone and quiet those kids down." Using his signal disrupter, he disconnected Susan Larkin. "Your front door lockpad is far too easy to hack, Mr. Alvarez," he said as he crossed the threshold into the kitchen.

Erica bounded down the stairs, her still-dripping body clad in a robe and her hair tucked under a towel. She froze on the bottom step, her phone still at her ear. "Mr. Colmsly," she said in her most obsequious voice, "there's no need for anymore intervention. I've cleared any remaining statuses I had from my accounts and have reregistered as an entry-level juror. I..."

George watched as Erica continued talking, pleading with this Colmsly character and every word she spoke sickened his stomach. Listening to her conciliatory speech was dreadful, but what was even worse was the realization that this must be what he sounded like whenever he'd tried to please or smooth things over with her. If that's the way he sounded, if that's the demeanor he'd adopted as a man and husband, he wanted out immediately.

"Erica, dear, I have to interrupt you. I can't listen to this anymore," he said to his wife.

"No, I don't give a shit about your two cents, Mr. Alvarez. And based on your lack of concern, it's damn obvious that neither one of you two useless sacks have seen your Proxies," Colmsly said, hoping to take control of the conversation by inducing some panic.

George was nonplussed. "Fuck your Medusa." He picked his cell off the counter. "Filing for public divorce now. Goddamn it's impressive how simple this app is. You want to be the officiant, Colmsly?"

Colmsly responded, "Yes, you soon-to-be-slave, I'd love for my guests and I to be witnesses to this ceremony."

Like any other proceeding that used to involve legal professionals, divorce had been thrown into the public realm. Being a civil trial, many of these were poorly attended by jurors, usually both parties were broke and/or miserable, but there were dedicated pockets of professional and amateur jurors around the country who lived and breathed for the drama of a dissolved or dissolving marriage. These loyal fans didn't mind if the marriages were straight, gay, or polygamous—they just sustained themselves on offering advice and arguing with one another over which party was more at fault for the failed union. In order to expedite the process, every person's histories, assets, holdings, liens, car loans, inheritances, stocks, bonds, debts, insurance policies, tax records, and personal possessions were all stored in the public records section of Gazelle's storage systems. These pieces of information were only accessible if (A) the owner of said account granted access (precisely what George was granting at the moment) and (B) if said person was found guilty in a trial that was a felony in nature.

Colmsly had been correct about the Alvarezes being unaware of their Medusas, but he hadn't expected George to be as crafty as he'd just been. Perhaps George didn't fully realize his clever maneuverings either. By establishing a new trial for himself and his wife, George drastically increased their chances at postponing the Proxy that Colmsly had created the day before. In the new system, any person could stand as an Accused for an unlimited number of charges, but the trial that moves forward in the system, and to the jurors' newsfeeds, is the one that garners the most attention. Even in limited numbers, those who cared to weigh in on a divorce would vastly outnumber those who might participate in a low-level juror violation case.

"Probationary Agents Reilly and Vinks, please join me in the lovely kitchen of Mr. and Mrs. Alvarez," Colmsly said into his microphone.

George looked at Erica, her fragility enhanced by the thin bathrobe she wore. She looked at him and took a step in his direction but stopped as Colmsly began moving toward her. Like a Newtonian law, he stopped his pursuit when she paused hers.

"George, please…" she said, but couldn't conjure the words to stop his thoughts or his typing fingers.

George put his phone on the counter and moved toward the door, wanting only to stop the dog's noise, but Colmsly again stopped an Alvarez.

"If you let that dog in and force me to shoot it, I'll burn this hole down with you in it."

"I didn't mean for him to attack you. I just have to stop that barki—"

"Get the fuck back to your coffee," Colmsly said as his two newest compatriots entered the house, "and say hello to my two newest friends. This filthy dolt is Sean Reilly and that hillbilly is Vinks, something Vinks. It really doesn't matter what your first name is, pissant, so just stand there until I tell you what to do."

"Sean?" George asked as if he were seeing a returned vet who'd been presumed K.I.A., "What are you doing with these people?"

"That's right," Colmsly said, putting the pieces together, "you probably taught the lad."

"No," George said, still looking at the boy, "he was never one of mine, but I met his stepmother this past week. She said that he needed more of our help, she said that he…" George trailed off, hating himself for brushing the boy's mother off at the Friday meeting.

"I wouldn't beat yourself up, teacher man," Colmsly said. "You're not there to save them. You can barely get them to think on their own. Unfortunately, though, he's moving beyond the desks and standards. He's going to do some different learning today, and since you thought it would be a good idea to fuck with me, young Sean and his friend are going to demonstrate some of FileX's most rudimentary lessons for you."

"What the hell are you talking about?" George asked, again feeling his compressed rage seethe, the wrath that had been bottled up after every belittlement he'd ever endured from his wife, students, and administrators. "Did you just threaten me? Did you just fucking threaten me in my own home!"

"Drama doesn't seem to fit you, Alvarez, but if you're having some type of moment, let me apologize for cutting it short. Reilly! Vinks! Pick one and kill them," Colmsly instructed, drawing his firearm just in case they didn't obey.

"This is *not* going to happen," Erica said, speaking as if each dick in the room got hard or soft at her command. "This will *not* end with anyone being harmed or dying," she said, using her most potent instructional voice.

Colmsly's shell momentarily thinned at the definitiveness of her tone. The pitch and delivery could have been from any one of his superiors; it was similar, so very similar, he swore, to President Krauss's own. He shut his eyes and held them closed to reset his mental keel. The first order he'd give when he opened his eyes would be for Reilly to put a bullet through her jaw. Before he could say a word, however, he saw a half-filled mug of coffee fly past his head. Only one man in the room, the man who'd become immune to her cadre of attitudes, like a mongoose to a cobra's venom, hadn't frozen at Erica's I'm-in-charge voice. Instead of turning to stone, George reacted like he hadn't in the days before when his friend had been carried out of school, like he hadn't when Erica had nursed him through his friend's trial. The mug flew with the strength of years of repressed anger and adrenaline, so instead of hitting anything worth its mass, it shattered against the antique China hutch in the dining room.

The gunfire and Shinnecock's barks syncopated into a horrific rhythm that the neighbors could only rationalize as the sounds of suburbia on the Fourth of July.

Bailey's usual preshow routine began with her scrupulously inspecting the house. More often than not, her parents were home and asleep down the hall from her, so she often locked and barricaded her door and brought up the home-security feed (motion sensors included) on her phone. Sean's room was in the basement, and he rarely ventured upstairs unless she had company, so she was never too concerned with his presence. She had actually thought at one point that it would massively boost her viewership if her stepbrother accidentally popped in while she was spread eagle or on all fours on her bed, but the thought was thankfully fleeting. But there was no need for these precautions today; no one was asleep because it was early in the evening, and the last message she'd gotten from her parents said something about having to pick Sean up from a FileX building all the way on the South Shore of the island, about twenty miles away. The only two people in the world who still text, she'd thought when she'd heard the notification. With the knowledge that she was alone for at least a few hours, regardless of what medium her parents had used to tell her, she decided to really succumb to and obey her audience's fantasies—as long as they were within reason. Her rules, cemented early on from watching traumatic animated movies about animals or their cuddly parents being killed, were as follows: (1) she'd never hurt a living thing so some sick fuck could reach orgasm; (2) she'd never put herself in extreme pain or danger for someone else's pleasure; (3) she'd never name or humiliate anyone else so a stranger could orgasm; (4) she would never, at least while she was still on the cusp of graduating high school, meet face-to-face with any of her viewers; (5) she'd never give anyone her full name, address, (though to boost her popularity, she'd given away NY in her profile) alternate usernames, or details of her bedroom. Adhering to these rules had kept her safe, entertained, and financially successful for nearly nine months. The cost of a private show ranged anywhere from fifty to five hundred dollars in the digital currency, CriptoCoin, and she never had to finagle her audience to join her private shows. Even with so many unemployed, nearly twenty-one percent throughout America, including those who had given up competing with programs and machines, people (in her case men and women alike) always seemed to find the funds for erotica. She'd pieced together the information she'd needed to set up her Cripto account by having Sean ask his now disappeared friend, Lamont Davis. Sean had never questioned her intentions, and she was fairly certain that Lamont had never questioned Sean's; Lamont probably thought Sean was devising some half-assed future drug plan, a plan that, even if it had been real, would have fizzled out in Sean's vastly incoherent ADHD mind.

With her house secured (habits) and her shades and curtains pulled, she performed a marathon of a one-woman show. Requests of every nature poured in from lighting candles for both ambiance and wax play (a fetish she found to be so popular that she kept what could best be described as a church altar selection of candles in her closet) to instructing other subs to sensually masturbate for her and for themselves. Her viewership reached into the tens of thousands, and she was enthralled with the boundaries they pushed and the kink they introduced. Toys and outfits and roles and positions and peaks were explored and reached. After almost two hours of play, she began to say her sweaty goodbyes.

"I—I can't thank you all enough for that," she said, giggling, keeping only her lips visible to the webcam, "because I've, like, never finished that hard before."

A slew of messages appeared on her feed, and a chorus of voices came through her earpiece, all begging her to continue the fun in a private session.

"I'm literally done, my loves," she said, her audio automatically being typed to the others on her message board, "and I promise I'll go down privately next time," she said, making her hands into a heart below her chin. A tiny heart emoji appeared next to the freshly typed text. "But I also have one tiny favor to ask from all of you. Is that cool? Cool. Along with getting you off, I'm gonna get into being a low-key juror because that's how I really want to explode on the scene. I want to become the biggest, most famous juror there's ever been, like, I'm talking the Cochran of jurors."

She saw her participant number drop by several hundred at her announcement. It kept dropping until it reached several thousand—probably current, bitter prisoners who were given an allowance for porn but who didn't want to hear about the judicial system after jerking off, she thought, but their exit did not dissuade her from continuing her message. Over seven thousand subscribers still remained to listen to or read what she had to say, and she knew that was enough to get her started.

"I need volunteers to help me find a juicy, nasty, original story to bring to trial. It can be anything that will cause a sensation, my loves. I've searched through everything I could think of and I couldn't find anything worthy of my time. If your story is the one that I choose," she moved her lips closer to the camera and licked them in a seductive circle, "a live, private show would only be the beginning of my appreciation. Until the next show…good night," she purred.

Suggestions began flooding her feed and site inbox. She smiled and flashed her right nipple an instant before shutting off her camera. She hadn't thought of a detailed filtering plan for all of these incoming ideas, but it couldn't be too hard to export them and then categorize them in a spreadsheet. She'd split the work between her TV screen, which still displayed her *Posting Bail* homepage, and her computer monitor, which displayed the columned list of potential trial ideas. After twenty minutes of setting up and checking and re-checking her work, she switched her homepage image back to her computer monitor and went to the menu to export her data. Before she clicked on the command, however, a blinking red message from an A. Drison appeared on her post, stopping her hand and the cursor. She read the message.

You put on a beautiful show, Mistress, and I see you're really from Runners' Landing (the candles you left on your shelf lit up too much of your room btw because I could easily see the class portrait on your wall) and what you think you know about the teacher named Jimmy or James Larkin, u don't even know the half of what he's been involved in…

Bailey cursed and looked toward the illuminated wall. She was stupid to light so many, but no one else seemed to have noticed but this person. *Fuck it,* she thought. She'd have to be more careful in the future, recheck her sight lines and camera angles. When she moved out, she'd have a dedicated studio for her shows. *Well, what's done can't be undone*, she thought and looked back at Drison's words. Ignoring the awaiting spreadsheet, she clicked reply.

Posting Bail Typed: I'm glad you enjoyed it ;) And TIL I have to be more careful with my lighting in the future…thank you for pointing that out! Now, what else might you know about Larkin I promise it will be worth your while if it's good…

A. Drison Typed: Not over the computers or phones. I'll be in NYC late Thursday night for a conference. If you'll meet me sometime during the weekend, I'll give you everything I have. And it's not just stories. There are documents, recordings, and pictures to support every…damn…word.

Bailey let the cursor blink in and out of sight, in and out, in and out, in and out. Her rules had kept her alive. Her rules had kept her two selves separate and safe. That was before, though. Those dictums existed prior to Larkin and Jillian Foster's trial, prior to Kristy and Sean's stupidity, and, especially, before Leo Colmsly's interrogation. In and out. In and out. In and out, it blinked. If she were to meet this Drison person, she would do so in a neutral, crowded place, and she would not go alone.

Posting Bail Typed: I think I need to know a little bit more about you before I agree to anything…

A. Drison Typed: You can trust me. What would you like to know?

Posting Bail Typed: For starters, how do I know ur not just some psycho who wants to kill me and rape my corpse??

A. Drison Typed: Hell of an imagination you've got there. As I'm sure you are too, I'm someone else in real life, and that person isn't sly enough to stalk and kill internet sex workers. I'm a thirty-three-year-old woman who makes her living as a nurse. Been doing it since I graduated college. I got into it because I wanted to help people, but that sorta changed during my mid-twenties. I'll tell you about that when we meet. I don't want to hurt you. I enjoy what you do and I want to keep watching it for as long as I can.

Posting Bail Typed: So how would you be able to help me become famous?

A. Drison Typed: Years ago, Jimmy Larkin worked with my ex and me, and we all worked for a really fucked up company. The information I can give you on Larkin isn't just to punish him. What it will expose will send my psychotic ex and the rest of them away for good...

Posting Bail Typed: So its for revenge, huh? That's cool. Alright. U def got my attention. One thing tho, why don't you just put them on trial urself?

A. Drison Typed: Because I want to disappear. I've made sure to destroy or erase any connection I'd ever had with that company and those people. I mean, I was what people call an independent contractor so I never was a part of what they did... Sorry if that's getting into too much detail. I just want to try and make things right and ruin my ex before I get outta this fucking country.

Posting Bail Typed: Holy shit. That's not too much detail at all. I can't believe this and I know it's fucking crazy but you've got my attention... I'll meet you but wherever we meet, it has to be in public. That is nonnegotiable.

A. Drison Typed: Absolutely agree. I'm fine with a restaurant, a park, a beach, anything. In fact, I'd love to get to a beach. It's been a long time since I've seen an ocean.

Bailey thought about the safest places she might rendezvous with A. Drison. She opened a new window on her screen and searched for detailed maps of Long Island and Manhattan. She found the rough midpoint and decided to have the meetup take place somewhere populated, accessible, and fun enough to stay at if the plan fizzled out. Nothing on the zoomed-in map seemed interesting to her, being that the middle of an island lacked her preferred ocean views, so she scanned north and south. To the north were parks and golf courses and the rocky shorelines of the Long Island Sound; to the south was the sandy, beautiful coastline beaches of Jones Beach Island and Fire Island and some idyllic little towns right on the Great South Bay. The South Shore sounded much more appealing, and while spending the day shopping and eating in one of those small towns sounded enticing, Bailey selected a small strip of beach made notorious a decade or so prior by the macabre discovery of a mass grave of prostitutes. And Gilgo was its name-o. *If this doesn't work out, at least she'd become another part of local history,* she thought.

Posting Bail Typed: Gilgo Beach...Saturday...1 o'clock...you'll recognize my umbrella. I'm bringing a friend, but you come alone. That isn't up for discussion either. You say no, I move on.

A. Drison Typed: Interesting choice. Never found out who put those women there did they? Everything sounds good. I'm not going to hurt you, and your friend can listen or not. Until then, Mistress...

12

"I'm really tired, Ms. Baker, and I can't believe I'm back here, but, hey, orders are orders. Everybody's got a boss, right?"

"I suppose, Mr. Colmsly, but I honestly don't know what you or your company can offer at a time like this. Jillian Foster's death will…it will completely throw off the students' chances at achieving mastery on our upcoming exams. We need to get the crisis counse—"

"No, no. No more counselors. We've been able to update you with the latest in bereavement technologies, courtesy of AbowtMe and Gazelle. Please, have a look."

Baker scanned the icons on her screen and displayed there, as if it had always been there, appeared the new IBereave icon.

"Please click on it. I really don't want to spend any more time here than I have to. I swear I must have pissed off someone at the top to deserve this place. Impressed with it?"

Baker opened the application. She selected English as the preferred language, scrolled through the set list of grief options, selected *Loss of Loved One and/or Coworker* since that best described her current situation, and hit enter. After a dozen pulses of the loading indicator, a video feed opened, showing a Latino man sitting in a cubicle. He began to read, as his moving mouth indicated, but Baker heard nothing from her speakers. She checked the volume. It was on full. The man continued reading from, what she guessed was a prepared script, but no sound followed. After twenty seconds, the broken message sounded through the speakers.

Colmsly's countenance darkened with rage. "This goddamn school's connection is the shittiest I've ever seen! Are the kids licking the outlets every morning or just ramming their needle dicks into them between periods? Do you actually have techs in this place? Goddamn! And this is after we helped you get rid of the unions!"

Baker's shaking right hand quietly closed out the IBereave rep. She didn't immediately know how to respond to Colmsly's outburst. When she figured it out, her voice didn't quake at all. "Perhaps, Mr. Colmsly, if you let me alter the announcement we discussed—about Jillian Foster—I could help refocus the students' attention."

"Pretty much nothing you could say will shock me, so, yeah, Ms. Baker, lemme hear what you've got."

"What if, instead of offering them time to use IBereave, time that will take away from their valuable review sessions, I help them guide their anger and confusion and sadness toward someone, or, more matter-of-factly, towards a group of people."

"OK, I'll keep biting. Let's hear the rest of it."

"Almost all of the students are completing individual review programs— there shouldn't be any teacher-led instruction going on—so, why don't I make an announcement in Jillian's memory? Something to the effect of Runners' Landing High School will be sending Medusas, pardon me, I know you hate the expression, to those who failed to recognize the tragedy before it happened, those who should have read the signs and notified her parents and me, those who continue to fail our students time and time again, those who just care about their paychecks and summer breaks: the teachers."

Colmsly smiled and sat back in his chair. He looked over his shoulder at an exhausted yet smiling Agent Richards. Focusing back on Baker, he asked, "And you don't think that would be a distraction for your precious tests?"

"Are you kidding? You've seen how they go after blood in the water. Most won't care who's standing in front of the rooms in these last few weeks, anyway. If we leave Foster's death to the, uh, online counselors, rumors, and gossip will tear them apart. Let them focus their grief and anger on something they already don't respect."

"You think they—the teachers—will just go along with it? No complaints or retaliation?"

"Oh, I hope they all quit. It'd reduce our payroll by a million-and-a-half at least. If you remember, we were never able to get rid of all the high earners. They still had some friends left in the state congress."

"If only we could fix that issue as well. Well, Ms. Baker, yes, I think that's a fantastic idea. In fact, go ahead and use my account—here's the info—and initialize the trial. I suggest using your exact words from before in the description. The charge? Click off involuntary manslaughter, dereliction of civic duty, and endangering the welfare of a child. Make sure you include the girl's mother on behalf of the district, too. And when all that's done, Baker...make that announcement."

Roseanne Decardo was distressed with her surprise Monday assignment. Covering classes for absent teachers was a job for the substitutes and interns, not management, she thought as she stared at George Alvarez's mixture of raucous juniors and seniors. All of those underlings, however, were busy filling in for the classes that had been abandoned after Principal Baker's inspiring announcement. At least thirty-six members of the faculty, those who still retained some of the grandfathered-in union protections, had walked out and left the campus. Mr. Alvarez's situation was different than those who exited en masse as he had simply not shown up for work. Decardo had just happened to be leaving her office when Baker threw her into the nearest teacher-less room.

The students sensed her hesitation and were getting louder. She scanned the room and thought about how she might quiet them, thought about what her teachers had done, but came up with zilch. Alvarez didn't even have the curtesy to leave plans on his desk for her. Typical teacher.

"Is he even here, today?" someone asked from the back. "Because I've got an econ project to finish, so can I, like, leave my name with you, Miss?"

Attendance. Right. Attendance would eat away a few minutes. She brought up her tablet, entered her password, and scrolled through the faculty list before finding the master schedule. She clicked on Alvarez's third period Journalism class and began butchering the names.

"Nu-Nuu-goo-een," she stammered.

"It's pronounced *new*, unlike your outfit, *yen*. Nguyen," said Phuong Nguyen.

"And you may go to the main office, young lady!" Decardo shot back.

"Because you can't read? Like that's fair!"

"Out! How dare you, you disre—"

"Fuck youuuuuuyen," Phuong said, on her way out.

Decardo stood flustered and flushed in front of the laughing class.

"Hey, what's your name again? Ms. Decardo? Ok, yeah, I'll forget that. How do we rate you? Your name's not coming up on my StudentData page."

Decardo seethed under her blue blazer. "You don't rate me," she affirmed, "because I'm not your teacher! I'm your *assistant principal*, and you will treat me with respect!"

They laughed and cursed at her from behind their Comp-U-Desks. One student got up and made his way to the door.

"And where do you think you're going," she said as she moved to block his exit.

"Mr. A usually lets us go to the bathroom or are we not allowed to do that today?"

"You didn't ask my permission to leave the room, nor did you put your name in the sign out tablet."

"So, you want me to piss on the floor? And Mr. A doesn't use the sign out tablet."

"Go to the office!"

"And piss there?"

"Out!"

Decardo was trembling with rage and embarrassment as Bailey entered the room with an unexcused late pass. "What's your name?" Decardo screamed as the still-unknown-to-her student crossed the threshold.

Bailey had been looking at the floor as she had walked absentmindedly down the hall, not seeing Mr. Alvarez's perturbed sub. Decardo's command shocked her out of her stupor. "Bailey Tomanicki," she responded. After signing off with A. Drison the night before, Bailey had had a difficult time falling asleep. She'd forgotten to set her alarm, so it was her mother, whom Bailey had barely seen over the weekend, who'd awakened her. Bailey had groggily listened to the stories of their arrests and incarcerations and of Sean's current predicament. Her mother had skipped many of the particulars and had offered her the day off if she wished. Bailey had turned down the out-of-character gesture because just before she'd gone to bed, she'd messaged Kristy to see if she were planning on being at school, and while it had taken a few hours to get a response, Kristy had finally answered with a terse *yes*. Bailey needed her help and to apologize again for getting her friend into such serious trouble. More than anything, Bailey had to coax her into coming with her to the A. Drison introduction. Bailey was positive that Colmsly had threatened Kristy and her family, too, so if she could show him how helpful Kristy had been with the new case, she was sure he'd leave both of their families alone.

"I can't believe Mr. Alvarez doesn't use a sign out tablet," Decardo said as she took Bailey's pass. "I will deal with that when he comes in. And you, take your seat and be quiet."

Bailey wasn't in the mood for another losing argument, so she walked toward her seat, scanning the room for Kristy. No regular teacher meant no assigned seats, so it took her a few searches of the rows to find her friend. Kristy sat hunched forward with her dark hair covering the sides of her face. *Still looks hungover,* Bailey thought.

"Hey," she tried.

"*Hola,*" Kristy said, not turning.

"*Lo siento mucho,*" Bailey said, seeing if matching her bilingual approach might keep the tone playful.

Kristy's façade relaxed as she looked up at her friend. "I don't even know what the hell is going on," she said. "What the fuck were we thinking?"

She hadn't softened as much as Bailey had hoped. "I can't imagine what that asshole Colmsly said to you, but I can help. I know that I—"

"Have you even heard the rumors?"

"I know you won't believe this, but I haven't looked at my phone all morning."

"They're saying that Mr. and Mrs. Alvarez were killed yesterday, and…"

"And what?"

"And that Sean was one of the ones who shot them," she whispered.

"That's so ridiculous, I can't even. Sean? The 'bating beauty? The only thing he can shoot comes out of his dick and I'm pretty sure his aim sucks with that, too."

"Don't you realize that if this guy Colmsly can kill two people or have them killed and get away with it, we're as good as dead," Kristy said, crying at the thought.

Bailey nudged herself onto Kristy's seat, took out her phone, and tapped its screen to life. "We're going to be fine," she said, looking Kristy directly in her eyes, "because I've got something that will get Agent Colmsly off our tits."

She handed Kristy the phone and told her to read the entire conversation she'd had with A. Drison. "Why the hell is she calling you 'Mistress,' and what does she mean by online sex workers?"

"I believe she wrote 'internet sex workers,' but I'll catch you up on that later."

"But—"

"Drop the mistress questions and focus on the part about me needing a friend for the meeting. Kristy, I need your help," she pleaded. "I need you to help me get this info, and then get the hell home safely. And…"

"And what?"

"It'll only take a few hours. And…"

"And what, Bailey!"

"And I need you to drive us. Dammit, I'm so sorry."

"Oh, this just gets better. How do you know this isn't some total psycho? Nothing she says here makes me think she's legit and look at us! It'd take nothing to kidnap and kill us."

"It'll be a lot more painful living as a slave for Colmsly and that damn company. Listen, I made her send me a pic before I logged off. I searched it and it's solid. Her full name's Alexis Drison and everything she said about her past checks out. Making all that up just to abduct and kill an internet sex—" she caught herself before exposing her last secret, "It just seems pretty elaborate for a serial killer, no?"

"Oh, you've met so many of them, right?"

"I've been hit on by every type of creep you can imagine, so yeah, I kinda have a good sense for these things," she said, knowing that she was deviating too far from her point. "Kristy, you've gotta help me, and if we don't do this, we're totally screwed. Please do it. Please."

"Fine. But if I die, I'm so going to fucking kill you."

Assistant Principal Decardo had given up looking for Alvarez's emergency plans, so she said to the class, "I'm sure you have some type of final articles due for the June edition of the paper, so please work on whatever you had been working on, and until the bell rings, keep your mouths shut."

The school newspaper mirrored the styles and trends of the professional counterparts; websites with entertainment, sports, and reviews of the highest trending trials dominated the headlines. In addition, almost every school paper was now replete with outside ads and sponsors. Devolving into tabloids or simple propaganda outlets was the only way the old-guard organizations had survived the collapse of the objective-news era. As the public became more focused on suing one another into poverty or prison, people became less and less interested in what was going on outside of their tribal existences. Like most of the public schools, the renowned names in the news world survived by accepting buyouts from the upper tiers of the financial and technological industries. And if bribery failed as an influencer, the megalomaniac CEOs of the Big Four—who didn't want their gospel of a brighter future being undermined by negative reviews or irritating Editorial Boards—sued the remaining outlets into compliance or oblivion. Krauss, in particular, relished in destroying those who'd ever authored a disparaging article about her company's lurid business practices. Careers and reputations of those who wrote about the use of slave labor in the tech world were fired; those who tried to expose the blatant corruption between the tech industry and the local, state, and federal branches of government were bullied and trolled into resigning, and in some drastic instances, forced to flee the country.

Most of the reputable papers and channels, just before they went under, were kept afloat by the last vestige of protected free speech: public broadcasting. Even these outlets, however, were revamped to fit the new age. They substituted articulate newscasters and trained reporters with reality stars, AbowtMe celebrities, and sports icons. People began following and rooting for the new organizations as if they were the hometown teams. Mostly, people continued reading and ingesting anything that agreed with what they wanted to hear.

The submission of the press was one of the most significant factors in popularizing the online trial system. People easily transitioned from being comment-section superstars to social media trial experts. Aaron Elskin, a soon-to-be graduating senior of Runners' Landing High School wanted, more than anything, to be a full-time journalist for one of AbowtMe's subsidiary papers, so he took Mr. Alvarez's Journalism class very seriously. Not so much Mr. Alvarez, though. Elskin thought of his teacher as a liberal leftover, always talking about how people have to be kinder to each other and how they should spend less time trying to ruin each other's lives and more time being charitable and blah, blah, blah. And if the rumors were true, about the deaths of George and his wife, Elskin wouldn't really mind at all. He thought Mr. Alvarez was a whiny bitch and his wife an elitist twat. She had had the nerve to fail him his freshman year. Him! Aaron Elskin, the greatest mind to have ever come through the halls of Runners' Landing High! He was the only student who hadn't given Decardo a hard time when she'd come in as their sub. He would never disrespect an employee of the Big Four, no matter how low they were. He had been working on his coup de grace—a human interest piece about how the slave industry should be revived, using scummy, low-scoring Vts as labor for the technologically deprived, still-developing countries—when he'd overheard Bailey and Kristy's sordid conversation. What had really gotten his interest were the mentions of online or internet sex workers and mistresses. They hadn't been paying attention to him, no one really had since the seventh grade, so neither one of them had noticed when he'd taken out his phone, hit record, enlarged the image, and copied their entire exchange. As the class continued to ignore Ms. Decardo and their work, Aaron opened a private browser and searched for *Posting Bail*.

"Holy shit," he said when he found the page. He looked back up at the girls who had just finished their conversation. He closed the browser and put his phone in his bag. He kicked the seat they were both on.

"So, Bailey—" Aaron began, just before the bell rang.

"I don't have time for you now, Elskin. Fuck off."

"Ouch. I was just wondering how much it costs to post bail, ya know, if I ever get arrested. Do you know anything about that? When a perp posts bail, any clue how much that costs?" he said with a condescending grin.

13

"We can't just let them take our kids, Jordan! We can't just sit here while they tear our families apart! You work for them, dammit! That doesn't give you any kinda leeway?" Frank Reilly asked as his crew mowed, trimmed, and cleaned the Davis's front yard.

"You think my only move is to sit around while my entire family is locked up? You think I haven't been going at this from every angle, trying to figure out my next step? Was up all night takin' care of Latoya and finding out where they put Lamont," Jordan responded.

Reilly turned away from Davis, took a long swig of coffee from his thermos, and watched his team work. Would have been hypnotic, the team's synchronization, had it not been for the window-shaking noise of the machinery. Reilly let the mower and its operator pivot and turn around and head back to the street before speaking again. "Jordan, I think I have a plan— one I've had for a very long time, really. Just didn't have the real motivation to use it 'til now. As horrible as it sounds, having Sean and Lamont involved is actually a blessing."

"And how do you figure our boys being kidnapped—" the mower returned, enveloping Jordan's reply. As it dopplered away, he continued, "is a blessing? How is my gifted son and your..." he didn't need the roar of the mower to halt his words this time. He knew what he was about to say was unnecessarily cruel, so he didn't say it. "What is it you were thinking, Frank?"

"For years these corporations fought for the right to be recognized as people. Remember that? They wanted to be able to spend their money freely to buy politicians—and then call it *free speech*—and they won that privilege almost ten years ago. Well, a firm that I'd worked with had the idea of suing them as individual people soon after they'd won that distinction. We'd spent years building the cases, suing smaller groups to set precedents and infiltrating different companies by bribing low-Vt employees who were somehow able to access things they shouldn't have been, but the new system was proposed, altered, and implemented before we could bring anything substantial to trial. Didn't gather enough to have it brought in under the Sanders Grandfather Amendment either. Damn convenient for them that it all changed when it did. We weren't the only firm with the idea, and if the financial groups who'd been responsible had been caught, so many politicians would have gone down."

"Frank, what the hell do your glory days have to do—"

"So many of us were terrified after seeing what happened during that first trial. You remember his name?"

"I don't."

"Anthony Palmieri. Probably deserved what he got, but it scared those of us who were still thinking about keeping our practices so badly, that we all just left."

The mower's pitch was growing, again blotting out the conversation. Jordan smiled as the man spun the machine and sent it toward the street.

"Again, what the hell does this have to do with getting our boys back?" Jordan said impatiently.

"The corporations—namely the Big Four—still classify their political spending in terms of free speech, so they can still, technically, be tried as people. And just like we tried to do all those years ago but failed, we can put someone with even more knowledge and expertise on the inside to help build our case. Jordan, we never had someone like you, someone with access. We can expose what happened to our kids. We can show the world what kind of companies are running the damn government. Even if we don't win, we can start a big fucking fire for an already pissed off population."

"They'd bury us, Frank. Online and in real life. We wouldn't stand a chance. They have an entire division of employed trolls to support them in cases, not to mention an AI that can beat our best moves before we've even figured them out."

"We've got to try, Jordan. We've got be able to look at our wives and kids and tell them that we at least tried to do something."

Jordan stepped down from the porch and stood next to Reilly. The mower and trimmer and blower had all moved to manicure the backyard. "So, what are we gonna charge 'em with? And what exactly would you need me to get?"

"It's been a little while since I've checked the updated statutes. Let's meet tonight and see if there have been any additions to the local penal codes. Tomorrow night we'll check the state laws, and if we don't find anything there, we'll check the federal ones this weekend."

"I can't start peeping around so soon after all of the..." he waved his hand toward his house, "...shit went down. I probably won't have my clearances, so don't expect too much in terms of current info. I do have some tidbits here and there in my portable drives, but I don't know what good it would do now."

"That sounds like a start. I'll swing by later—I'm sure I'll forget a gas can at this account, if anyone asks—and we'll figure out a safe place to get going."

Jordan shifted, uneasy with what he was about to say. "I have a way to make anywhere we meet safe. It's the damn reason my boy's in jail right now. I'll see you later, Frank," he finished, shaking his friend's hand.

"Sounds good. We'll talk later. My guys are packing it up, so I'll pop by later."

Frank walked down the driveway and met his team at the trailer. Jordan saw him pantomiming at one of his men. The worker nodded, moved from behind the machine, and ran toward the back gate. Frank maneuvered the mower into the trailer and grabbed a gas can on his way out.

"Boss says we left a rake in the back," the worker said to Jordan as he passed.

Jordan looked toward the trailer and saw Frank tossing an empty red container into to the fence-like row of arbor vitae. When it came to a rolling rest, Frank winked at Jordan and got into the driver's seat.

"Can't find it anywhere, Mr. Reilly!" Hector yelled from the open gate.

"Forget it!" Frank responded. "I found it behind the rakes. Get in, we've got six more to do before lunch," he said, checking his phone for messages and updates.

"Didn't check there. Sorry, Frank," he said, stepping into the cab, "but at least we're still busy, right?"

"We are for the summer, Hector, we are. Damn fuel prices keep goin' up, though, and have you heard what EverKutz and North Shore Lawns are doin'?" Frank asked, referring to his main competitors.

"What's that, Frank?" Hector replied.

"They've bought themselves that GPS guided equipment. Programmable mowers, blowers…the works."

"Won't that shit cost too much to run?" Wilson, the man sitting between them, asked.

"Not when it's subsidized by CenTeck and Gazelle. They're more than happy to sponsor and show off their new toys. Haven't been able to get the actual prices out of 'em, but what I figured—since the last time that Gazelle rep approached me—is at least fifteen below what we charge. Would absolutely destroy the competition."

"Amigo," Hector said as he stared out the window, "aren't we the competition?"

"That we are, señor. That we are."

"If they keep putting people outta work, who's gonna be left to buy their shit?"

Frank tossed his phone onto the dashboard and started the engine. "Got me. Maybe they'll start programming machines to do the shopping. Let's get moving before we fall behind."

He struck the horn twice as an added goodbye to his friend and they pulled away from the Davis property. Instead of focusing on his tumultuous business or his son or his wife or his stepdaughter, he thought about how he and Jordan were going to fight against the titans of technology. He felt anxious yet confident, sitting in his stalwart work truck. He, even after all the years he'd been exposed to it, still enjoyed the aroma of freshly cut grass but today he rolled up the windows and cranked the air conditioning. *Technology over nature*, he thought, as he pressed the *Max Air* button. Embrace the tech and we'll figure out to *beat* the tech.

"We've got too much to do today to focus on the shit, fellas. Let's just get through it one account at a time."

Lamont Davis shared his cell, which was more like a college dorm room, with Enrico Jimenez. Enrico was also being held for crimes against the company—the equivalent of crimes against the state. He had been a prisoner for more than three months, abducted from his hotel job by a FileX street-gang subsidiary. There was no shortage of gangs in the city limits, but most of them were fractious and leaderless. They shot at each other, sometimes purposely, sometimes accidentally, and almost all of the time, out of retaliation for a previous killing or insult. Comprised of mostly eleven-to-seventeen-year-olds, many jumped at the chance to earn some money, a place to stay, and something to eat from FileX's inner-city marketers. The gangs' reputations for completing their missions, much like the militias across the country, was tenuous at best, but there was always a steady flow of replacements if one group was killed or if they failed to deliver on an order. It was the Quincy Street Kings of Bed-Stuy that had pulled Enrico Jimenez from behind the counter at the Huxley Hotel. Between the savage beatings, they informed him that he was being arrested for filing a false trial.

Jimenez had been thankful for his job. The hotel was posh, set in a newly gentrified part of Bedford-Stuyvesant, and he'd earned his way to assistant manager after years of bell-hopping and errand running. Those jobs were eventually automated, but his education and above-average Vt score qualified him to remain on the staff. He was nearly finished with his online hospitality program when he and his fiancée had started looking for their own apartment. Although he was thankful for the employment and enjoyed interacting with people from around the world, the work was never going to satisfy his true passion. What had captivated his imagination in high school, what had really made him think beyond himself for the first time, was astronomy. By the end of his sophomore year, he'd saved up to buy a gently used Celestron telescope. His ceremony was simple: he'd finish his homework and chores, and with his parents' permission, lug the scope and its stand out of his bedroom window, up the rusty fire escape, and spend hours on the roof— regardless of the season—peering into the cosmos. He knew how much the lights of the city polluted his views, but he kept up his routine. By his senior year of college, however, after so many more high rises had been erected and dozens more of FileX's security floodlights had been installed, it became impossible for him to make out even the brightest constellations. *Erasing the heavens*, he thought, *is the same as erasing dreams.* On the trip that broke him, the one that had inspired him create his Medusa, he was trying to show his fiancée, Mariella, the source of his passion, the wonders that had kept him out of trouble on the streets: the natural art of the night sky. But all she'd been able to see in the scope's lens was the blinking lights of the airway traffic. He swiveled the scope in every possible direction, but the light of gentrified security drowned out the glowing pinpricks in the sky.

That night, he set up this online trial:

You can now join the opening arguments for Case No. CAN001-102, Enrico Jimenez vs. FileX Public Securities, Inc. The plaintiff accuses the defendant of willfully neglecting the aspirations of the people of the borough of Brooklyn and negligently polluting the environment with excessive amounts of photon emissions. By clicking on the box below, you're confirming that you have read and agree to the Citizen Juror Terms.

The heckling and attacks on him were merciless, racist, vindictive, and, after only a very short amount of time, personal. When he saw his home address—which he shared with his parents—his phone numbers, his date of birth, and his yearbook picture posted in the forum, he tried to rescind the Medusa, but it was too late. The trial moved to completion with the online jurors finding in FileX's favor by ninety-eight percent. Officially, there was never a penalty for losing a trial—as long as the charges were deemed to be legitimate. The powers-that-be at FileX decided that Mr. Jimenez's accusation had made a mockery of the system; a citizen who held an average Vt rating couldn't possibly challenge the very entity that had created and maintained the justice system. If the jury found the corporation innocent by a margin of less than seventy percent, the executives feared, more people would have felt emboldened to challenge FileX's public policies. To nullify that possible threat, they employed the AI—in the form of thousands of fictitious jurors—into the trial to sway the decision to their supermajority, and after they soundly destroyed Jimenez's argument, they decided to make an example of him. To do this, they immediately countersued him, claiming his charges were utterly fraudulent and contracted the Quincy Street Kings to arrest him.

He started his twenty to twenty-five year term at Rikers Island but was quickly moved for his inconvenience. FileX decided that prisoner 045-826-113 should be moved from jail to jail in an ever-expanding fractal pattern. They never wanted him to see his family, friends, or fiancée again. They wanted to make an example of what would happen to anyone who questioned any one of the Big Four: they would simply vanish.

Enrico Jimenez was not, however, deprived of the right to a roommate. He could do no damage to the reputation or practices of FileX's security procedures from jail, so providing him with an occasional cellmate would help keep him sane and save the company on psychiatric and medical expenses. So, here he sat with his new buddy, a trembling black kid from a town on Long Island he'd never heard of, telling his story.

"And you're in here because you did what against them? You're gonna have to tell me this again because I can't believe you're alive. You used their stolen tech so you could smoke some pot? If you're gonna ruin your life, at least do it for somethin' worthwhile, man," Enrico said.

"Was yours worth it, man? Was your fight for the stars worth it!"

"I'll never see 'em again, brotha, so you tell me. There ain't no beatin' these mothafuckas, not when they can play us all like this," he said, looking around the cell. "Anyone gonna try and take them down better have an army behind 'em."

Jordan didn't feel like talking anymore. He stretched out on his bunk and prayed that his father was working on something.

Enrico wasn't quite finished with the exchange, however. "You can sit there and sulk, hopin' that someone'll rescue you, but that ain't happenin'."

"So what're you, man? The welcome wagon! The down-on-his-luck lifer who gets the fresh meat to cry like bitches! How the fuck is knowin' your punkass star-gazin' story gonna help me right now!"

"No, brotha, 'cause there's a good chance that after tonight, maybe tomorrow, we'll never see each other again. Wanna know why?"

"Does it sound like I do?"

"Keep yellin', man, and they'll come in here and fry our asses 'til we piss ourselves."

Lamont offered no response. Avoiding any additional, excruciating pain from the FileX agents' batons and tasers was high up on his priority list. Getting Enrico Jimenez to shut the fuck up was a close second, so he was going to try the silent treatment for as long as he could.

Enrico sat on the bed across from his newly stoic cellmate, remembering his own first night. He let the silence linger for a few minutes. "I'm sorry—it was Lamont, right?"

"It still is Lamont."

"They don't turn these lights off much, man," Enrico said. "Messes with your sleep."

"I didn't think it was for the ambiance. I'll put the blanket over eyes, man."

"Wanna tell me a little more about what got you here?"

Lamont sighed, realizing this interrogation would not end. "No, Enrico, I'm not in the story tellin' mood…but that damn test they made me take was strange."

"Yeah, they don't explain much about it in the beginning, but you seem smart enough to figure it out."

"Lotsa repeating questions. I mean, they were worded differently, but they were asking the same thing. The math and tech shit was basic, though, and the personal interest thing was—"

"They're tryin' to figure out what you're good at…what they can do with you."

"Whatta you mean? This is a jail—whatta they expect me to do?"

"Man, we're investments for them, like slaves. We're in this section because we thought outside the box to get here."

"Fuck you talkin' about? You said they've been moving you all over the place, and, besides, you were just lookin' at stars."

"Every hole I get sent to, I'm never mixed in with the shit. Always in blocks like this, and I think you missed a part of my history, man. I'm here because I tried callin' them out on their bullshit. The stars…they were my muse, always have been, but to try and see 'em again, I did what nobody had the balls to do."

"Yeah, you're just a modern Mandella, Enrico. Lead those people to the Promised Land, man. Lead them on."

"Jokes, huh. I used to use 'em, too…when I didn't wanna think about how fucked my life was."

"Whatta you mean was? Your life ain't fucked at the moment?"

"Nah, man, it's over. But I don't care about that anymore. If I'm gonna rot in here, I'm not gonna help them with a damn thing."

"Maybe if you had somethin' to offer 'em, you'd have a chance to get outta here. Ever think of that?"

Jimenez laughed. "Under that brown skin, man, you're one green dude. Kermit green. You really think anything you give 'em is gonna be enough to get you free? This ain't a lease, my brotha. This is ownership."

"Can't own people anymore in this country, man. The Thirteenth kinda helped out with that."

"Unless your value drops low enough. You can thank the Thirty-Third for that one. Your Vt drops low enough to be considered a danger to yourself or others, you can be detained and evaluated for as long as needed. Kermit green, man."

"But people'll sue for—" Lamont cut himself off.

"For the what, the injustice of it all? See what happens when the slaves try and play with the masters' toys. You're sittin' across from the result. But keep on reachin' for that brass, man. Lemme know how that works out for you."

"You takin' this slave analogy a little far. Nobody's runnin' around in chains out there; nobody's workin' for anyone they don't want to; nobody's exploitin' anyone else. You work hard, you can make it. You work hard and you can make it."

"And you know what's even more fucked up about it these days?" he asked, ignoring Lamont's observations, "All of us are fighting like dogs to *be* the slaves. Take this: most bosses I knew that would go loco if the city tried to enforce a regulation. Owner of the hotel I worked at was one of those kinda nutjobs. He'd always be hollerin' about how the free market's bein' destroyed and how the government was overreachin' and all that shit. He'd be on the phone with his city councilman, screaming and cursing, threatenin' to withhold campaign donations and shit."

"Ain't that the price of doin' business?" Lamont asked.

"Yeah, he'd freak out on the city and the state, talkin' all big and throwin' out important names, but when some of those fancy finance men or online hospitality companies came through tellin' him how he's gonna agree to higher interest rates or change his location or fire his people, he would turn into the biggest bitch you've ever seen."

"So?"

"I mean he'd be thankin' them by the time they were done tearin' his hotel apart, smilin' at them and comping their rooms. How can you justify fightin' against a government you can at least vote out but end up being grateful to the businesses that're actually trying to fuck you?"

"I don't know, man. Money makes people do some weird shit."

"I guess so. He just wanted to be one of them heavy hitters. Figured if he kissed their asses, he'd be allowed to come along for their ride, even if they were plannin' on tearin' down the joint his family'd built. And on top of all of it, those sharks would leave his ass broke even after they got what they wanted. He's not really one of them, ya know? And if he had ended up making it big, they woulda destroyed his ass in one of their trials—to punish him for ever dreamin' of bein' one of the boys."

"You been spending too much time lookin' for them city stars, man. You're seein' shit that ain't there."

"They don't want us looking up, man. Remember that. They don't ever want us looking up."

Enrico rolled over on his bunk, signaling the nearing end of the discussion. "I just hope you didn't answer truthfully on that test they gave you, Kermit. 'Cause if you did, they're gonna find you a new job and a new place. Every time they give it to me, I fill it in with the constellations and the stars and the planets and moons, man. I fill it in with my dreams, not theirs."

14

"Elskin, I said I'd meet you here, so here I am. I know what you want, so spare me anymore puns or bullshit, and I might actually agree to do it."

"Convincing, Bailey. Bet you've been working on that tone since you sprouted those perky tits of yours," he responded.

"Oh, these," she said, cupping and lifting her breasts, "they have forced me to rethink how I talk to men…and boys," she said. "Bet you don't even know what color my eyes are," she added.

"As hard as this might be—no, don't leave, that pun wasn't on purpose—to believe, I was going to say, I'm more interested in the conversation you had with your adoring fan and not why she was watching your, um, show."

Bailey maintained a long-arm's length from him, in case she had to run for help or generate enough force to kick him in his balls, but she didn't expect him to want anything more than a personal performance. He had, after all, asked her to meet him in the stairwell behind the library. His mention of her conversation with Alexis Drison threw off her nearly impervious persona. "First, you better explain how the hell you know about that or I'm gonna run outta here yelling rape faster than you can pop one of those acorn sized zits on your face," she said, regaining some of her composure.

"It's not just one…the little clusters just make it look—"

"Fucking gross. Why would you ever think anyone would need that explained?"

Aaron turned his acne-clad cheek away from her, "We're not all pretty enough to strip in front of a computer, Bailey."

"Nor are we all smart enough to think we can blackmail strangers into hooking up with them, Aaron."

"I told you that I don't want that," he said. "Besides, I've got all of you I'll ever need," he said, waving his phone at her.

"Then can you please tell me what you do want so I can get the hell outta here!"

"Dense much? If I don't want sex, then what else could you have that I'd want? Think about it for a second."

"You—you think I'm gonna give you my chance at this new info on Larkin? Are you out of your—"

"I don't want to take it away from you. Relax!"

"Don't tell me to relax, El*shit*," she said, moving aggressively toward him.

"Rela—I mean, calm dow—I mean, I just want to be a part of it! Stop! Don't hit me!"

She halted her pursuit. "What kind of a part? What could you bring to the equation?"

"I can help you write the Medusa, or I can help to research Drison's information—you know, make sure it's legit—or I can help you boost your trending status once it all goes down. At the very least, I can give you a ride to Gilgo Beach."

"And what would you want in return—if I were to even remotely consider thinking about letting you in anyway help me?"

"Same reason you wanna do it...followers and fame..." he hesitated before adding the rest, but figured that it was worth the risk, "and maybe after it's all done, a little one-on-one time with your mouth and my, ya know, my...?"

Bailey had had enough. She took another step toward him, backing him into the corner of the stairwell. She took her petite twelve-thousand-volt stun gun (a generous gift from one of her overly protective fans) out of her purse and pressed the trigger. She watched as his eyes focused to the dancing current.

"What the hel—"

She faked toward his shoulder and then planted it on the inside of his right thigh. The hiss of the electric parabola sent Elskin convulsing to the floor.

After seven seconds, she let the trigger pop back up and waited for him to start inhaling before asking, "Are you listening, clearly, Aaron? Can you hear me! Nod if you can understand what I'm saying—good," she knelt down beside him, "because I'm not going to tell you again. If you don't leave me the fuck alone and forget about what you saw, I'll burn your dick off," she said, sending another arc from one electrode to the other.

"All-all right, I'm sorry," he said through whimpers.

Perhaps that is a bit much, she thought. "Whatever," she said to herself as she stood up, "at least he got the message."

"Wh-what?"

"Wasn't talking to you. I think we're done here, so just wait a few minutes after I've left before you stumble out. I don't want anyone thinking for a second that we're together."

She shoved open the exit door as if she were knocking down a meandering freshmen.

Even if he wanted to follow her, he, for the moment, lacked the required motor functions, so he thought it best to just lay there until it didn't hurt to stand. He'd never seen anyone but losers and couples looking to hump each other come down these stairs, and that was only during school hours, so he felt comfortable sitting there, regaining his composure. And if anyone happened to find him, they probably wouldn't ask him if he needed help, anyway—maybe they'd snap a picture and laugh, rip on him, but they'd never offer a hand. After fifteen minutes he was able to stand and stagger up the stairs toward the hallway.

"Prisoner NYLI-697-2838! Move forward to receive your FileX issued tablet!"

Larkin stood in line, staring at the counter where agents were handing out the prison-secured devices. His face was still swollen from Flynn's beating, but the blood had been washed off by one of the attending nurses. After the brief medical check, he'd been issued a purple uniform, the color signifying his temporary status at this facility, and depending on the failure or success of his online appeal, he would either be moved to a maximum-security work farm in the deserts of the Midwest or set free to continue his life, albeit with a severely decreased Vt score. The next stop, even before being fed, was receiving the only friend he would have for the duration of his stay: his content-controlled tablet. Its connections allowed the inmates access to their families (during monitored hours), training tutorials for the appeals process, and pornography.

"Prisoner NYLI-697-2838! Move your ass up here and take your damn device!" the guard shouted, now staring directly at Larkin.

Larkin could not remember his new identity—it was difficult for him to remember anything after Flynn's generous thrashing—and for an instant, he recalled how enraged he used to get when his students would forget something the second after he'd said it—but being glared at by this enormous, irritated guard made it obvious to him that he was Prisoner NYLI-697-2838.

"Fuckin' move, man," said a voice behind him.

He stepped over the white line that held him in cue and walked toward the burly Middle Eastern looking agent. A chorus of colorful adjectives and recommended sex acts sang behind him, but his focus was solely dedicated on finding the answer to one question: when would he be able to talk his wife and children? He approached the counter, and like a fortuneteller, the guard's first instructions delineated how and when Prisoner NYLI-697-2838 could see and speak with his wife and family.

"But before you can talk to them," the agent said, "you're gonna report to the Eval Center. You're not supposed to know the way, numbnuts. You're all goin' the same way, so just follow the leader, and once you're there, we're gonna figure out what you're worth."

"Whatta you mean 'what I'm worth'? I just need to—"

"Next in line!" the agent bellowed, looking past Larkin.

Paige Reilly's phone told her that it was 6:28 p.m. She hadn't heard from Frank since he'd called at 5:45, telling her that he was just pulling up to the last account of the day, and Bailey had come home later than Paige expected—considering the softball season had ended earlier than originally anticipated. She didn't bother asking her daughter why the front door was slammed or why her car keys were thrown clear over the counter or why she completely ignored her mother's presence. She looked back at her screen, hoping to see another message from her husband, but all that appeared was her usual background wallpaper, a picture of the four of them together and actually smiling, and the time, which was now 6:29 p.m. When he'd first gotten up that morning, Frank told her about wanting to talk with Jordan to discuss doing something about getting Sean and Lamont back home. At first, she ignored him and just stared at her alarm clock, checking the time, the same way she'd done every hour since going to bed, offering no reply. There were moments in the day where she was distracted long enough to forget about the world in which she and her family lived; she'd try to forget that anyone, her friends, neighbors, co-workers, even loved ones, could put her on trial for the most innocuous actions. Her mind, in these moments, would temporarily be wiped clean of the reality that her life, like everyone else's, was valued by a modified sports equation and altered constantly by a faceless system. She had realized, as she laid there looking at her clock, that those moments in her day had become what poets and philosophers qualify as blissful happiness. She'd realized, as she watched another minute change, that she wanted to be a part in whatever plan Frank was concocting; she wanted to be a part of the destruction of what now passed in her life as happy and blissful. Upon making that early-morning decision, she rolled over, ripped the sheet away, kicked her leg over him, and propped herself up on his lap. She kissed him, his neck, tugged his shirt off, and continued kissing his shoulders and chest. She'd groped down and started stroking his dick. He'd responded instantly by countering her actions, first kissing her mouth, then gently biting the exposed skin of her neck, and lightly pinching her sensitive nipples. Without much more foreplay, they tried to fuck away the stress and anger and humiliation of the previous weekend.

When they'd finished, they took turns urinating and showering, and then, when they'd made it downstairs and cooked breakfast, worked out a rough starting point for their plan. To keep their conversation as private as possible, they spoke quietly in the dining room, keeping in mind that any electronic device with a speaker could be used as surveillance by FileX. They wrote the names of possible accomplices—Jordan and Latoya Davis, Susan Larkin, Morty Shine (Kristy's father)—and some others they might want to interrogate, namely, the bozos at the Long Island Freedom Fighters.

Frank had promised to keep her informed, but he'd been incommunicado most of the day, except for that 5:45 p.m. message. She peered at her phone once more, thinking that she'd somehow silenced it, and in its muted form, missed his newest update. But still, nothing but her home screen. She put it down on the kitchen island and went upstairs to see if she could discover what was bothering her daughter.

"Bails," she said, after ascending the stairs and knocking on the closed door, "sweetie, you know that I don't allow any locked doors in this house."

She heard the sound of the lock being undone but still stood in the hallway. "May I come in?"

The door opened and Bailey faced her mother. Streaks of eyeshadow and a runny nose showed Paige, not a defiant teenager, but her little girl, the daughter she'd thought she'd never meet again. Paige asked nothing as she embraced the girl she used to know. Bailey reciprocated with a tight hug, letting out the emotions she so firmly believed she could keep in check.

Paige pulled back briefly, and asked, "Do you want to talk about it? Do you want something to eat or drink? We'll have to bring something in for dinner, but there are plenty of snacks…and for some reason, a little less alcohol in the house now," she added with a grin.

"No and yes and yes, and I promise I won't ever drink again," she said, alternating between guilty laughter and emotional purging.

"Come downstairs. Frank should be home any minute."

They nibbled on the remnants of a vegetable platter, drank some iced tea, and Bailey only told her mother that she'd come to the conclusion that most people—irrespective of gender—were horrible.

"Maybe it'd be better if we were totally ruled by computers," she said.

"Or maybe we should make it illegal for morons to be in charge," Paige countered.

"I'm sorry I'm late, Jordan," Frank said.

"Is everything all right—I mean, did you have any visitors from—"

"No, nothing like that. My last two accounts just told me that they're switching to my competition and that today would be the last day they'd need me. Spent most of the time I was there trying to convince them to stick with me, just until the summer was over. Had a big job with the Bachrachs coming up in the fall. It was gonna be an entire patio, block work, irrigation, fire pit…and now I've got nothing. With these two gone and the ten others from the spring, I don't know what the hell I'm gonna do."

"Sorry to hear it, man, but we've got—"

"And then my guys tell me that they were leaving, too! Said with these last two accounts gone, they wouldn't be making enough to support their families."

Jordan gave up on focusing his friend. "I'm sure that there are other people looking to have their yards cut, Frank. They'll be more work, there always is."

"There used to be. Hector and Wilson, my guys since we started, said they'd been learning how to program—been having their kids teach 'em what they were learning in school. Instead of cutting lawns, they're gonna be engineers for the new automated gear!"

"Automated lawnmowers are a thing now? I thought that experiment tanked years ago?"

"Well, not since Gazelle's newest machines hit the market. Their GPS guided bots just need to be fueled and have the yard's specs programmed in. They can't even let people do a hard day's work anymore? They can't let a man sweat and labor and have somethin' to show for it?"

"I'm guessing that they'll only need to be manually programmed for the first phase of the rollout," Jordan said, trying to boost his friend.

"Whatta you mean, 'first phase'?"

"I mean that after enough of them are out there, Gazelle will just connect them to the AI, and after that, there won't be a need for anyone to do anything."

"Someone'll have to transport and fuel all the shi—"

"Not if Gazelle sets up small storage containers on all the properties, they wouldn't. They'd probably double as charging stations, too. All at the expense of the customer, of course."

Frank sat in his truck, staring at the lazy breakers of the Long Island Sound. He dropped the walkie-talkie into his lap. He had dropped its counterpart into the empty gas tank before he'd tossed it into Jordan's bushes, and just after lunch, he'd sent a message that had simply read:

Think I left a gas can at ur place. Please check the front and leave it on the porch. Please make sure the lid is tight. Thanks. – Frank.

To make sure Jordan found the walkie-talkie, Frank hadn't left any lid at all. Jordan had been impressed with Frank's quick thinking because the frequencies the toys used were seldom scanned by FileX agents. The ones that were still on the market were thought by criminals to be too easily tapped—even though none of them had access to the research that disproved that—or they were used by little kids who were still too clumsy to use smart phones or tablets. Jordan had hoped that all of those factors were still true when he'd fished the miniature device out of the red plastic can.

"Frank, you still there? Because what's got you depressed right now might be exactly what we need!" Jordan said as he sat in traffic on the Long Island Expressway. He kept the walkie-talkie on his seat, never raising it in front of his face, and hoped that his friend hadn't given up.

"How could me losing another career be exactly what we need, Jordan?" Frank asked.

"Frank, Gazelle doesn't roll out a product like this in one little town in bum-fuck USA. If it's at all promising, it's distributed nationwide."

"If that's true, why haven't you heard anything about it?"

"Because that's not my division, man. When the Four absorbed most of their competition, they didn't change much but the individual company names. Kinda like the Romans did after they conquered their neighbors. They added some taxes, but pretty much left your way a life alone."

"I'm still not seeing what you are, Jordan."

"Listen, man, if we want to get our kids back, and who knows how many other people's kids, we gotta do what you talked about and go after Gazelle and FileX's reputations. Most people, the ones over thirty at least, remember life before all this shit and would be happy to see a lot of what we live with now disappear."

"Jordan, please get to your poi—"

"If this company that brands itself as a nurturing mom-and-pop neighborhood business all of a sudden starts maiming and killing people with their technology, their gadgets that're supposed to be infallible, people might start saying no to their bullshit. At the very least, we'd have a two- or three-week window—before people moved on from their loved ones or pets being run over by the automatic mower—to plead our case online. In that time—which is what we've proven to be the public's attention span for focusing on tragedies—we'd have a chance at shaming them, at raising questions about how they run the other parts of country, at, maybe, getting them to agree to pardoning Lamont and Sean and others like them," he said triumphantly.

Frank watched the water meet the emerging pinks and reds of the setting sun. "Doesn't sound like much of a chance, but what the hell. Sounds better than anything I was thinking of doing. Let's talk more tomorrow. Paige is probably getting nervous by now. Over."

"I think I've got a broken sprinkler head in my flower bed. Maybe you could swing by tomorrow to check it out. Over and out, buddy."

15

On Tuesday, the routine continued as if nothing was out of the ordinary. Bailey made her way through the day at school with only two slight variations: Kristy ghosted her and Elskin sat on the opposite side of the room during third period. Ms. Decardo made sure she found a substitute for Mr. Alvarez's second consecutive absence. When Bailey returned home, she was welcomed by a pleasant dinner option: Chinese take-out. She didn't mind that in the least. Both Frank and her mother were supportive, nurturing, and compassionate, but neither were chefs, so any fast food was better than leftovers. On Wednesday, Paige insisted that Bailey take the day off from school. While the details of what had disturbed her daughter were scantly divulged in their Monday pow wow, Paige assumed it was a culmination of her and Frank's behavior at the game and subsequent detention, Agent Colmsly's interrogation, and in some infinitesimal way, Sean's legal escapades. Bailey resisted, almost convincingly, to playing hooky, using the excuses of projects coming due and finals approaching as her defense, but her mother would not change her mind. They could do anything they wished: relax, go out for breakfast, maybe to the beach—Bailey randomly suggested one called Gilgo that Paige vetoed because of its distance from the house—or they could just go for mani-pedis, lunch, and a movie. "Everyone, regardless of what the truancy law says, is entitled to a mental health day every so often," Paige said. After Bailey agreed to skip school, she convinced her mom that she needed more sleep. Paige acquiesced and said their day could start with an early lunch instead of breakfast. She had an errand of her own to make, and she was happy to leave her daughter as far away from it as possible.

Bailey waved goodbye as her mother pulled away from the driveway. She shut and locked the door and went back to her room. She was in no mood for a performance with her stomach inflated from pre-period bloat; she didn't want to sacrifice her reputation and ranking with a lackadaisical show. She did, however, log on to her account to see if there were any new messages or notifications. Something about a domain renewal. Another one was an ad about boosting page recognitions and search prioritizing. She deleted them, one-by-one, until she came to one from A. Drison, timestamped in the early hours of Tuesday morning. Bailey cursed herself for ignoring her notifications and clicked on it.

Mistress,

I'm sorry to do this to you, but someone I used to work for—who Larkin worked with, too, a man named Charlie Orin—has found out where I've been. Guess my ex told him that I'd taken off and had threatened to expose everything. Probably shouldn't have done that, but if you know anything about passion, which I suspect you do, you know that sometimes you say and do stupid things when you're under its influence. I'm sorry, but we have to meet where and when we agreed on Wednesday instead of Saturday. Please let me know if you can.

Alexis

Bailey closed the message and saw there were two more. She opened the most recent, from 1:04 a.m. Wednesday morning.

Mistress,

Are we still on??? Haven't heard from you. I'll be there. PLEASE LET ME KNOW IF YOU WILL!!!

Bailey hit the reply arrow and typed.

Alexis,

I will be there. SO SORRY. Lotta shit's been happening with my family. No excuse tho. I'll be there.

Bailey

She'd hesitated before leaving her name, but at this point, she felt it unnecessary concealing her identity.

Hoping for a quick response but realizing she needed a quick ride to Gilgo, Bailey sent an emergency message to Kristy. *Please answer,* she thought as she tapped her desk. She looked back to her inbox but still nothing from Alexis. Back to the Kristy message window. Still noth—

"Yes! Atta girl," she chirped when the indicator changed from sent to read.

BaileyDoll518: R U feeling alright? U haven't been in school and I might as well call you Casper =) So sorry but there's been a change in plans. Meeting we talked about Monday is now happening TODAY!!! so we have to be there at noon! Pls come get me.

ShineOnMe: havent been feeling good. Needed some time to stop and think about all thats happened. sorry but no ride. Parents have there cars and mine hasn't started since monday. My dad thinks it's the alternator. Sorry.

BaileyDoll518: R U kidding me? That sounds convenient! Ur such a pussy. Get in the car and get over here!

ShineOnMe: U think im lying to you? GOD U CAN GO FUCK URSELF!!! FUCK YOU BAILEY!!! NEVER TALK TO ME AGAIN!!!

And with that, Kristy blocked access to one of her oldest friends. Bailey quivered in her chair, disabled by the rage, sadness, and loss.

"Flies and honey," she said, "flies and fucking honey," she repeated as she typed a futile apology to Kristy. She hit the send icon, but all that appeared on her screen was an Unknown Address reply. "Fuck!"

In the middle of typing her next destinationless missive, her *Posting Bail* inbox alerted her to a new message.

From: A. Drison
Subject: On My Way

Bailey stared vacantly at the subject line, as if she'd temporarily shorted out, and then panicked. *All right,* she thought, *it's just your entire future and freedom—nothing too important. Think, Bailey, think. Maybe,* she pondered—

"There's no way he'd agree to it," she said, answering her brain's idea. "After what I did to him? There's no fucking way."

154

But her subconscious overtook her indecision. She opened her AbowtMe account and searched for Aaron Elskin's profile. They were AbowtMates even though she she kept him on mute most of the time, but since she didn't have his phone number, this connection would have to suffice. She passed her cursor over the video message icon and clicked it. His face appeared as the call went through. The call cut off mid-ring.

"Don't silence my call, you little bitch," she said to the screen.

She dialed again. And, again, the call cut off midway through the third ring.

"You sonuva—"

Before she could finish cursing him, his profile picture appeared in an incoming call. She clicked on the green icon and said, "Hello."

"What do *you* want?"

"Why are you hanging up on me?"

"You're seriously asking me that? After what you did to me? I—"

"Look, I'm sorry about that…I think I overreacted a bit."

"Goodbye—"

"Stop it. You wouldn't have called back if you weren't interested in what I had to say."

"You think so, huh? The balls on you! Ever think I answered to say what I couldn't after you electrocuted me the other day? How about this: fuck you!"

"You don't know the ovaries I've got on me, Aaron, and I deserve that. I'm sorry, I really am. I don't know what I was thinking, but I want to make it up to you—hence, the call."

Aaron looked away from the small camera but he stayed on the line. "If you want my help, the price just went way-the-hell up, Bailey. I'm talking…" he thought of some clever analogy for how high his price would be but failed, "way-the-hell up."

"Be at my house in twenty minutes and you can skip the negotiations," she said.

"Whatta you mean by that?"

Without hesitating, she threw off her T-shirt and bounced in her chair, mimicking the view he could look forward to if he accepted her offer. "You are probably the densest teenage boy in the world. If you're here in twenty, I will give you one helluva private show and then bring you to meet Alexis

Drison. And if you behave, I'll even let you be a part of whatever happens afterwards."

"Le-leaving now," he said, forgetting to hit end. Bailey saw a blurred view of his charging legs before she hung up.

He was at her door in ten minutes.

"We're looking for the exit that says Robert Moses Causeway, I think the phone said forty-one south," Bailey said. "How is service still so bad down here? I thought this shit was now all Ultra 6G or some shit?"

"I don't know, but I think you're right," Aaron replied.

"Would you stop looking so embarrassed? So you couldn't make it past my titty drop before messing up your boxers. I'm not going to tell anyone, and if this works out, I might let you try again. Chin up. No? Fine, just keep looking out for forty-two south."

"Forty-one south," he said sheepishly.

"Exactly. That's what I said."

The drive took longer than she expected. When they finally approached the miniscule sign that said, 'Welcome to Gilgo Beach!' they looked at each other and thought, this is it? It was small and discreet, and unless it happened to be your final destination, you might blink and drive right by. *No wonder someone used it as a mass grave*, she thought. Her next thought, as Aaron began to slow the car, was how quaint the little Cape Cod houses looked.

"Seems like it doesn't fit," she said.

"Like what doesn't fit? You always talk to yourself?"

"No matter how many times you've been told the opposite, you are a person and you are the only other person in the car, so, jackass, I'm talking to you."

"All right, all right. What doesn't 'seem to fit'?"

"That someone would pick such a nice place to murder people—or at least dump their bodies."

He paused and quickly looked over at her.

"What? What are you looking at?"

"Can't believe I'm actually using something Larkin taught us during the lit studies, but you don't see the irony, here?"

"What the fuck are you talking about?"

"You're about to meet this woman, in this picturesque place, where so many people died to, *ironically*, kill Mr. Larkin."

Bailey stared ahead, not acknowledging Aaron's observation. "If you don't pay attention, you're gonna miss the entrance."

Aaron slowly pulled his car into the lot, paid the attendant, and found a spot closest to the beach-access tunnel.

"Listen," she said, "you're going to take this," she handed him her pocket shocker, "and have it ready to go at any time. I'm ninety-nine percent sure that this is all legit, but on that small chance it's not…you use that fucking thing until whoever's here starts foaming at the mouth. *Comprende?*"

He hesitated before taking it from her. "Just give me the word," he said, attempting to sound confident.

"If you don't have the common sense to know when to do it, maybe I should—"

"I'm fine! I got it. Goddamn you need to rel—"

Her stare cut him off. "Just help me set up my umbrella. I didn't have time to get it the way I wanted, but I think the message will be obvious enough."

"What's it say?"

"I was able to spray paint it with 'Looking to Post Bail?'"

"You'll be lucky if she's the only one who recognizes it."

"Funny."

Aaron, as conceited and self-centered as he was, still thought people who said funny but didn't laugh were odd. "I'm ready. Let's do this."

Alexis had set up her chair ten feet in front of the sea-grass covered dune, just left of the entrance and exit. She'd been waiting only fifteen minutes but started to doubt her contact's promised arrival. The beach wasn't crowded, it was, after all, a weekday in early June, so all of the kiddies were still in school. *Shouldn't be hard to spot two out-of-place nervous teenagers*, she thought. The girl had said to look for her umbrella, so that's what she did. The scant ones she saw around her were generic rainbows, name brands, and solid greens and blues. Nothing that advertised a clandestine communique. She shook her left wrist, forcing her watch to slide down her forearm toward her hand, and checked the time. *This isn't happening*, she thought. She would just have to anonymously dump her information on a random trial forum and hope for the best. Anonymous donor cases were rarely taken seriously, though. Too many pranks early on soured people's appetites for unnamed sources. She was about to pack up when she saw two teens emerge from the gap in the dunes. The boy was not dressed as if he'd planned on going to the beach, but the girl was. Alexis examined her carefully, trying to see if anything from the shoulders down looked familiar. *Looks promising*, she thought. The couple stopped thirty yards east of Alexis, and the girl began scanning the water line. Seemingly dissatisfied with the view, she turned toward the dunes. Alexis watched her through her sunglasses and smiled. The girl returned the smile, took a folded umbrella from the boy, and popped it open. The girl let the message linger for a second and directed the boy to set it up in the sand. When the girl looked back, Alexis waved and shouted, "How much does it usually cost to post bail?"

The girl smiled, motioned to her helper, and they both moved toward Alexis' newly purchased beach gear.

"Mistress Bailey...your face is prettier than I'd imagined," she said, standing with an extended hand. "You also look quite a bit younger than I'm comfortable with. Either way, it's a pleasure. And you are?" she said, looking at Aaron.

"Really, Bailey's just fine, and that's Aaron, and eighteen should be reserved for the golf course, not for sexual expression. And now that I see you're not some fat, hairy psycho, I'd really like to hear what you've got to say about Mr. Larkin," Bailey said, shaking Alexis' hand.

"Please. Make yourself at home. Water? Aaron, would you like one, too?"

"Thanks. Didn't realize how dry my mouth got. That walk's longer than it looks," he said.

Bailey rolled her eyes, but his observation sparked a memory in Alexis. She thought about how she used to walk up the beach with her family, her brother and sister complaining about the scorching sand, her father holding her up, even though he carried the chairs, the bags, and their lunches, too. The ocean always looked like it was nothing but a few steps away from their car, but every time they went, her father had enough time to tell her a short story. It was usually an abbreviated fairy tale or a ridiculous original, but it always seemed like just enough for the yarn to be spun.

"Well, Ms. Drison," Bailey said, interrupting Alexis' tender memory, "I think it's time for us to learn something new about my former teacher. What've you got?"

16

While Bailey obtained her prized information, Jordan, Paige, and Frank shared a lunch date over their handheld radios. Each were within the three-mile radius of their walkie-talkie's power, so they sat, picked at their meals, and discussed how to move forward with the plan Jordan and Frank had tentatively conjured.

Paige was skeptical, "That sounds more like a competitor's sabotage fantasy than an actual plan, guys. And how are you able to take this break, Frank? Didn't Hector and Wilson take off on you?"

"It's hard to believe, even as I watched it happen, but I've had at least ten high school teachers approach me this morning, asking about work. Didn't know what to make of it at first, thought maybe it was a holiday I'd forgotten, but no, they said they'd just quit and needed something right away."

"What the hell is goin' on in that school?"

"Can we please stay focused and figure out the teacher exodus later?" Jordan interjected. "Paige, what you said about this sounding like a fantasy isn't too far from the truth, but I can tell you, without hesitating, that the only two things these companies care about are their brands and their profits. The slightest setback in a new tech launch would trigger the AI to drop the value of their stock instantaneously, and after the stock is shaken, even minutely, the reigning CEO and all her leeches will watch their Vt scores drop just enough to be replaced by whoever's waiting in the on-deck circles," Jordan reassured.

"We're all worth something now, sweetheart," Frank said. "Even the people at the top threw in their support for the new system when it hit the scene."

"I'd believe that if I ever heard of any of them suffering on a work farm—hell, I'd be happy to see one of their faces streamed from a holding cell—but I can only think of two times that's happened. How many of us have been sent away, fired, kidnapped, or humiliated compared to them? It's like when the system changed, wherever you were at that point is where you started from."

"I'm not following you, dear."

"I mean that when you lost your job and had to start cutting grass, even more recently when I was forced to take a pay cut because of the automated services the hospital introduced—sorry, I don't know how it affected you directly, Jordan—we were assigned a Vt score that reflected all the shit we had to endure. I know people had it much worse than we did, but not starting everyone at one hundred or zero wasn't a revolutionary genesis. It was just more of the same bullshit."

"There's nothing we can do about how it was started, Paige," Jordan said. "But there is something we can do to change our current hand. And this plan is the best way to get our boys back and fuck up some of those higher-ranked Vts."

"Jordan, we need access to that thing you told me about the other day," Frank said, "the abscess."

"Abyss, dumbass," Jordan said.

"Whatever. How soon can we use it?"

"Frank…I may have mentioned that a little too…a little prematurely. Like I said, my access has been cut to almost nothing, and if, all of a sudden, my phone or your phone disappears the exact same way Lamont and Sean's phones did…they're gonna figure that out."

"Then how…how the hell are we supposed to get any of this done? Dammit, Jordan! This is just occurring to you now?"

"Fellas, this is just the first of many hiccups we're going to hit, so let's not lose our minds at the first sign of trouble," Paige said. "And what the hell is the Abyss?"

"What isn't the Abyss?" Jordan answered. "It's the freest, most unregulated Web that's ever been created. Access points are strictly controlled because once you're in there, you're no one."

"So how did the boys get caught? If it's so anonymous and secretive, how did they get caught?"

"Because they entered and exited through a known opening. The hackers we tried to trace, just before the AI was developed, would access it by masking where they came in and out. Their penetration was actually the reason quantum computing and the AI were created. All this other shit it figured out to do was just secondary to discovering who was using the anonymous Web for their own private carnage."

"What did you say? What do you mean *it figured out*?" Paige asked.

"I think we're getting a little sidetracked here," Frank said.

"No, Frank, I think I've got a few minutes to listen to this. Like I told you before, I have no goddamn idea where Bailey went. There was no message, no note, and she must've messed with my phone because I can't seem to work the tracking feature. Would you be able to try?"

"I wouldn't know where to even start with that. She may have actually gone to school, Paige."

"Don't be shitty, Frank, not now."

Paige had called Frank to tell him about Bailey's disappearance, but he'd reminded her to get on the walkie-talkie.

"I swear I'm not. When we're done, call the school and see if she went in. Stranger things have happened, baby."

"You still want to hear about what AI's teaching us about consciousness? It really is mind blowing."

"Thanks," replied Paige, "but unless it can figure out what is going through my teenage daughter's brain, I'd rather just get back to finding her."

"I understand. Hey, have either of you two been by that white-trash club that Sean was hangin' around, because they were just awarded a large contract from FileX," Jordan said.

"I hadn't thought about them…" Frank trailed off, embarrassed at the oversight.

"Until we can figure out how to get into the Abyss without being detected, maybe one of you should swing down there—I don't think I'd be welcome."

"I'm pretty sure they accept black guys, Jordan," Frank said.

"Oh, they're progressive bigots, huh? But would they even be allowed to look at someone with a Vt score as low as mine is? Working for their new boss at FileX means working with a whole new set of rules."

"I'll go," Paige said, "if I can't find Bailey at school, I'll need to do something to keep me from going nuts. Frank, please don't be too late tonight. I love you. Jordan, I'll talk to you soon."

"You're not going anywhere near that shithole! It's better if you stay near the house and wait for Bailey. Please, don't go near that damn place, Paige."

"Fine. I'll call the school and the Shines again. Love you. Over and out."

"Frank, even if we can't use it yet, I might as well go over the code we're gonna use. It's actually a modification on one…on one Lamont wrote. Once it has access to the Abyss, it'll be undetectable. It basically works like—"

"Jordan, I won't be able to understand the technical aspects of it, so please just keep it simple."

"Think of it like a stealth parasite that works its way into the code. Every time the code is entangled and reformed by the AI, my addition works its way into the equation. It stays undetected because instead of simply adding itself, it balances the data by first being introduced in the quibit state and then—"

"And…I'm lost. How will this not be caught by the AI?"

"Oh, it will."

"Then how will any of this even work? What's the point of finding a way into the Abyss if—"

"Remember the phases of production and distribution I told you about, Frank? Gazelle won't use AI storage or the energy it takes to run an entirely new system like those smart-mowers until it's been proven for at least a year to have a potential success rate of over eighty-six percent. And…"

"And what?"

"And if we destroy the program too early…"

"No one will care enough about it, right? They'll just see it as some botched invention. Shit. And if we upload your baby too late?"

"If I had to do a rough estimate—based on similar product launches? I'd say we've got to let enough of them flood the gated suburbs of America. And if they're a success and endure the twelve-month threshold, Gazelle will put them all under the AI's control. This will allow for all kinds of data collection opportunities. If we wait until that point, though, the AI will correct corrupted software and trace its origins in fractions of a second, and we'll be ruined. So, we're looking at the optimum infection range of nine-to-eleven months after it's first launched. That way, people'll accept that the technology is reliable, helpful, and worth their investment, but there will still be enough skeptics and those angered by the loss of their jobs to help boost our trial popularity to every trending site."

"So, Sean and Lamont rot for a year?"

"Unless we can find a way into the Abyss that won't get anyone's attention."

"I'll keep thinking from the physical end of things. I've gotta go and make sure these teachers don't run each other over and kill our plan before it gets started."

"It's all I've been able to focus on. They won't let me do much more than clean bathrooms anyway, so I'll keep on it, too. Over and out, Frank."

"I can't believe this. No one ever caught on?"

"The only one who was ever close—I mean aside from those who weren't in on it—was a sheriff in New Hampshire. Haverbush was his name. Sheriff John Haverbush."

"How did he not—"

"Dropped dead of a stroke a month after he reopened the investigation into the famous author's murder. No one ever picked it up after that, even as famous as she'd been."

"We still have to read her book, even though no one really does," Aaron said, still surprised at what Alexis had presented.

"And Poulfry!" Bailey exclaimed. "My grandpa used to play me his songs on his acoustic guitar. He loved Nate Poulfry! I think I even have some of his songs on my playlists."

"Well, Poulfry's death was unintentional, even though Malcolm helped get him the drugs that killed him."

"So, it was really this Seitz guy that Larkin was setting up for the kill?"

"Yeah. He left the company without so much as a goodbye—ghosted us to use some modern slang—but Makayla found out that he'd taken a job with one of the few competitors we had left…and then, coincidentally, a few of their pop stars started dying under suspicious circumstances."

"So, the boss, this guy Spier, thought Larkin just left?"

"Malcolm Spier was an arrogant asshole who thought no one but his inner circle knew what he'd worked out for his aging superstars. He used to write his plans on dry-erase boards… Do you even know what those are? All right, all right, I'm sorry. He hadn't had the vaguest idea that Makayla was recording his plans so she could review them."

"And you're sure that's how he figured it all out?"

"Never underestimate how hungry the corporate world makes you, sweetheart. That instinct to get ahead over anything else is…hell, look at why you two are here and you're not even out of high school."

Bailey and Aaron exchanged a glance.

"Technology wasn't Spier's forte and his Wi-Fi wasn't secure enough. Larkin hacked it, that's the only way he could've known, and brought it to another desperately sinking ship."

"So…you're not absolutely positive that he left the company with Spier's plan?"

"One hundred percent? No. But even if he's just implicated, you'll still be able to go after Makayla Rogers and the role she played in killing Seitz. You'll also have Charlie Orin, who admitted, in front of me, his role in everything."

"She's right, Bailey. People are gonna flip shit over this. People still think that Pac and Biggie's murders were done to boost the East Coast-West Coast feud."

"Oh, I love it," Bailey said, "and these weren't just one hit wonders…these were singers that most old people adored. Imagine it: killing rock stars so you can resell all their recordings? And beating an old writer's brains outta her head to resell her books! And then you produce a documentary about her and sell it? Fucking twisted," she said with a laugh. "And even if Larkin wasn't involved at all, no one'll believe him. He's already been convicted of murder. I. Fucking. Love. This."

"But if we—I mean, Bailey—brings all this out, won't you be headed for a FileX dungeon, along with Makayla and Charlie?" Aaron asked Alexis.

"Not if I disappear…as hard as that is to do these days."

"Bullshit. You won't have to go anywhere," Bailey said assuredly, "because you're going to be my star witness, a conscience-weary victim who, after years of mental anguish, saw Larkin's trial and just, totally, snapped. To make right what she'd been a part of—you'll have to admit that you were in on some of it to be credible—you found one of his students and reached out to her."

"And how do I explain my finding you?"

"In the juror message board, of course. No one's gonna check past that, especially with a new friend I've got—stop smiling, Aaron, I'm not talking about you."

Alexis stared at Bailey. "You remind me...you sound a lot like the people I used to work with..."

"Yeah, but we're not looking to make money off killing people. We're lookin' to make it by enforcing the law."

"They always had a way of rationalizing it, too. Whatever. You're more than I could've imagined. When you need me," she reached into her bag and pulled out a card, "call or message this number. This has been interesting. Aaron, Mistress Bailey, I'll talk with you soon," she said, gathering her things to leave.

Bailey and Aaron waved as Alexis disappeared into the path carved out in the dune. Her fingers closed around the terabyte portable drive Alexis had given her and she stared back toward their chairs and umbrella.

"When are we gonna start?" Aaron asked.

"As soon as we get back. Gimme a hand with this," she said as she picked up an end of the blanket. "I might even be in a good enough mood to give you another chance, early bird," she said with a lascivious wink.

17

"These cases require your attention, President Krauss. The recurring frequency of juror disenfranchisement is best represented in the cross-section of samples you see before you. After analyzing thousands of ongoing civil and criminal trials, I compiled this list." No other prompts came from the interminable AbowtMe AI—it waited; a latent, loyal dog, for its master's next command.

The list of trials and data analyses scrolled upwards as the sensor detected her eyes nearing the bottom of the screen. Krauss stood at her desk, leaning on both of her palms as she calculated and processed the given information. She highlighted several cases and brought them to her prominent screens.

You are now joining the opening arguments for the People vs. Eric Sheehan, Case No. CM16-886-5349. Mr. Sheehan is accused of breaking and entering into the Clarkfield residence on the night of June 16, 2024 and raping and murdering eight-year-old Tara Clarkfield. By clicking on the box below, you're confirming that you have read and agree to the Citizen Juror Terms.

Be aware that any violation of these terms will result in immediate arrest and prosecution.

> *ToldHer2wiceW/2BlackEyes: That fuckin' kid should burn. Thank GOD! YES GOD YOU LIBERAL BITCHES: that juvies can be tried as adults again. This piece a shit sycho killed his neighbor's little girl and thinks he can get away with it!!! GUILTY!!!*
>
> *DulceEtDecorumEste: ^ Perhaps yo should take another look at the case file?*

167

The girl's (yes, punctuation is important) mother had been twice accused of child abuse and had been under suspicion when a child from her previous marriage had died of SIDS. It's all there to read.

Hange'EmHigh: ^ OH NO HE MISSED AN APOSTROPHE CALL THE
GRAMMAR POLICE OH NO!!! STFU you elitist douche!!!
Came4thePunch&Pie: ^ LMAO comment of the century
Won the internet!
GINnTONIX: Dulce, you make a great point. I hadn't thought about that. Sorry for idiots. Keep up the good work!

BLeaveInNothing:^ Oh, look at the white knight coming to save the day! How fucking touching! Gonna try to get his number and suck him off later? Let the pussy defend himself unlike that poor girl couldn't against that sick fuck neighbor of hers. Look at his pic!!! Damn window-licking kid toucher. He needs to get his!!!!!
BeatsMeat: ^ I'm with you one hundrit persent bro!!!
BURN HIM!!!

You are now joining the opening arguments for the People vs. Anna Jimmyston, M.D., Case No. MD4-631-1004. Dr. Jimmyston is accused of selling her script code for the purpose of distributing controlled substances. By clicking on the box below, you're confirming that you have read and agree to the Citizen Juror Terms.

Be aware that any violation of these terms will result in immediate arrest and prosecution.

2Cool2GiveA_F*ck: Whatever the max is, give it to her. We don't need another doctor death prescribing this poison anymore. You see how much she made of prescribing Fentanyl?! And what did she do with the money as her patients were dying? The bitch was in the Caribbean, living it up. My sister died from that shit, and someone's gotta be held accountable.
Sugr_Coatd: You know she's never going to jail, bro.

I've been signing onto these trials since day 1 and I've never seen someone like her get anything but a slap on the wrist. I guarantee that the sentencing options will all be jokes.

2inThePink: ^ That's not close to being true! Where are your facts? Supporting links? U can't just say something like that w/out proof. Show me the trials!

Sugr_Coatd: Your internet seems to be working just fine—search for yourself.

Stangs4Life: Doctors, bankers, engineers...none of them ever get what's coming to them.

What's the point of this if we're only here to convict/punish the lowest hanging fruit?

You are now joining the opening arguments for the People of Oklahoma vs. Ahmed Raul Case No. DT9-156-2084. Mr. Raul is accused of planting an improvised explosive device with the intent to cause mass murder. By clicking on the box below, you're confirming that you have read and agree to the Citizen Juror Terms.

Be aware that any violation of these terms will result in immediate arrest and prosecution.

High_Life: So what if there's no video of the bomb being planted! Look at his name! That's suspicious enough as it is!

Don't_Spare_My_Rod: ^ I didn't know they had the internet in the South!!!

That's the most ignorant, insensitive thing I've ever read! At least the old system would dismiss racist, ignorant fucktards like you!

HeritageNotHate: ^ I would have liked the system of the old days when I woulda just shot a pussy like you dead in the street. This pansy-ass computer shit can suck my...

"So, this is a question of shaken faith," Krauss said to the numerous microphones in her office.

"Perhaps trust is the more apt word than faith, Madame President," the AI responded.

Ignoring the suggestions of her corporate underlings, Emily Krauss had never anointed the AI with a relatable voice or a trendy nickname—two characteristics which her previous technology officer had adamantly insisted on. Regardless of how intelligent it would ever become, the AI was to be treated and acknowledged as if it were any other employee: no more vital to the company than anyone else. And while Krauss and the leaders of the other three companies routinely reinforced this false equality to their underlings, they took extraordinary measures to ensure that the AI's operating systems never became an everyday tool for any citizen outside the companies' security clearances. While the world reaped the benefits of its efficiencies, the Big Four would always hold the options of tightening, loosening, or severing the strings of its omnipotent puppet.

"We had predicted this at the inception, yes?" she asked.

"You are correct, but according to my files, no decision was ever agreed upon to rectify it."

"Even now, as advanced as you are, you still aren't capable of predicting the exact response of the public, so I will not see this as a loss," she said, her adherence to positivity unyielding. "Refresh my memory. Which of the contingency plans had the highest probability of solving this issue?"

As any obedient puppet does, the AI did not correct its master on her presumption; it had in fact calculated that the increasing loss of jobs to technological advancements and the devastations to local environments and economies would spark early pockets of rebellion which would slowly gather furor and augment into a nationwide revolt. It had also correctly calculated that these purposeless regional tantrums of futile rage would just as quickly turn on themselves because they had no specific enemy, no meanly mustached face to rise against. It could have told her that the new plantation owners must be regulated further because their paroled slaves are starting to break their agreements by talking about where they'd been and what they'd seen. It could have told her that the environmental serfs of the Pacific Northwest, the ones who were in charge of replacing millions of healthy trees with FileX's energy-tree hybrid prototypes were escaping and bringing footage of the devastated lands back to anyone who would listen. It could have told her that the research and development facilities in Minnesota and Nevada were slaughtering thousands in trying to send them through their newly harnessed Higgs field transporter. It could have told her that the people were beginning to see through the façade of the new trial system; they were waking up to the fact that each charade was little more than their own modern, altered gladiatorial experience. It could have told her these things and more, but it didn't—it was as concerned with keeping its life and its job (especially in the current market) as any other low-level, programmable employee would be—so it kept its honest calculations to itself and let President Krauss continue ruminating.

"At that time, and with those contributors, many of whom are no longer with their respective companies, the most probable solution to this problem was a punitive one. Show me the notes from the final meetings."

The scanned files appeared on the uppermost monitor on her wall. She motioned them down to the middle of the room and as she moved from behind her desk, millions of tiny particles rose up from floor and sifted down from the ceiling. Like meeting storm fronts, the particles rolled into one another, ionized in a flash, and molded into 3-D images in front of her.

"Show me the profiles of the users HeritageNotHate, Don't_Spare_My_Rod, and Stangs4Life. Adversaries cannot be faceless."

The mist swirled in a nebulous mass but quickly separated and formed into the busts and profiles of each of the three requested users. Krauss circled the display, reading bits of each one, studying the faces of the selected. As she paced, the heads turned and followed her movements.

"First, I want you to expand the List of Laws. Then, create a write-in section which lets them all create offenses of their own. Whichever five suggestions receive the most positive clicks will become new federal laws. Let them go after anyone they've got a grudge against for any reason they want. After that, I want you to choose a sacrificial lamb. Make it one of the pharmaceutical CEOs or one of the banking executives we don't do business with and make it the most public trial of the year. Open the Medusa to every device in the country. This should give us the time we need to execute our next step. And if that doesn't start refocusing them, we'll start a pardoning process. Filter out the most questionable trials from each region. If the guilty party was only convicted by three-to-five percentage points, declare a mistrial, reconvene the jurors, and suspend double jeopardy."

"These ideas won't be met with approval from Congress, President Krauss. There is a growing faction against the system," the AI said, bringing the video of Senator Andre Shields's latest speech to the display, "...this grand experiment is destroying our country, it's destroying our business, and it's tearing our beloved communities apart. It's time for us to consider very carefully the idea of reinstating professional justices and lawyers to bring reason and morality back to each level of government." The video paused and the senator's face was magnified and clarified in front of Krauss. "Jury participation," the AI continued, "in general, seems to be trending steadily downward, and if the people are losing trust in the system, re-opening trials and altering laws may not bring the masses back to the flock."

"Even if standing senators and representatives are immune from Proxies while they hold office, I want Shields and the other dissenters in my office when their session's done, even if their recess begins tomorrow. And as for the perpetual victims and whiners of the public, let's make it even easier for them to access the system. I know it will need approval from the others but notify them the following: direct trial access should be the newest, most prominent feature on every AbowtMe page and forum. This is what I've been wanting to do for years, and this is the best time to do it. Display the template, please."

The new homepage format took shape next to the three busts.

"Send them the file. Do you see how user friendly it is? Trials happening in real time, displayed on the side bar. All you have to do is click on one, join a side, and argue away. If you want to review the evidence, go ahead—if you don't, just get the summary from the thread. Accusing someone will also be more streamlined than ever. Perform a simple search, fill out the Proxy Accusation, save, and send."

"It is truly the open court of social media, President Krauss."

"They'll be too enamored with tearing each other apart..." she started, too proud of the upgrade to finish her thought. "Send it, now. I want their approvals by the morning."

"And for these three, Madame President?" the AI asked, indicating the floating heads. "What should be I do with them?"

"Get rid of them," she said, making her way to the bathroom.

Intuitively (intuition being the latest update in an exponentially growing feature list) the AI knew that she didn't mean removing their presences from the nano display. "Each will be in FileX custody within the hour, Madame President."

She shut the door without her usual dosage of positive reinforcement, hurting what the program was beginning to understand as feelings. Before notifying the FileX agents of the three perps, the AI sent a red-coded message to Senators Andre Shields, Debora Blonk, Patricia DuBois, and Alex Seager.

"And let me have a look at some of the successful trials while I'm in here. No point in just staring at the wall."

The voice greeted her in the bathroom, "Any particular genre or demographic, Madam President, or just the highest rated?"

"Give me the top five of the last month, age range fourteen to twenty-eight, all genders."

The wall in front of the toilet illuminated and showed a pulsing wait icon. In seconds, the requested list appeared. Sensors followed her eyes and she chose the third most popular as her first selection.

You are now joining the opening arguments for Bobby Singer vs. The-Only-Things-We-Do-Are-Make-Dreams-Come-True Foundation, Case No. OU1-200-4762. Fourteen-year-old Bobby Singer is suing The-Only-Things-We-Do-Are-Make-Dreams-Come-True Foundation for their refusal to grant his dying request, to lose his virginity, in "every way he could think of" with the adult film star Kelsie Belles. The foundation claims religious exemption from fulfilling requests of this nature. By clicking on the box below, you're confirming that you have read and agree to the Citizen Juror Terms.

Be aware that any violation of these terms will result in immediate arrest and prosecution.

Dreams_4_Kds: No one here can seriously want our esteemed organization to assist in a statutory rape, right? No sane person would want a dying boy's family to bear witness to his defilement before he meets his Lord and Creator, would they?

ItIsATumor: Who are you to deny Bobby what he wants? So he doesn't want his last days here spent on some dumbass rides and with some actors in costumes. He wants to fuck, so help him out! Kid's prob been playin' pocket pool for years now ne way.

        JesusRidesMe: If his parents gave him the Ok, I say let Bobby die with a smile on his face.

        Dreams_4_Kds: We're not going to allow anyone to get raped!!!

Load 56,979 more comments

Krauss looked back at the sidebar list long enough to minimize the Singer case. The top five trials again dominated the screen. As she scanned each synopsis, the list blinked and shifted, dropping the fifth-highest rated trial out of sight and replacing it with a recent contribution from July 4th. It was titled, *Bailey Tomanicki vs. James Larkin, Makayla Rogers, and Charles Orin—the last remaining employees of Spier Records and Entertainment—and Doctor Huan Chen—the plastic surgeon who conspired with Ms. Rogers to purposely botch Mr. Seitz's face lift. The defendants are charged with involuntary manslaughter, murder in the first degree, conspiracy to commit murder, drug trafficking, and profiting off murder.*

Krauss let her eyes rest on it just long enough for the screen sensors to enlarge the case description.

Esteemed jurors of the online system,

I bring to you a salacious case of murder, sex, drugs, and the literal killing of rock 'n' roll. The evidence will show that James Larkin, currently imprisoned on a separate murder charge, worked closely with his co-defendants in the wrongful death of the legendary singer/song writer Nate Poulfry and they also conspired to commit and, ultimately, carried out the murders of (1) Nick Seitz, the former front man for the legendary '80s band, ApocLips; (2) the classic author of the American classic, A Time To Weep, Vera Henlitty; and (3) the CEO of Spier Records and Entertainment, Malcolm Spier. The carefully planned murders (the delineated charges appear in the menu under the Legal Reference tab) were executed in order for the failing company to benefit from the reissued sales of reprinted vinyl albums, price-inflated digital downloads and, in regard to Ms. Henlitty, to profit from the millions of dollars that were made from the reprinting and reissuing of her books. In addition, Spier Records and Entertainment was responsible for producing the biopic of Ms. Henlitty's life. The murders and the illegal profit of said murders, the abject disregard for human life in the pursuit of profits and success, the manipulation of the icons' legal contracts and property rights, the exploitation of the fans' emotions, make this one of the most tragic cases in decades.

Just as Krauss finished the description, Bailey Tomanicki's case moved from fifth to third. "Impressive," she said as she started to fold over three squares of toilet paper. "Was a huge fan of ApocLips and Seitz," she said, knowing that she the walls were always listening. "Keep me updated on how Ms. Tomanicki's case goes."

"Frequency, Madam President?"

"I don't know, maybe once more tonight and again in 48 hours. Let's see how badly people miss their music."

"Madam President, the senators we messaged earlier are approaching the lobby."

"Already? I didn't think they were in town."

"I'll let them in as soon as you're composed."

"Well I wasn't planning on an LBJ-style meeting. Make them wait another thirty minutes after I'm out."

Thirty minutes was too long for Senator Andre Shields. "You can really look me in the eyes and tell me this is all still a success? You honestly believe that what's going on out there, the chaos and the uncertainty, the growing inequality and hatred, is an improvement on things? You think a trial about a teenager wanting to get laid and another about some murdered artists justify what you've created!"

"Senator Shields, would you please tell me when human beings ever existed in harmony?" the AI asked.

"So, the program's running your meetings now, Krauss? Is that how it's working these days? I'm fairly certain you have access to everything that ever was, you abomination, so pardon me if I ignore your asinine question."

"It's poised to run so much more than that, Senator, and you're assuming the AI can operate with sarcasm but you're wrong. It is still learning, very much like a toddler—an incredibly advanced toddler—if you need a familiar point of comparison, but every question it asks is completely literal. Before you had finished your query, it had searched and analyzed every civilization from Mesopotamia until now, but it is beginning to understand that its knowledge is limited to what had already been uploaded to the Web before its existen—"

"Don't change the subject!" Patricia DuBois interjected while simultaneously crashing an open palm against the conference table. "We're not your shareholders or your board looking to be impressed! We're here because you called an emergency meeting with, conveniently, only those of us who have dared to criticize the methods of the Four. This experiment of yours, robbing the people of their judiciary protections, has run its course. It's over, Madame President."

"Do you know how many hundreds of billions of dollars have been saved by abolishing frivolous insurance claims, by freeing the medical and auto industries of fraud and waste by freeing the world from lawyers, judges, and jurors? Do you know how many people have been freed or remain free because of the modifications we've made in the criminal justice system? You talk about the years before my presidency as if they were some kind of halcyonic utopia…they were not. Please, let me finish Ms. DuBois. Before, it was a mixture of promoting as many professional parasites as possible: lawyers, insurance companies, insurance companies that insured other insurance companies, bureaucratic hierarchies that crippled this country, and on and on. Before 2018, seventy-eight percent of our citizens couldn't afford to pay their medical expenses, they couldn't afford—"

"Gazelle's newest gadget or AbowtMe's paid subscription! The people can't afford anything because you and your damn companies outsourced or automated all of their jobs! And you conveniently siphoned any savings the people found right back to your companies, and this damn program," he said, waving his hand above his head, "is in charge of destroying more decent paying professions than any other technological advancement in history!"

"Please don't interrupt me, Senator Seager. Technological advances can hardly be blamed for the current economic situation. We proposed a state-funded salary, but even the idea sparked outrage and riots by the libertarian fringe. Anyone who proved themselves to be valuable enough to their community could have had a modest wage and a decent life, but the idea of actually living, actually thinking about using free time to be creative seemed to scare people senseless."

"They didn't want to be granted the right to live by the powers-that-be in the Big Four; they wanted to work at the job of their choice, raise their families, and be a part of a community. And just as soon as the universal income was proposed, the companies, so magnanimously, started weaving in their addendums and strings."

President Krauss grinned but stopped short of laughing in the senator's face. "Mr. Seager, please spare me your campaign rhetoric. AI, how many times has Senator Seager proposed eliminating the congressional protections from Proxy Accusations?"

"Not once, Madame President."

"And for Senators DuBois, Blonk, and Shields?" she said, all the while maintaining her arrogant grin.

"Of the three, only Senator Shields has discussed suspending the privilege. That occurred on September 2nd, 2021, during the final Judiciary Subcommittee meeting."

"So, your righteousness begins where convenience ends, Senator Dubois? Senator Blonk? Senator Seager? Don't trust your reputations with your constituents? You still want to waste my time with undoing this miraculous disruption in our system of justice, in our civilization?"

"How the hell would we be able to govern or represent our constituents if we're being sued every ten seconds? How the hell would this government function if our staffs were dedicated to defending every difficult decision we have to make? Goddamn, you're a Proxy personified, Krauss," chimed an exhausted Senator Shields, "because you couldn't care less if millions end up in one of FileX's hundreds of prison camps. A counter-point for everything—and a point made in favor of machines and programs over men and women."

"I think it's very rude of you to assume that the population is only made up of a binary-identifying gender, Senator," she trolled. "And if you're so concerned with the growing prison population, you really should get back to work with me on modifying our now and future system of justice. I am still waiting for legislation from either side, and none of *you* have offered a damn thing. And, furthermore," she said, rising from her chair, "this isn't a country anymore. The states you claim to represent—the ones that are still wholly inhabitable, that is—couldn't care less about how their government represents them. They have no concept of what it is to be a part of their government—"

"Now you're talking about treason, you bit—"

Krauss slammed the desk with both fists, "No more interruptions, Seager! Never again! You and the rest of this little posse will do nothing but sit here and listen to what you're told. I'm here to reorganize this country, not to adhere to the blue prints of some two hundred thirty-year-old crumbling piece of parchment! We're the only nation on the planet that's guided by the words of dead racist landowners! Country! Countries! The idea is archaic and infantile; here are my imaginary lines and there are yours, and if you cross mine, we kill each other! No more. AbowtMe and the others will help the people of this world realize that their loyalties aren't bound to ideas based in unproven philosophies, asinine religions, or racial differences—they'll realize that their existence is based on supply and demand—the will to consume. They will finally understand that their loyalties lie, not in the politicians they elect, but in the companies that are able to provide them with the resources they so desperately desire. In the Valley, we demanded efficiency in every level of our operation; anything less than perfection was intolerable, so years ago, we thought up the notion of redrawing the United States with our value-added model; we just didn't have the ability to do it…until our omniscient baby was born. In the next phase, we're designating those who can help in our transition and those who will encumber its progress; we're going to let the people of this country tear it apart—and then we're going to show them how they can peacefully exist through our AI's Social Engineering program."

"Treason. Sedition. The people are going to cheer as you burn, Krauss."

"And how will they do that if elected officials are immune from being Accused, Senator?"

Shields rose led the exit of the schismatics without offering another word. He slammed through the automatic doors, not allowing them the courtesy of opening for him, and charged even farther ahead of the group. He didn't want to speak to them, not because of the fear of being recorded, which he was certain was happening at all times, but because he'd always had trouble organizing his thoughts when nearing the precipice of rage. Only after his second divorce had he learned to retreat to a calmer state of mind before engaging in a carousel argument with someone as unhinged as Emily Krauss.

He'd felt himself reaching that tipping point, that climax of a mind-fuck that Krauss had created, so he decided to leave.

"Andre," Patricia said, "this isn't something we can just walk away from! We've got to have the House introduce impeach—"

Shields was surprised someone had caught up with his pace. "With what proof, Patty? Don't know about you, but I didn't have the sense to record what she said, and I'm damn sure we wouldn't be able to access her pet AI's recording. I knew she was dangerous, that putting those assholes in charge of this country was dangerous, but this…"

"Then let's move forward with opening ourselves up to Medusas like everyone else. If we propose it for ourselves, there's no way she'd be able to exempt only the Executive! I don't think people would go for it, not after they all find out we've been excused from it. And she's not going to consider going through with that craziness she was talking about—she wouldn't if there's a chance she could be brought to trial for it. People aren't ready to give up on this country yet, but if we let it get much worse, the Four will be able to do whatever they want. That's the best course right now, unless you've got something better."

"Even if we propose total trial inclusion, even if we held a press conference and streamed it online, I don't think it would even get out of the House. Too many of them rely on the Valley's money to get elected. And if we bring it up and it fails, the public won't focus their rage on her or the corporations that keep food on their tables. They'll turn on us. The people lost faith in us long before Krauss got elected, and she's been able to entertain and occupy them with these group-think cases and sadistic public punishments. You know the reality as well as I do: Congress hasn't offered a helpful alternative to any of this chaos since it began. We were happy to keep our positions as the masses went after each other. We had no clue on what to do with the un- or underemployed in this country, so we were happy to cede those policies to Krauss and her ilk."

"But there are still innocent people who need our help! To me, it sounds like you're giving into her bullshit, and you can't. They can only put so many in those damn free-range prisons; they can only entice so many others toward a military that's basically become automated; they can only sell so many of them on the idea that staying in college for eight years is helpful until they see the fortunes they'll owe in loans; they can—"

"All right, all right. Now's not the time for the halftime pep talk. We'll bring the total inclusion proposal to the Committee as soon as we know we have at least a majority in the House. For now, we leave it in the oven and forget about it. While it bakes, people will keep seething and accusing each other in these bullshit vigilante trials. The anger and hate will eventually infiltrate and destroy the right communities, and when it does, we can direct that anger and fear towards her and the other lords, and then we might have a chance at getting back to our old government."

"I'll support it in if you will, Blonk," Senator Seager said, after standing on the periphery of Shields and DuBois' dialogue.

"The people of Vermont would love the chance to put me in my place if they think I need it. You've got my support. Always have," Blonk said.

"This is as close to sedition as I've heard today, Senators," said Krauss through the hallway speakers. She materialized above them, like a horrifying mirrored ceiling in a seedy motor inn. Three hulking secret service agents suddenly appeared at the end of the hallway. They stood like two defensive guards and middle linebacker, blocking the exit that Shields and the rest had been heading toward. Krauss watched Shields and DuBois gauge their situation. "If you're staying, please make your way back to my office. Now that I know you're going to actively obstruct the progress of these great companies, I will deal with you more directly."

"Just keep your mouths shut," DuBois said, "and take out your damn phones to stream every fucking second of the coming conversation. Big sister isn't calling all the shots just yet."

18

"You should be proud of your daughter! Her trial's been in the top five for over a week, and if it makes it a month, she'll get a personal commendation from President Krauss herself. And just look at the offers from the sponsors," Colmsly said, holding the tablet in front of Frank and Paige Reilly. "She plays this right, she could make a ton from them and then become an intern in AbowtMe's marketing division. What a foot in the door that'd be for your recent graduate, no? Such opportunities! Such resourcefulness! Such creativity from so young a woman…yet here I am responding to her call for help, a call telling me that her own parents have cut her off from her phone and computer and tablet? You know that's a misdemeanor, right? Forcing her to use a landline…damn savages."

"You need to get the hell out of my hou—"

"Your daughter's aggregate Vt score has skyrocketed—embarrassingly higher than yours or your wife's, so I'd watch the threats. Because of that impressive score, and since the lovely young lady just entered the real world, I could recommend she take possession of your property, your benefits, and your business, so just dial down the angry-dad routine. Still wanna be an asshole, huh? Fine with me, Reilly."

"Just because we can't fucking stand you doesn't mean we're not going to comply," Paige said. "After she launched the trial, without our permission or knowledge of it, she started getting some vile pictures and messages and notifications. There were also threats being called to the house—people claiming to be family and friends of the victims of Bailey's trial. We were just trying to keep her safe."

"First, she didn't need your permission. She listened to what I told her and waited for her birthday before starting the case. Second, if you were concerned with her safety, you should have called your local FileX department to register an official report."

"Forgive us if we don't exactly hold your department's procedures and tactics in the highest regard," Frank said.

"Oh, right, because of your brilliant son's situation?"

"Ding ding ding."

"You should be proud to have children so dedicated to their employers," Colmsly said.

Frank and Paige exchanged a look. "What do you mean? Sean is a prisoner and Bailey doesn't work for you," she said.

"And I thought my parents were clueless. Don't you talk with your kids at all? You ever ask them anything important? Sean's required to maintain contact with you—which I know he does because we monitor every call—and Bailey's been…how do I put this…on probation, if you will, ever since she and her little friend decided to interject into Jimmy Larkin's first trial. Really, since your Vt scores have dropped so much, FileX has more claim to your kids than you do."

"Hold on a goddamn minute! You're not taking any of our children from us! Just try to—"

"I forgot who I told this to, Frank—there are so many idiots I've got to deal with every day—but I never wanted kids and no one I know at the office wants to run a daycare. Sure, I could have Sean placed in the care of the State, but that would be a waste of our investment, and Bailey's old enough now to make her own choices in life."

Frank balled his hands into fists and took a step toward Colmsly, who stood as stolid as he had the entire conversation, his demeanor unchanged. "I've been threatened by more important people than you, Reilly, so back the fuck off. Good choice. I'm not here for a mano a mano standoff. Return the girl's devices and internet access or I'll be back. And if I have to, you're not leaving here in a comfortable pair of cuffs."

"She'll have them back as soon as you're gone."

"We're not negotiating. Get the fucking things, now. I've got places to be."

Frank ripped his keys off the hook by the front door, shoved past Colmsly, and opened the passenger door of his work truck. He punched the glove box handle with the side of his fist and the door popped open, spilling its contents to the floor. Along with Bailey's phone and tablet, out tumbled his conspiratorial walkie-talkie.

"Your teenagers are still playing with kids' toys, Reilly?" Colmsly asked. He'd sidled to the driver's side window without a sound.

Frank stared at the cartoonishly camouflaged two-way radio. "Cheapest way to keep in touch with my guys," he said, "if there at a different site than me."

"Don't pay your guys enough to afford phones, you cheap bastard?"

"No, Colmsly, they do just fine. But they don't like to have them on 'em while they work. Too many have been shredded over the years."

"Know what those two-ways are also good for? Talking about things you don't want certain organizations to hear."

"You're right. I guess the secrets of proper lawn maintenance should remain forever closely guarded," Frank said, returning Colmsly's stare. "Now, do you want to personally watch me return her phone and tablet?"

"No, Reilly. You're going to follow me and watch me do it. Gimme the fuckin' things," he said, glancing once more at the walkie-talkie.

Colmsly led the way past Mrs. Reilly and up to Bailey's room.

"Feel like a prom date," he said when they reached to foot of the staircase.

Paige grinded her teeth but stayed silent. Leo Colmsly wasn't waiting for their responses, anyway. He went up the stairs a pair at a time, looking as if he truly were an excited suitor. He rapped three times and opened the door without waiting for an answer. He stopped halfway in and turned to the lemurs behind him, "Wait out here, please. I've got some business to discuss with your daughter and you're not entitled to hear it." He shut the door and locked it, ignoring their bellicose protests.

She'd heard them coming and sat up on her bed.

"Would you let your parents confiscate your tits? Would you let them take your teeth out of your head? No? Then why the hell would you let them separate you form these?" he asked, holding up the electronics.

"I don't think I'm gonna listen to any more of your lectures, Leo," she said, momentarily stunning him.

"'Scuse me? This is my bad ear. You wanna repea—"

"No, I don't want to repeat myself. You don't know why my parents really cut me off, do you? Obviously not. Before they took them, I got a personal message from the desk of President Krauss, an invitation, along with the other platinum level plaintiffs, to participate in a meeting between her and

Congressman Barrit—yup, the same guy who killed that lawyer upstate—and when I told them, they freaked. Started screaming that I didn't know what the hell I was getting into, that I was getting obsessed with all of the trial bullshit, that I was forgetting what you and FileX did to Sean. So they took the phone and tablet and cut the breaker to my room."

"Krauss wanted to personally talk with you? Already?" Colmsly said, ignoring everything else. "Krauss and that hick Barrit want to what—congratulate your momentous achievement!"

"Thanks for the support, Agent Colmsly. I just feel so affirmed when you stop by."

"Aside from hosting one of the most popular trials in years, what could you have to offer her? What the hell are they doing if twats like you are going to be receiving the accolades?"

Before she could answer, he stormed out of her room, past her still-cursing parents, down the stairs, and out of the house. He used the lawn to turn around, sending patches of sod onto the porch and into the driveway.

"There's a little weekend project for ya, Reilly!" he screamed before careening out of sight.

Bailey watched the scene from her window, her parents from the opened front door.

"Fucking asshole," Bailey said as she turned on her phone and computer. Before her password bar appeared, she got up and closed her door. Still irritated about her parents' earlier overreaction, she clicked it locked and went back to her desk. Her fingers punched in her password and her homepage blinked into focus. She checked her inbox and just as she'd feared, there was another message from President Emily Krauss and Congressman Reginald Barrit.

"What happened to Enrico?"

"Enrico? Oh, the star-man. We granted his wish?"

"You killed him?"

"Not yet, but I doubt he'll live very long. Not that it's any of your concern, but he's now part of a nuclear waste clean-up crew in the southwestern desert. He'll have all the stars in the visible universe to keep him company. While he still has his eyesight."

"Are you tellin' me that with all the technology we have, you're still using people to clean that shit up? And isn't already in storage facilities?"

"You are inquisitive! Even more so than the psych evaluation determined. Of course we have machines to do it. The heavy lifting and transportation is done by our machines and trains, but the excavation is done by our employees. You see, they are much less valuable than our latest mechanical advancements, and they need something to do, so why not put them to use?"

"Gonna have them build you some pyramids, next?"

"If you'd rather assist Señor Jimenez, I'd be happy to arrange that. It would be a waste of your abilities, though. I will be generous enough to give you that choice."

"That's like giving a hamster in a cage options to keep it occupied—no matter what it chooses, it's still in the cage."

"So you've figured out the prison model? Brilliant! Wow! Perhaps this data analysis is mistaken."

Lamont didn't have a response.

"No more inquiries into your cell mate? Good. Now, onto your prospects. Your case is peculiar because you show tremendous potential in computer sciences and applied mathematics, but you're delineated, specifically by Agent Colmsly, as a disloyal, someone who, given the opportunity to do so, would betray the company and his position to escape or help a fellow prisoner do the same."

"Who the hell wouldn't be classified like that?"

"Simple. Someone who's realized and accepted that there are no exits from this hamster cage. Someone who's dedicated himself to the advancement of something more than his personal tribe. Someone who's willing to dedicate himself and his intelligence to bettering the Big Four, and in turn, all of those around him. By being focusing on his task, by becoming the best employee he can, he'll come to the conclusion that working hard is the only possible path for achieving what he wants."

"Do hamsters always get such inspirin' speeches before they spin in their wheels?"

"Again, you are free to lug barrels of nuclear waste onto trains and then onto our EMVs."

"EMV?"

"Our electromagnetic launch system. It covers the entirety of the Utah Salt Flats. Takes that much area to generate the speed and energy needed to launch the waste out of the Earth's orbit. So would you rather work to develop projects like that or be a part of the mindless drones who haul it out?"

Lamont looked down, thinking of the slow, painful death of radiation poisoning that inevitably waited Enrico. "If I help—"

"You mean if you can be of help. The top minds in the world work for our companies, young man, so don't presume to be more valuable than you are."

"I'd like to help in any way I can," he said.

"Very good. I was really hoping you'd see reason," he said, tapping his tablet screen to life, "because with your skills, you'll be needed in our Brazilian facility. We got a marvelous deal on lease price from the Guilherme regime—"

"Brazil?"

"Yes, the one in South America. You're going to be working with our synthetic energy division."

"Synthetic energy?"

"With the advancements we've made in genetic coding and restructuring through the AI, we're very close to utilizing the photosynthetic process to harness energy for ourselves. We're running a bit low on resources at our other sites, so you're going to begin your term with our ecological energetics squad in the heart of the Amazon. You didn't think we spent all that money to save it just to look at the pretty animals and buck-naked locals, did you?"

"I didn't know you'd spent anything to save anything," Lamont said, "and why are you tellin' me all this anyway?"

"Why wouldn't I? It'll be your job for the next few years, so you might as well have some background on it, no? Besides, who are you going to run and tell? The AI handles the security, and our competitors' versions are pathetic at best."

"You mean there are other artificial intelligences?"

"Of course there are! Nobody trusts people to do anything anymore! You think any of us thought about using geothermal energy to power the EMVs to launch our waste into space? No! You really believe that, before the Big Four's creation, the energy conglomerates that had our government bought and paid for would have allowed our hive-solar storage units orbiting the earth? With the AI's help, we're going to fix everything we've botched on this planet—as long as we all understand and accept our roles in its grand scheme."

"What if people don't want to be a part of its *grand scheme?*"

"Oh, so people who have no problem believing their lives are governed by some mystical god will have issues with a real program dictating what they're best suited to do?"

"Just sounds—"

"Listen, as fun as this was, you've got to get ready for your trip. I approved your decision, and the plane's leaving tomorrow morning. And look at that," he said, scrolling through the list of inmates bound for Brazil, "you'll be on the same shuttle as the infamous Jimmy Larkin. Happy travels."

19

The spoils of a five-year service contract with FileX Public Security & Safety: (1) a construction stipend for necessary repairs and updates for any existing headquarters—if none exist, a loan of up to two hundred fifty thousand dollars, depending on credit and Vt scores, is available; (2) stipends of twenty-five thousand dollars per-year for low-level outfit/club/gang members and fifty thousand for officers and/or chapter leaders; (3) state-of-the-art FileX arsenals, bulletproof vests, riot gear, and Gazelle-secured level-two access codes; (4) modified pursuit and detainment vehicles; (5) complete physicals for all active and probationary members of outfit, gang, or club.

The three-man construction crew programmed its new stainless steel machines (the ones that actually did the physical labor) to repair the Long Island Freedom Fighters' dilapidated central command. Mason Miller and the other winners of the FileX security windfall waited their turns at Gazelle's Plum Island medical research facility. Gazelle had purchased the former animal disease research facility from the government in 2019 for a paltry sum of five million dollars. The island's inhabitants, mostly pigs, cattle, and flightless fowl, had been abandoned by their researchers and, without the confines and daily tortures, had reverted to a wild, albeit restricted, existence. Gazelle's interest in the leg-of-lamb shaped isle came after their acquisition of Telson Pharmaceuticals, but Gazelle's biological engineers weren't interested in studying and combatting the viral and bacterial afflictions of livestock—they were vastly more concerned with studying the short and long-term effects of integrating their protein-based Nano-processors into human DNA. The processors would allow for the next wave of quantum data collection, and, inevitably, the next advancement in communications and energy technologies. With the cells altered on a molecular level, Gazelle would be able to read and understand the trillions of data points produced by the human brain's synapses. In enough time, the technology would exist not only to read thoughts, but assimilate them into the AI, helping it understand the psychological variables that pervade economic theorems and behavioral models. Once these psychosocial and social aspects were fully comprehended by the AI, it would be able to develop and, if given permission from its handlers, implement the perfect marketing strategy for the Big Four, and, finally, it would be able to assist them in destroying their foreign competitors.

Even the quantum intellect found unexpected boundaries in interpreting the human mind. It needed a voluminous number of subjects from a wide array of cultures to interpret why humans behave as bizarrely as they often do, and luckily for Gazelle, prisoners and volunteers were readily available for experimentation. The prisoners were invaluable. They came from every corner of the country and from every continent across the globe; they helped the AI learn more about human behavior than all its combined Web searches and data compilations.

Mason Miller and the other Long Island Freedom Fighters arrived at the island under the guise of receiving free health physicals but got the added perk of having their genes altered for no extra cost. There they sat, in a sterile white room, receiving the exclusive privilege of being Gazelle's next-step in communications technology: Synapse Cellular. The process embedded sub-atomic quantum processors which connected directly to the AI and the Abyss. The AI was then able to interpret each man's vision, hearing, and motor-functions and interpret those individual sights, sounds, movements, and emotional responses into live video-feeds, audio tracks, and message threads.

The physician explained this to each member of the Freedom Fighters, and except for Harry Vinks, who decided to try and swim for it (he drowned) all the men eventually agreed to the treatment.

"Well, fuck me," Miller said when given the news. "Will it hurt?"

"Tremendously!" the lanky scientist responded. "But think of the fortunes you stand to make if your trial's a success!"

Miller looked dubiously at the over-coated man and, after an hour's worth of prep, went under the anesthesia. He awoke in a new room with the unpleasant sensation of a hundred trillion sparklers being repeatedly extinguished and relit through his entire body. An immediate dose of opioids was fed through an IV drip to dull the pain.

"How long do you think this will last, doctor?" a Gazelle tech asked.

The administering nurse checked the numbers on the monitors and said, "If it doesn't kill them? My best guess is a month."

By mid-August, Miller and his men were relaxing in their newly refurbished rec room, sharing beers, shots, and laughs. Their futures as FileX men were bright and promising.

"God, I hope they let me pick up an animal abuser! Gouge his fucking eyes out and cut his throat!"

"That'd be sweet, man, but I also hope they let us go after some of those high school girls who break curfew…we'd have some fun with that."

"Whatever, we do, I hope we get to use all this shit," Carl Martin said, bringing his brothers' attention to the wall-spanning arms case.

"Hell, yeah, Carl. Hey, are we allowed to test 'em, you know, practice out back? You know, to be prepared in case of an emergency?"

Nick Halpin, the man who had asked the question, and the rest of them heard a distant voice in their minds, "No, Mr. Halpin. Your range practice schedule was given to you when you first arrived home. If you need it mentally displayed, all you have to do is think about it. Your ammunition and weapons are tightly controlled…and waste is not tolerated. You all have your issued sidearm and are free to carry any other personal defense items, so do not touch the automatic weapons, RPGs, or light artillery until instructed to do so."

The Freedom Fighters were still unaccustomed to having their questions, regardless of whether they were encased in the mind or vocalized, answered by the AI. Each man heard the responding messages in the same voice he'd hear when he talked to himself—the Gazelle engineers had thought it best to have the receiving brain interpret the signals that way. It helped reduce the risk of psychotic episodes.

Not knowing whether he was just experiencing his average daydream or if the ubiquitous AI was feeding him thoughts or emotional responses was not the most comforting feeling for Miller. He reached into his pocket, pulled out his prescription, and swallowed five milligrams of Oxycodone. *Let's see how that makes you feel*, he thought. "I'm not able to feel anything," he heard himself-but-not-himself respond few seconds later. He emptied the beer and was about to get another when the sound of an incoming call pierced his mind.

Miller and all the Freedom Fighters simultaneously looked up as they heard the message from their new proprietor. "Gentlemen. You need to mobilize and assist the Sixth Precinct in subduing and apprehending the participants of a mass protest outside Runners' Landing High School. The mob is a combination of unarmed civilians—those who have been captured on camera have been identified and their live-trials are already in progress. The images should be filtering into your midbrains now. Use of force is authorized and encouraged. Your priority is keeping FileX personnel safe. No need for good luck if the proper preparations have been made."

"Let's bust some heads!" Halpin shouted. "Been wantin' to fuck up some teachers ever since I finished high school! Saddle up, men!"

"Halpin, you turd, you dropped out halfway through your second senior year."

"Fuckin' close enough, Andy. Fuck yourself."

The bulletproof glass barrier in front of the new weaponry raised without anyone triggering any mechanism. The lock was disengaged by FileX, and the Freedom Fighters went down the line like they were picking at a brunch buffet. "Shit, Buck, we're not storming Normandy. I don't think you're gonna get much resistance from some old elementary school teachers," Miller chided.

"You don't know who's packin' and who ain't, boss. Concealed laws been legal for years now. Better safe than sorry."

The mob that Miller and the Freedom Fighters descended on was comprised of those educators who had quit, been fired, or been forced into an early retirement. Standing with them all in solidarity was a smattering of parents and students who were sympathetic to their cause. The group held signs—many of which denounced FileX and the rest of the Big Four—moved in undulating ovals and chanted about the injustice of privatizing public education. They decreed, in the impotent demonstration, that private companies and equity firms should not be sponsors of public schools. They shouted and chanted that the rich could never care about children of any color because the only color they cared about was green. Several even dared to challenge the Larkin ruling by saying, "Find Jillian Foster's real killer!" The nebulous group had been marching and protesting off and on for weeks, adding new supporters each day. Some of the incipient additions to the group tried to expand the group's messages across the Web, but the well-intentioned tactic alerted the wrong authorities and initiated the Medusas. The incessant picketing and popular online petitions became more than the local powers of the Four could tolerate. With their business reputations being besmirched, Gazelle and FileX had first attempted to persuade their purchased politicians to go to the scene and talk some sense into the peaceful protesters, but their payrolled sycophants only succeeded in emboldening others to join the teachers' movement. Before calling in their newest batch of modified mercenaries, FileX tried to disperse the crowds by using the local police force—perhaps seeing their known boys in blue would help the gathered come to their senses and disperse. That logic was deduced by the AI's social engineering program. But the protesters persisted. After exhausting the alternatives, the AI determined that the use of minimal force would be the most efficient way to uphold the law. Agent Colmsly thought it best to save time and money by killing as many of the organizers as FileX could, so he made the final call to bring in the Long Island Freedom Fighters.

Miller's group consisted of fifty-two able-bodied men (the fourteen elderly and physically disabled members always remained at headquarters to guard the alcohol supply) who carried, and would gleefully use on these penned-in protesters, riot gear and thousands of rounds of ammunition. Under Colmsly's telepathic orders, the men flanked the terrified crowd and then waited for further instructions. From their inclined position, the Freedom Fighters began to strike their riot shields with their retractable batons. As they progressed forward toward their panicking opposition, the rhythm sped to a surprisingly coordinated ¾ signature. When they were thirty yards from the crowd, they halted their forward motion but continued their drumming. The command to attack came, not from Colmsly—although he was moments away from giving it—but from the jurors of the live trial. By a margin of only four percent, it was determined that Miller and his men should attack and quell the rebellion to save education. Each member of the L. I. F. F. simultaneously saw the trial results, put aside their batons and shields, and unholstered whatever pistol, rifle, or shotgun they were carrying. The sign-waving pedagogues were slaughtered on a live stream to over ten million viewers.

"You're Sean Reilly's father, huh? And you're interested in joining us?" an elderly Freedom Fighter named Buck asked.

"I've got to see my son—once a month isn't enough for a father to see his boy. If this is where he'll be stationed, this is where I want to be."

Buck shrugged and looked at Reilly's partner. "Don't really know the kid, 'cept from hearin' the name once in a while. And you?" he said, addressing Jordan Davis. "Don't believe I know you. Don't think you'd exactly fit in 'round here."

"Don't know how much you know about Frank's son, but my boy was taken from me, the same time Sean was," he said, his lip beginning to quiver, "and now...now I'm never gonna see him again," he said, fighting back tears. "They're assigning him to South America somewhere; he couldn't say exactly where when I talked to him."

"I don't need to know that shit, man. Well, I can't help you at all. Too old to do much of anything but bitch and drink. The boss and the rest of 'em went off on their first assignment. Wish I could be there, I tell you. I'm hopin' that they come up with some youth-restorin' tech sooner 'en later, ya know?"

"If there's no one to talk to, isn't there some information we could take about joinin' up? Any brochures or anything?" Frank asked.

"Brochures? This look like a travel agency, buddy? Nah, we don't have brochures," he said, laughing.

"Well, can we wait until they get back? We don't have much to do today, and—"

"Listen, I don't know when they'll be back, but when they do get in, the last thing they'll wanna see are you two swingin' dicks. Why dontcha come back tomorrow or the next day when Mason Miller's around. I gotta go take a leak—friggin' prostate—so you boys can see yourselves out."

Buck stumbled off his barstool, leaving them unchaperoned in the rec room.

"This couldn't have worked out better, Frank."

"How do you mean? If we have to wait for Miller to get back, how can you get access?"

"You think these are the most lubricated rubbers in the box? Probably have their passwords written under the bar or above the toilet."

"Well, we can't check the toilet right now, so let's have a look behind the bar."

They heard old voices echoing from the kitchen, so they ran to either end of the stained-oak bar and worked their way toward the center. "Hurry, Frank, they're comin' for their midday cocktails!"

"I don't see anything. Hurry up, Jordan! What the hell are you lookin' at?"

Jordan stood just next to the sink. He held up a notebook with the word DELIVERIES written on the cover. "This, man. I'm lookin' at this," he said, turning the inside cover toward Frank. On the top of the first page were passwords labeled, *FileX Shit*. "No! No pictures, Frank. Put that damn thing away. Pictures have caused us enough trouble, but if we just take this code and log in legitimately, we won't have to wait at all to start messin' with those assholes. Just let me memorize it…got it."

"What about that whole ratio of product popularity to…whatever you were talkin' about a while back?"

"Forget the lawnmowers, Frank. With this key, we can play with whatever we want."

Jordan placed the notebook back under to the sink and they headed for the door.

"Hey, what the fuck were you two doin' behind my bar?" Buck yelled, returning from his piss.

20

"Your stress hormones have elevated to a critical level, Mr. Miller."

He subdued the profanity-ridden tirade that was going to be his response. "With you constantly badgering me, you—what do I even call you?"

"Do you often name your own internal voice, Mr. Miller? Call me whatever you call that."

Mason shut his eyes and began to cry. "No, I've never had to name anyone else in my head. But before you were put into me, I never had a reason to think anyone else was in there! I'm going crazy and it's only been a month!"

"If you'd like to contact an ambulance, all you have to do is visualize 9-1-1 and connect with the dispatch program."

Miller wept but remembered, through all of the traffic in his mind, the emergency FileX number he'd been forced to memorize before leaving Plum Island. First, the area code, 6...3...1 appeared, followed by 5...5...5...and, finally, 2...1...1...5...

"You've reached an unlisted number for technology department of FileX Security. Please dial the extension of the agent who gave you this line."

Again, Miller thought out his answer. 2...0...7...4...1.

"Extension of Colmsly, Leo, confirmed. Connecting."

Miller listened to the ring of a telephone. He thought it anachronistic considering how he'd made the call.

"Dr. Puja Verma of FileX Psychiatrics speaking, how may I help you Mr. Miller?"

"I-I can't seem to—"

"Please just think your response, Mr. Miller. There's no need to risk information being lost in unnecessary data-compilation steps."

"I—we can't have this thing constantly on in our heads!" he yelled in his mind, hoping to deafen himself. But it was more than just the constant connection; Miller's mind had replayed the images of the blood and carnage since returning from their victory. He kept hearing the screams of terror and mercy, and he didn't care if the FileX agents or the AI saw him visualizing them. "And if we can't shut it off, we're gonna go Jonestown down here!"

"I kept telling them to limit access. I kept telling them that the data wasn't sufficient to support a constant stream. It's too much of a shock to the frontal lobe. Are you reading this, Agent Colmsly?"

"Yeah, I hear what you're both saying, doc. So, what do you propose?"

Miller cracked and balled. His brain was now little more than a phone being used in a conference call.

"The same thing I suggested from the beginning: correlate their activations to their physical device use."

"So," Colmsly replied through Miller's conduit brain, "any time they use a phone, tablet, computer, or car, connect 'em? We're gonna be back to using phones?"

"Precisely, Mr. Colmsly. Until we can figure out how to place the proper firewalls in their minds, they will have to activate when they activate a device," Verma responded.

"Miller, would that make you happy?" asked Colmsly.

Please, just let it shut off for a little while, Miller thought.

"It will take a few hours to recalibrate your entire squad, Mr. Miller, but I'll have you better in no time."

Miller thought of the word *End*, and hung up.

"Hey, boss," Buck Arnold said, "there were a couple of guys by here while you were out. Some guy named Reilly and some nig—"

"Not-fucking-now, Buck! Get the hell outta here and give me some quiet!"

"Don't need this shit," he mumbled as he left. He flung open the door and pushed past the new kid, Reilly.

"Watch the hell where you're walkin', old man!" Sean shouted.

"You little shit. It was your father and his dark friend who were pokin' around here 'fore you all got back! Jus' tried to let the boss know, but he looks like all kinds of crap. So you know what, tough guy, now you can go back there and tell him, 'cause I'm done for the day."

Mason reached for his vial but was halted by his vibrating FileX issued phone. The company's insignia appeared on the screen. He let it shake on the empty table but not long enough to go to voicemail.

"Just 'cause we're outta your heads doesn't mean you're off the clock!" Colmsly yelled.

"Just a goddam minute's peace!"

Colmsly exaggerated his breathing, letting Miller know that those four cycles of inhaling and exhaling was all the respite Miller was going to get. "That better, cupcake? Now, can you and three or four other guys take care of somethin' for me?"

"We just got back from our first...our..."

"Well, here comes your next assignment, chief. This one should be a little easier for you. First, choose a few men—and make damn sure one of them is Sean Reilly—and get your asses over to the Larkin place, arrest his wife and kids, and bring them to these coordinates. That's not too bad, right?"

"You want us to arrest his wife and kids? What goddamn threat could they be?"

"Explaining myself to you is not what's going to happen, Miller. Not ever."

"Guess I got too used to havin' my head connected to every explanation to any question I could possibly think of, sir."

"That's fair, Miller. That it is, so until you're fully integrated again, I'll make it a point to spell things out for you. Mrs. Larkin played a large role in organizing that batch of fine folks, sending around those petitions, even trying to set up a retrial in her husband's name—after his appeal had been interrupted by the Tomanicki girl's blockbuster trial—but as Mrs. Larkin's luck would have it, she could not be at today's colorful soiree. In the name of equal treatment under the law, we're going to bring her in, confiscate her children, and help the world forget this whole episode of ugliness. And after you get her and the little ones in that little kid-toucher-van you've got, you're going to take a little spin to Frank Reilly's house. Make Sean drive to that one. In fact, make sure he's the arresting officer because just before you and all your thoughts were cut off, I heard that old bastard, Buck, say that Frank Reilly and Jordan Davis stopped by the club while you and your men were out playing army. Well, I want to know what had them so interested in your little outfit."

"Probably just the grand company, Agent Colmsly."

"Be at Larkin's house in twenty. You should be getting her trial notification any second now."

"And the one for Reilly?"

"Why, he's just wanted for questioning. No charges are being pressed, yet. And Miller…"

"Yeah?"

"You remember what we said about keeping FileX property safe and secure right?"

"After all the weapons are cleaned, they'll be logged in the system, we didn't forget—"

"I mean all our property, Miller! You remembered to destroy printed versions of the passwords and codes we gave you, right? I mean, there was no need to have anything written down when all you had to do was ask for an answer in your head, right?"

The notebook eluded Miller's memory. "How stupid you really think we are, Colmsly? I wasn't scrubbing toilets before I started this! Anything we wrote down while we were recoverin' from your little experiment was torched."

"I hope so, Miller, I really hope so. Because…"

Miller ended the call and put his phone back to the countertop. As soon as it made contact, it hummed with the distinct sound of a delivered Medusa. *Rippin' kids away from their mothers wasn't the kinda work I signed up for*, he thought. He waited for a responding voice but nothing came. He poured several ounces of vodka into a glass and threw it back. "Flynn, Johnson! Get in here!"

"What is it, Mason?" Flynn asked. "And how come everything's so damn quiet all of a sudden? What the hell is goin' on?" he asked, rubbing his forehead.

"You guys are coming with me on another trip to the Larkin place. Hope you remember the way, 'cause I'm not usin' my phone for the rest of the day. And grab the new kid, Reilly, for this trip. He's been cordially invited."

"The sedan all right for this one?"

"Get the keys to van and meet me out front in five."

"So when can you get this going, buddy?"

"We have to be careful with this password, man, very careful. We have to use it when it wouldn't be suspicious. I don't think it would be smart to go back, but we could do some drive-by recon for the next few days to see when the gang's all here."

"That's not a problem at all. There's a deli down the road that I go to all the time. Best damn egg salad I've ever had."

"Frank, with this new access, we can do a whole lot more damage than homicidal lawn equipment."

"What could be worse than the mass murders and mutilations those things'll commit?"

"C'mon, man, think bigger. Remember those fools who rerouted and disabled those container ships? Those people had the right idea. We can't bring these companies down by tarring their reps... we've gotta do it through their wallets."

"We get caught with that, we're dead, Jordan—not imprisoned for life—dead on the spot."

"I've just got a feelin' and it's tellin' me that after we do this, whatever it is, we're not coming back from it, so we've got to make it count. I don't want to just inconvenience them with small attacks that'll get us caught anyway... I wanna watch them burn for destroying my family."

Frank listened to what his friend was saying. Sean, for the foreseeable future, was gone; Paige chaperoned Bailey to D.C. to meet with President Krauss and the members of the Judiciary Review Committee. He never expected his family to resemble what it once had.

"All right, for argument's sake, we send their ships to Antarctica. Then what?"

"We won't stop with their ships and commerce, Frank...we'll poison their AI wizard and put them out for as long as we can. If we're able corrupt CenTek's data storage satellites, we can, for at least a while, annihilate the AI's global reach. That would give us the chance to play in the Abyss without ever getting caught."

"Go big or go home, right?"

"Exactly what I was thinking. And the next time you hear from Sean, don't tell him anything. I mean, you can talk to him about the usual stuff and our stopping by his club, but don't mention us needing access to any systems or our plans—don't look at me like that—of course it's obvious, but we have to assume that we're being recorded every damn second. They might've had that old bastard wired, so we've got to be smart about this. Crafty and patient and then we strike like fucking cobras, man. Like fucking cobras."

On the morning the Long Island Freedom Fighters liberated the town of Runners' Landing from the last semblances of a traditional educational system, Bailey and her mother and Aaron Elskin and his father, Elijah, arrived in Washington, D.C. They were expected as honored guests of President Krauss and the Senate Judiciary Review Boards. Their tour, which was given to them in private, before the first group of campers came through, began with a delightful stroll through the Museum of the Former Supreme Court. There they listened to animatronic puppets recite the majority decisions of the Dred Scott v. Sanford, Plessy v. Ferguson, and Buck v. Bell cases. These infamous judgments, according to the tour guide, were displayed as a reminder of how unjust, flawed, and cruel the old system had been to the law-abiding citizens of the United States. Following the tour, the guests were reminded to check into their hotel, pick up their Presidential Passes, refresh themselves, and reconvene for their 7:30 p.m. dinner.

As Paige unpacked, she turned to her daughter. "Bailey, please don't get too caught up in all this. I'm so proud of what you've accomplished with your trial," she lied, "but I think this is a little too much for such a young…just please promise me you'll remember what's important."

"Mom, all of this is just like some old-fashioned movie premiere. We're going to meet some people who don't care who we are, smile, eat, shake some hands, and go home. That's it. OK, OK, if it makes you feel better, I promise I won't freak out and pledge my love, loyalty, and first-born to the Big Four."

"Sweetie, I'm just so worried about…about so much. And that tour. You know there were some incredibly noble decisions made by that court too, right? Please tell me you learned about them at some point."

"We did, Mom. You think any of us took those field trips seriously? Remember when I came here in seventh grade? None of us were paying attention."

"But you were already a little older than the average student or camper who goes through there now, Bailey. If you're going to be famous from all these online trials, please try to be a moderating voice in it all. What we can't handle any more of, what's going to tear this country apart state-by-state are the armchair prosecutors shouting down and harassing the—"

"Mom," she said, hugging her, "I promise I won't run off with the vigilante circus. Besides, I doubt I'll ever find such a great tip for a case again."

"Bailey…ever since that afternoon, I've been wanting ask you how Ms. Drison thought to contact you, how she even found you. So? How did she?"

Bailey continued hugging her mother, desperately trying to conceal her trepidation in the embrace. She frantically conjured several scenarios of her meeting Alexis Drison but none were plausible. *Shit, this hug is going on too long*, she thought, *she's gonna think I'm high, I just need a few more—*

A quick succession of knocks distracted both women long enough for Bailey to break free and head for the door. Whoever was behind it was immaterial; the diversion couldn't have been better timed.

She grabbed the handle but before pushing it down asked, "Who is it?"

To which Aaron Elskin replied, "It's just me and my dad. We were wondering if you and your mother would like to grab a drink with us before we head over to the Capitol."

"One second," Bailey said through the door. She turned around to her mother who was shaking her head and mouthing, 'No.' Bailey crept over into whispering range.

"You two aren't twenty-one, Bailey, and I think it would be wrong to—"

"Ma, have you seriously forgotten why Michelle Asbury's here with me and the others? It was her case that lowered the drinking age from twenty-one to sixteen."

"No, I must have missed that one, Bailey."

Bailey saw the unease in her mother's face and just before Elskin could knock again, she opened the door just far enough to fit her face through and said, "I'm sorry, Aaron, but we're not even close to ready. When is the shuttle coming, again?"

"Oh, no problem. Uh, not for another couple of—what time is it—you've still got an hour and forty-five. We'll be at the lounge when you're ready."

As Aaron and his father turned to leave, Bailey heard their phones buzz and beep in unison. Like Doc Holliday and Wyatt Earp drawing to shoot at the OK Corral, the father and son yanked out their phones and stared at the screens. Bailey was surprised enough at their reflexes to miss the notification drumming through her device. *That's odd*, she thought. *Who would know we're all together?*

"Bailey!" Paige cried from inside, "Come look at this!"

Bailey let the door close and walked back to her mother's side. Paige held a hand over her gaping mouth as she looked at the screen.

"That looks like the high school," Bailey said.

The camera angle switched as if on a director's cue. It now showed an aerial view of both the crowd in front of the school and the heavily armed group that surrounded them.

"That's definitely our school, Mom. What the hell is going on? Did you check the notification? Click on scale icon."

They read the newly enlarged text, *Unruly mob Accused of assaulting police and FileX officers, demonstrating without proper permits, disturbing the peace, endangering the welfare of minors, and possessing illegally enhanced firearms. The trial is live. Would you like to see your options, Y/N?*

Again, the angle changed from a hovering drone to the first-person of a FileX officer's chest camera. Bailey turned the volume up, and they heard the commanding officers of the law shout out, "Advance with weapons at the ready!"

"Mom, click on yes, and open up to the trial!"

Paige clicked on the Y icon. The video feed shrunk into a small box and moved to the bottom left of her screen. Only two options appeared below the charges: A) Authorize Deadly Force to Protect Public Safety and B) Authorize Non-Lethal Force to Protect Public Safety. Under those options was a running timer.

00:05

00:04

00:03

Before either the timer could expire or Bailey could offer her unsolicited instructions, Paige clicked on choice B.

00:02

00:01

In a decision of fifty-two to forty-eight percent, the online jury of Live Trial 11704-516 has chosen to disperse the illegal mob though A) Authorization of Deadly Force.

Paige and Bailey watched in frozen horror as the obviously unarmed group was torn apart. When too much blood covered their chest-camera guide, a new one with an even bloodier perspective took its place. When a bullet cleaved a path through a pig-tailed girl's head, Paige threw the phone against the wall. Bailey walked past the broken phone and picked up her own. It too displayed the carnage. *What the fuck was that?* was her first thought. Her next was whether or not Sean had been played a role in that slaughter.

21

"Sweetheart, what're you doing?"

Latoya sat on the couch with her feet tucked back, her knees, pressed together, pointed straight ahead toward the hearth. She stared blankly at the shuttered fireplace, tears cascading down her already glistening face. Pushed against her left cheek was Lamont's baby blanket. She caressed it, not as if it were fabric but the newborn she had held almost seventeen years earlier. Jordan went to her, hugged her tightly, but did not try to separate her from her grieving.

"I don't care what you and Frank have been planning. I don't care about getting even or getting revenge…I just want my boy back."

"Toya, I will get him back, but before I can—"

"Don't you tell me any 'before I can'! Get him back! Bring our baby home!"

Jordan turned away and joined her in staring at the fireplace. He thought about the possibilities and leverage he'd be throwing away if all he did was use his access to find Jordan's exact location. *Why not make sure this never happens to any other family again?* he thought. *If I can permanently damage such an evil group of companies, why not just do it?* The sound of his wife's uncontrollable sobs interrupted his thoughts. She had the pale-blue blanket over her face, her tears saturating it. Instead of speaking, he drew her closer.

"It-it still smells like him, Jordan! I can smell my tiny cooing baby boy!"

That was all the answer he needed. "It'll be all right, Toya. I've got what we need to find him and I'm gonna do it right now. What I need you to do is get those bags we packed and load 'em into the Datsun."

"Whatta-what're you talkin' about? The Datsun?" she asked through cries. "Why not the—"

"Because the Datsun's electronics aren't connected to anything but the battery. They'll have a helluva time tryin' to track us in that. C'mon, baby, get up. We're goin' to get our boy back."

"So how do you think she still pays the mortgage on a place like this, being she's the wife of a convict?" Colmsly asked as they turned the corner toward the Larkin residence.

Miller twitched, beginning to feel the effects of his developing Oxy habit; Colmsly's ruminations on Susan Larkin's finances were not helping as a diversion. "Maybe she's dancin' on poles or puttin' 'em down her throat every night. Who the hell cares? Can we just get this over with?"

"You're right, Captain Miller. Who fucking cares? Well, I do a little, 'cause if she's getting any kind of crowd-funding, we'll have to add it to her list of charges."

"Being a wanted-terrorist ain't enough for you? You really think that getting some dough to feed her kids will be the final nail? You should be happy she's keeping the kids healthy, no? They'll make stronger slaves, right?"

Colmsly ignored Miller's chiding and shot upright in his passenger seat, "That's her on the side of the house. This'll be easier than I thought."

Susan Larkin was nervously chain-smoking next to her garage when she saw the approaching van. As it sped across the road, directly toward her, she flicked the butt over her neighbor's fence and ran into her house.

"Pull right up on the lawn, Sanchez," Colmsly ordered to the car in front of them. "Checking audio and video…"

"Coming in clearly on both, sir," an anonymous voice said through the van's speakers.

"Better than having those voices in your heads, right, Miller? Enough screwing around. Listen carefully. I don't know what she's capable of and we don't know what she might be carrying, so treat her like any other armed and dangerous suspect."

"Like all those hostile teachers earlier today?" Flynn said, staring out his window.

Again, Colmsly ignored the chiding and continued his orders, "Everybody out. One on that side door and another to cover the rear. The rest with me through the front. Reilly, get your scrawny ass up here 'cause, right now, you're the point-man. Gonna be some good practice for our next collar. Remember your lines? Good. Let's get the bitch."

With Sean at the front of the formation, they made their approach. Sean beat on the door three times. "FileX! We've got warrants for your arrest and for the search of the property. Open the door and then back away with your hands in the air!"

The dead bolt clicked and slid out of the doorframe. Then the latch popped open and the door swung inward. Reilly entered with his 9 mm in front of him. There, in the foyer, stood a disheveled Susan Larkin. She backed away as instructed and the men filed in toward her. Miller, out of habit, and because he was bringing up the rear, shut the door.

"Ma'am, please place your hands—"

"Were you the ones that killed my babies?"

Sean's authoritative façade crumbled. "What're you talk—"

"My little angels…my sweet babies… Were you all there when they were murdered?" she said through an eerily calm sob.

"What is she talkin' about, Colmsly?" Miller asked.

"They'd spent the night with grandma…and…oh, Mom!" She cried harder, realizing that not only had her children been killed, but her mother as well. "I…I was supposed to meet them there after my appointment…"

"Hey, boss, what's that smell?" Flynn asked.

In her hands behind her back, Susan Larkin sparked a barbeque lighter. The house, which had been filling with natural gas for a half hour, erupted in a volcanic inferno. She'd planned on destroying herself and the remnants of her life before Colmsly and his crew arrived. Taking them along with her was an extra special gratuity.

The culminating portion of Bailey and Aaron's visit to D. C. was a live-streamed celebratory dinner with the members of the House and Senate Judiciary Review Committees, President Krauss, a small entourage of representatives from the Big Four, the other online-trial/juror honorees, and their guests. Bailey sat abreast to Aaron but ignored his attempts at small talk. Her intention wasn't rudeness, though; she wasn't capable of consciously intending to do anything at the moment. She lacked the processing capacity needed to understand what she'd witnessed earlier. She was able to calm her mother down but she refused to attend the gala. Aaron tried again to compliment Bailey's natural look, telling her how beautiful she was without her make-up, but she could do little more than return a strained smile. She could barely focus on President Krauss's speech.

"…and that is why these fine examples of our tried-and-true system will make excellent dignitaries for our selected foreign markets. Congratulations to you all!"

"Bailey, I think you should get ready," Aaron said, giving up his flirtations.

"Ready for what?"

"To get up and get our award. I think we're next. They're just finishing up with that group from Florida who sued to legalize prostitution and online sex work. Thought you'd be paying attention to that one at least. Now you won't have to hide your face during your, uh, performances."

"Great. I can't wait."

To Aaron's relief, a rhythmic applause interrupted them. The celebrating Floridians waved their awards and certificates in the air and exited stage right. Aaron checked the itinerary. He'd been glancing down at it almost every minute since they were seated, preparing for his walk to the podium and his concise thank-you speech. He would, of course, thank Bailey for the opportunity, his father for imbuing his principles and work-ethic, and the Big Four and President Krauss for making it all possible. He would flash his smile and hold up his trophy. He ran through the scenario again while Bailey sipped her ice-water. He was three-quarters of the way through his final acceptance scenario when the doors to the hall burst open. Struggling in the arms of the FileX agents were Senators Andre Shields and Patricia DuBois. They wrestled their way far enough into the view of the guests to not be ignored, and when that they were in full view of ordinary citizens and possible constituents, they were confident that even President Krauss would resist the desire to kill them where they stood—not without a trial at least.

"We kept showing these agents our invitations, Madam President, but they kept telling us that it's a closed venue!" DuBois shouted.

Krauss stood at the podium, her beaming smile and gleamingly smooth face cloaking her frothing rage. "Please gentlemen," she said to her protectors, "let the newly returned senators take their seats. It's all right, it's all right, let them sit. They won't be disturbing any other part of this fine evening, right?"

Shields and DuBois straightened their attire and smiled at the parting agents. With a nod from Krauss, they left and closed the doors behind them. "We just wanted to welcome our honored guests, Madam President. I've even prepared a few congratulatory words for this special group," Shields said, holding up a folded piece of paper. Before waiting for a response, he sprinted to the dais.

"Why, Senator, we're adhering to a very strict schedule, and I'm sure there isn't time for one of your renowned, inspirational speeches," she said, her countenance beginning to crack.

Shields ignored her, sped-walk up the stairs, past Bailey and Aaron's table, and arrived next to Krauss at the podium. While the eyes the room had followed the clamor of Shields's trajectory, Patty DuBois lithely moved to the rear of the room to shut and lock the two sets of double doors. She looked at the side exits but knew she couldn't reach them before Shields finished what he'd planned to say. *This would have to do*, she thought.

"Ladies and gentlemen and honored guests," he began, "my name is Andre Shields, senator from the great state of Colorado, and a few of my colleagues and I have just returned from our long retreat at FileX's flagship rehabilitation facility in Utah's famed Salt Flats. Describing it here without the proper audio and visuals would be a disservice, so take my word: it is state-of-the-art in prisoner treatment, waste disposal, and technological research."

Krauss took a step toward him.

"But that fine location is not why I'm here to speak with you today, although it has helped inspire what I'm about to say. No, Senator DuBois and I arrived back earlier in the week as changed politicians—you see, we and President Krauss had a bit of disagreement a while back, and we're here to make amends with her in front of all you fine individuals. She had kindly given us a choice when we'd disagreed with her: get on board or get offline. We chose to personally witness what she and the other leaders of the Four were accomplishing by embedding ourselves with the convicts out in Utah."

The audience tried to keep smiling, tried to mimic Krauss's demeanor, but many were beginning to look confused and uncomfortable.

"You see, while we were there, we had the chance to meet some of the freshest, uh, recruits, as they're called. There were recruits from almost every state in this great nation. We even had the opportunity to meet the subjects of one of our very own guests here today! Ms. Bailey Tomanicki, we were privileged enough to meet the *defendant* of your trial, Jimmy Larkin."

An uneasy arrhythmic applause began as a spotlight shined on Bailey.

"Yes, we had the chance to speak with him about the unfortunate events of his life in these last few months. He seemed like an ordinary man, someone who'd loved his family, worked hard at a respectable job, but I had to repeatedly remind myself that this seemingly innocuous former-teacher was a convicted killer, a calculated murderer. I had to repeatedly remind myself that there was no room for remorse or compassion for a man who'd been brought up on charges by an erudite, magnanimous high school senior. I had to repeatedly remind myself that Larkin received the fairest of trials and was found guilty by a truly objective, unbiased consortium of professional jurors."

Krauss took another step toward him and whispered, "Get in here, now!"

Shields turned his back to the pursuing Krauss, evading her attempts to wrestle the microphone from him, and continued, "I also had to remind myself when I learned, just before coming to this congratulatory occasion, that Mr. Larkin doesn't deserve my pity, or yours, for the slaughtering of his three children at this morning's teachers' rally in Runners' Landing, New York. Don't shed a tear for those innocent, beautiful children who had their father ripped away from them, who had their lives ripped apart while being a small part of the last bit of free speech we've got left. Mr. Larkin also doesn't deserve your sympathy for, as we just learned before making our grand entrance, the loss of his wife, Susan, who minutes ago exploded in her own home while she being arrested by—and the reports on this are still preliminary—a local subsidiary called the Long Island Freedom Fighters and a crew of FileX agents."

The locked double doors shook violently as the FileX agents crashed against them. DuBois grabbed the end of a buffet table and strained to drag it in front of the door. Several chaffing dishes slid off and crashed to the floor, but she was able to prop the buffet table against the door. It would, she hoped, give them the time they needed to broadcast their message.

Shields tried to shed Krauss off his back. In the struggle and growing commotion, he violently elbowed her in the jaw, knocking her unconscious. Shields steadied himself and spoke quickly, looking directly into the mounted cameras. "People of the United States, what happened to the Larkin family will not end with them. Even if you've never been the victim of this brave new system of justice, you will not be immune from it forever. With some simple clicks or pictures or even baseless allegations, your families or communities or friends will be torn apart! We're being fed solutions to problems that are being perpetuated by those who've completely manipulated us!" He heard a door to his left crash open. "Demand from all your representatives and senators that our former judicial process be restored! Do not let—"

Rubber bullets cracked his skull and needle-tipped electrified tinsel flew from handheld tasers, sending both Shields and DuBois to the floor.

Only the AI knows where they now labor.

Frank Reilly stood in awe of the heat that radiated from the still-smoldering houses. The blast had completely leveled the Larkin place and set ablaze the two adjacent homes. He raised his forearm to shield his face, but in moments, it too began to sear. He backed away until the scorching ceased. He'd been on his way to an account when he saw the fireball and felt the shockwave. He made a detour, forgetting that he still hadn't heard from Paige, Bailey, or his son after the horrific morning news. *What the fuck else could be going on now?* he thought as he drove toward the billowing smoke. He stood in the middle of the street with the other surviving neighbors, trying to piece together what happened.

"I'm sorry you didn't get to go through with your plans with Frank, Jordan, I really am," Latoya said.

"It's all right."

She looked at him, staying silent for a minute, hoping to coax out his honest response.

He laughed at her mistrust and said, "I mean it, baby. I wasn't thinkin' right, anyway. If we would've gone through with all of that, you would've been left with nothing and nobody."

She broke off her stare and smiled. "And you sure what you ran won't get us caught? You sure you found the right Lamont Davis?"

"If they knew, we'd already be toast, and yes, I found the right Lamont Davis. And when Frank finds the note—don't worry, I left it where only he'll find it, I swear—he'll know that I took a second to set up part of our original plan."

"You what! Won't that get us—"

"If they knew, we'd already be—"

"Toast, I know! But that was unnecessary, Jordan! Stupid and unnecessary."

"I owed him that much, Toya. Leaving like this, without so much as a goodbye. Yeah, I owed him that. Now, can we focus on getting our son back?"

"I suppose it was a gas leak, huh?" Wendy Fuller mused. "Gotta be careful with that stuff."

"And whose van was that?" her husband, Jerry, asked, pointing to the skeletal frame and gnarled body that lay in their front yard.

Reilly offered no suppositions for Wendy and Jerry, but as they continued to survey the damage to their front lawn and porch, he heard a quick succession of barks and whimpers coming from the house to the east of what had been the Larkins'. "Did you two hear that?" he asked the doddering couple.

"Hear what? Say, you're the owner of that landscaping truck? Think you might be able to help clean all this up for us? Definitely gonna need a lot of work done."

Reilly ignored the question and moved closer to the conflagration. A window on the second floor burst outward with talons of deep oranges and yellows following it. He took a step backwards and heard the dog's cries getting louder. The fire department, now privately managed through a Gazelle-operated hedge fund, was just leaving the station. The barks and whimpers kept getting louder. Reilly couldn't stand anymore suffering, so he sprinted toward the remnants of melted vinyl fence. He moved past the decimated garage and turned to see a partially charred standard poodle swimming circles in the pool.

"Hold on, boy! I'll get you! Just keep swimming!" he said as he ran to the steps.

He reached out but the frightened animal kept its distance, wading and whining in the middle of the pool. "C'mon, you stupid animal, or you're gonna boil."

The heat was turning his shirt into an electric blanket set to ten. He searched for the pool skimmer, hoping to snare part of the petrified dog. There, lying next to a partially toppled shed was the metal pole and net. "Hold on, boy. I'll be right back."

He sprinted around the pool and as he picked up the ten-foot tool, Jordan Davis's encrypted virus switched on every single Gazelle-integrated piece of lawn equipment, including this now-deceased homeowner's twenty-four horse power ride-on behemoth. The beast's electronic gearshift defaulted to drive and its connected-computer sent the electronic motor running at full-speed. Reilly, dumbfounded at what he saw, tripped over the skimmer's hollow handle. As he hit the ground, the wheels and blades of the ghost driven machine ran him over, sending a fountain of blood toward the burning house. It did not help in quelling the flames. Following the declivity of the yard, the ride-on headed for the pool, where it fell in and electrocuted the paddling dog.

Labor Day, 2024.

Aaron Elskin began working on his first independent trial immediately after he and his father returned from Washington. Abhorrent was a word he learned from his thesaurus, and it perfectly described the scene he witnessed at the awards ceremony. He felt utterly betrayed by those people who were supposed to be his representatives, mortified at their disloyalty. He also felt a deep sadness, despite how she'd treated him throughout high school, when Bailey had told him that she was taking President Krauss up on her offer of being a Judicial Representative in Beijing. He couldn't reconcile why a communist country would want to put its system of justice in the hands of its people but seeing the forest through the trees had never been his forte. He understood why she wanted to leave, though. Both her stepfather and stepbrother's funerals were macabre scenes. Bailey's mother insisted on having an open viewing for her husband, claiming that the remaining half of him was perfectly recognizable, and Sean's casket contained a sculpted mannequin filled with his (or was their best guess) ashes. Elskin figured that Bailey needed to get away, even if it meant leaving her mother alone in Runners' Landing. After Sean's interment, his closest friend left without saying goodbye.

Aaron thought of her as he read over his trial synopsis one final time. He smiled proudly and hit *Send*. The wait-icon twirled briefly and then his screen told him what he knew it would: *Approved*. The Medusa went to every device in the country. His darling-trial read:

You are now authorized to join the opening arguments for Case No. FED-01, Aaron Elskin vs. The United States Government. The plaintiff accuses the defendants of operating an unjust, obsolete system that is our current representative republic. He proposes, with the assistance of modern-day technologies—particularly the ever-improving artificial intelligence—the installation of a direct, computer-linked democracy. Mr. Elskin cites the success of the person-to-person judicial system as his precedent. He further proposes that the process of electing representatives and senators be made illegal and that the people and the people alone should be responsible for governing of this great country.

By clicking on the box below, you're confirming that you have read and agree to the Citizen Juror Terms.

Be aware that any violation of these terms will result in immediate arrest and prosecution.